BOUND

THE PLAYGROUND CLUB
BOOK 2

SHANNON ELLIOT

Bound

The Playground Club Series

By Shannon Elliot

To request permission or for more information, contact the publisher at pa@authorshannonelliot.com.

Paperback ISBN 978-1-964117-19-5

Ebook ASIN B0CVYHLXW6

Second edition December 2025

Edited by Bookcase Media

Proofed by Bookcase Media

Cover Art by Eve Graphic Designs

Formatting by Creative Shannonigans

CONTENT AWARENESS

Please take the following under advisement before reading.

Your mental health matters.
<u>Hate, Discrimination & Oppression</u>
Fatphobia, Misogynistic white men
<u>Abuse and Relationships</u>
Intimate partner abuse (in the past)
<u>Mental Health and Suicide</u>
Anxiety & anxiety attacks, Depression, Dissociation & dissociative
episodes, Intrusive thoughts, Self-harm (threats), Suicidal ideation
<u>Alcohol and Drugs</u>
Alcohol consumption
<u>Blood, Injury & Medical</u>
Blood depiction, Bodily fluids, Emergency services,
Hospitalization, Medical treatment & procedures, Physical injuries
<u>Kink Related</u>
BDSM & Kink, Bondage, Forced orgasms, Toys

This book contains "spice", or graphic sexual content, and is

RESOURCES

Your mental health and safety matters to me.

Please make note of the resources below if any content in this book is triggering for you:

Dial 988 for the Suicide & Crisis Helpline or visit their website for more resources. (https://988lifeline.org)

For support after losing a loved one to suicide, call 1-800-646-7322 or visit the Friends for Survival website. (https://findahelpline. com/organizations/friends-for-survival-suicide-loss-helpline)

Call 1-800-662-HELP (4357) for SAMHSA'S national helpline (Substance Abuse and Mental Health Services Administration) or visit the website for more resources. (http://www.samhsa.gov/find-help/national-helpline)

To everyone who's tired of being "good." I see you.
Welcome to The Playground, you sinners.

WELCOME TO THE...

Playground Club

1

BEX

January 12

"I swear to all that is holy if the package of condoms and lube is late when we have Selene's engagement party this weekend? I will scream until I shatter windows, Alvie. No one can stop me." I huff as I shove the last of my toiletries into my overnight bag.

"Birdie, we have a few hours before we need to head over to the club to set up. It's gonna be fine." Alvaro says calmly before mumbling under his breath. "And you could have just had them shipped directly to the club."

I glare at him, but he pointedly ignores me, instead focusing on meticulously packing the bag of whips, floggers, and other goodies for this weekend.

"This is an important weekend for Selene." I sigh, hopping up onto the bed beside the bag he's packing. "I just want it to be perfect."

"I know you do, and I admire you for it," he says. "But the group knows this is all hands on deck and it's going to go smoothly with everyone stepping up."

His small smile is reassuring, but it's the glimmer in his emerald eyes that has my pulse picking up pace.

Alvie is a cowboy, through-and-through. His body is proof of all the time he spends outdoors. His cheeks are the perfect shade of pinked by the sun and his natural deep sienna complexion is only deepened by all the hours outside. To the point where his tan is so deep, the smile lines on his face are prominently pale when he's not grinning at me.

His body, too, is exquisitely chiseled just for my enjoyment. Every curve on his body is pure muscle, built from hard labor on the ranch. There's not an inch of him that I haven't touched or tasted.

Watching him now, so entirely focused on his task, has me drooling over my own husband.

"Your confidence is reassuring and I appreciate you helping me ground myself." I shake out my shoulders to pull me from my thoughts, which are quickly turning dirty.

"Anytime, birdie," he says, finally looking up at me giving me a kiss on my temple. "Now, are you all packed for the club?"

The Playground Club & Resort opened three years ago, and, since it's opening day, we've been patrons, attending nearly every weekend we can. There are plenty of lifestyle clubs in the city, but living as far out as we do, it's just more convenient to go to The Playground. Plus, every time we visit, we're met with three years of memories and friends who've come to mean the world to us.

The Playground is an escape for those who live unique lifestyles and enjoy taking part in specific activities of a more erotic nature, namely swingers and kinksters. The owners, Juliana Morgan and the rest of her polycule, have curated a non-judg-mental space, and community, that is supportive of non-tradi-tional lifestyles and interests.

Alvaro and I have lived an alternative lifestyle together for nearly a decade, but living in the country on our ranch can be isolating from not just people but others who have similar outlooks on relationships. Finding the club when we did was a saving grace and a breath of fresh air we needed. We've found an incredible community of people who have similar values and interests to our own.

This weekend is a celebration of that community.

Selene Solis de Estrella is getting engaged to her partner, Gunnar Rees, who met at the clubs opening party and have been inseparable ever since. Seeing their relationship blossom over the years has been an honor, but this weekend has to be perfect, as she deserves.

It's bizarre to think about how a bond formed over shared interests like flogging and rope play, but nonetheless, Selene is one of my closest friends.

The doorbell draws my attention to the front door, and I'm hopping off the bed and sprinting out of the bedroom to answer it before Alvie can yell at me not to run in the house.

Swinging the door open, I see the delivery driver retreating to their truck.

"Thank you!" I call out.

The woman tips their hat to me in acknowledgement and continues to get in their truck.

I look down at the box and immediately abandon it, instead turning back to yell, "Alvie! I can't lift this."

I may be an experienced yoga instructor, and far stronger than my size 22 might lead others to assume, still, I'd rather watch my husband's ass as he lifts the massive box than do it myself.

I'm bouncing on my toes when he comes into the living room. He takes one look at the box and his eyes widen.

"I thought you ordered condoms and lube? What the hell is in there?"

"Condoms and lube! And a few other things." I wave off his concern. "Now put it in the truck so we can leave."

His side eye hints at a spanking coming my way, but I knew that when I placed the order.

Within the hour, we're all packed up and headed to the club.

Pulling up at the property always sparks something in my soul. It's the calm of coming home with the excitement of new things to happen.

The entire property is immaculately lain out to take guests on a journey and provide them with ample space to relax or play. Whoever designed the resort took every feature of the land, from the natural pecan tree's that grow abundant, to the river that runs along the back of the land, to create an oasis among an otherwise flat landscape.

The Playground is both modern and elegant, yet still maintains the rustic charm that is associated with the architecture of rural Texas. The main resort is built of steel and stone. A foundation of limestone contrasts the black metal pillars that form the main frame of the building, which allow for long stretches of windows that let light into all of the rooms. There are accents of wood throughout which look like they've come from the land themselves.

Driving up under the awning of the main building, we're greeted by a team of staff members ready to assist with our every need.

"Mr. and Mrs. Silva, welcome back to The Playground." Mark greets us.

"Good to see you, Mark." Alvie smiles at the man. "How are the kids?"

"Doing well. Natalie is a few months away from graduation, and then she's going to do a European backpacking tour. June-bug is finishing her sophomore year now and already planning for her junior prom." The man laughs.

"Oh wow! That's so exciting." I smile.

"You're staying in the villas this weekend, correct?" He asks.

"I believe so. The group of us should all be together." Alvie confirms.

"Perfect. Juliana, let us know about this weekend. We're all very excited to celebrate." Mark grins. "If you go on ahead inside, we'll get everything taken to your villa."

"Oh, and the boxes go to the club for the party!" I chime in.

"Yes, Mrs. Silva." He says as I give him a brief kiss on the cheek. "Thank you, Mark."

2

NAOMI

January 13 — One week into the new semester, and there's already a three-day weekend

Online friends are weird.

I've known Selene for over a year. We message back and forth from sunup to sundown, and a little further into the night, too. It's weird when I don't hear from her every day.

Selene is easily my best friend. She's my soul twin.

But, despite still living in the same state, we've never met.

Texas is fucking huge y'all.

My excuses for why I can't make the four-hour drive to visit my best friend have run out, though. So, I've spent the entire drive on this Saturday morning to some town outside Houston trying to keep from turning my ass around to go home and hide in my apartment by myself, studying, for the first three day weekend of the semester, like I always do.

There's no way I'm missing such an important day for her, though. Selene would kill me, and she is nothing if not persistent. It's how we became friends in the first place.

When I was finishing my master's program, the pressure became so bad at one point I came very near to harming myself in a permanent way. I'd been thinking about it all semester, I was one semester from graduating with my degree, but all I could think about was how much easier things could be if I just stopped for a minute, stopped existing. It was around this time of year that I actually put together a plan. I was just waiting to do it.

There was one particularly low day where the world felt like it was collapsing. I had everything I needed. I had the supplies and the note all printed out. Nothing could stop me.

Nothing except the stupid reflex to reach for my phone anytime it chimed with a Discord notification.

A friend request and a one-word message.

OVERTHEMOON

Hey!

That's all it took to divert months of planning.

MINDFUCKMASTER

Hey.

Now we're here, a year later, and I'm pulling up to some resort in small town Texas to meet a semi-random woman for the first time. Of course I know her, I know everything about her, but knowing a person online versus in person could be two different things. I'm doing this all so I can be there to celebrate her engagement to a man I only know as a voice in the background of our near-daily calls.

My grandma is terrified I'm being catfished and Selene is actually an old man and serial killer, at that. Though I'm really not sure how you fake something like a video call. Plus, judging from the exterior of the resort I'm pulling up to, this is not some place you lure someone you're murdering to.

The Playground Club and Resort.

A woman owned, woman run business outside of Columbus, Texas, catering to people in the swinger and BDSM lifestyles. One that my best friend of a year calls the home of her second family.

I've only spoken with Selene's fiancé, Gunnar, a handful of times without Selene and all of those times have been about her. So, it wasn't entirely unusual when he called me to plan their engagement. Selene had been planting hints and suggestions for both of us for months. It was only a matter of time before he reached out to arrange everything for a proposal at the club, which I thought was a little odd at first. Unfortunately, I wasn't able to attend, but it would have been a dead give-away if I was there anyway since Selene and I had yet to meet. What I wasn't expecting was how adamant she would be about celebrating her engagement to her future husband at the club too.

But what my best friend wants, my best friend gets. Including my presence at a sex club.

Approaching the main building of the resort is entirely unexpected. The exterior of the resort looks like any other getaway in this area. It's a gorgeous resort for sure, but it doesn't scream "swingers resort" or "BDSM club" at all.

I put my car in park and reach for my purse, but jump when I turn back to open my door and find a staff member already standing outside my drivers side door.

"Ms. Hall. Welcome to The Playground," says the man as I crack open my door.

"Hi..." I say, a little shocked he knows who I am already.

"Ms. Selene is waiting inside for you. Please let us take care of your car and bags." He explains, holding out his hand for my keys as I crack the door open further.

"Oh. Okay."

A high-pitched squeal comes from behind the man, and he's barely taken two steps away from me when I'm tackled by a petite, curvy Puerto Rican woman.

"¡Oh, por Dios! ¡Estás aquí! Realmente estás aquí. Eres más alto de lo que esperaba. ¡Pero estás aquí!" *Oh, my Goddess! You're here! You're taller than I expected. But you're here!* She rapid fires.

"Selene?" I ask, as though I don't already know from the koala-hug.

Her smack to my arm as she pulls away is all the confirmation I really need.

"¡Tonta!" *Silly!* "Of course it's me. I've been tracking your phone for the past hour and a half. I knew the second you started driving up the road to the club." She rasps.

"I really regret giving you access to that." I chuckle before diving in for another hug. "It's so good to meet you in person!"

"I know! It's taken too long, but you're here! I can't wait to show you everything and introduce you to everyone."

Already she's moving at a million miles a minute, like she normally is, and I'm just happy to be swept up in the enthusiastic storm that is Selene.

"Gunnar!" She calls out as she turns to the building's main doors. "I found her."

"I can see that." A tall blonde, Viking-like man chuckles. "Naomi, it's nice to meet you, finally."

The way he looks down at Selene with stars in his eyes causes a pang of longing to shoot through my chest at such a sweet sight.

I've known for a while that they're perfect for each other. Their appearances are the perfect deception. Her dark features and tan complexion are the perfect light to his hulking, golden boy darkness. Their personalities balance each other in every word that's bickered back and forth between them. But seeing how Gunnar looks at my best friend in the universe, a woman I would protect with my last breath, solidifies the trust I've put in him to handle her heart.

"Come on." The sparkly woman demands. "Let's go get you settled in and then we can start getting ready for tonight."

"Selene, it's like two o'clock. We have hours until anyone is heading to the club tonight." Gunnar says in his smooth bass.

"Yes. And that's hours of primping that we need to do before we get dressed and meet up with the rest of the group," she says with a glare in his direction.

I can't help the chuckle that escapes, earning me my own scathing look from Selene.

"If you gang up on me with him, I'm cutting you off." She snarks.

"Cutting me off?" I gasp in horror. "You wouldn't."

"Yup. You heard me. No more fluff photos."

"You wouldn't. You'd never take away my time with Beef Cake."

"I wouldn't, but it's a damn good threat, cariña. Cat photo withdrawal is a serious condition." She quips before turning on her heel and marching to the entrance. "¡Vamos! *Onward!*"

Looking at Gunnar, I glance toward my bags, wondering if I'm supposed to do anything with them. "Do I?"

"Nope. Staff here are amazing." Selene supplies without missing a beat. "They'll bring everything to our villas. Gunnar tip the nice men who are helping us. Gracias." *Thanks.*

"Yes, ma'am." He smirks, then walks off to chat with the valet and bellman.

Before my brain can really register, Selene goes back to pulling me toward the great doors.

Walking into the lobby is like walking through a looking glass. On the other side of the doors is a whole different world. The Texas heat and building's modern rustic exterior are traded in for a sleek version of its outer charm. The hill country limestone and black steel is carried throughout, but now with a chiseled precision that gives everything a new elegance.

Selene calls out to a tall blonde woman with lush curves much like my own, "Juliana! Look who I found!"

The woman turns to us with a broad smile and a sway in her step when she approaches.

"You must be Naomi," Juliana says, extending a hand toward me.

"Um. Yes. Hi." I manage to get out while taking her hand to shake.

"Welcome to The Playground. Selene's been looking forward to your visit for quite a while. It's nice to match a name to a face," she says with a genuine humor in her tone. "I hope you enjoy your stay with us."

"I'm looking forward to it." I smile back.

"You're gonna be there tonight, right?" Selene asks eagerly.

"Of course!" Juliana replies.

"Perfect. I want everyone there." Selene says more seriously.

"The kids are looking after each other tonight, so all six of us will be there. We wouldn't miss it." Juliana reassures.

"Good. Griff already missed my birthday, and I'm still mad at him." Selene says flatly, which earns her a chuckle from Juliana.

"I've got a few things to do before tonight, though. I'll see you later, love." The blonde says. "It was lovely to meet you, Naomi. I hope you enjoy your time here."

A quick exchange of hugs later and the blonde beauty is sauntering away from us in her towering heels.

"Juliana's one of the owners. She was a stripper in a past life, and she's one-hundred percent badass. I want to be her when I grow up." Selene gushes.

"Isn't she our age?" I ask.

"Probably, but she's larger than life."

"I'm not sure that's possible with you around, Lena." I laugh as Selene drags me in a new direction.

She leads me through immaculately kept grounds, which are clearly designed intentionally to allow guests a plethora of spaces to gather.

The main resort backs up to a massive pool with swim-up bar and multiple spaces for outdoor cooking and grilling. All around in the distance are smaller buildings, which I assume are the villas where we will be staying. But the main feature that draws my eye in the distance is what can only be the club that The Playground is well known for.

"Is that the club?" I ask Selene, pointing at the building.

"Hmm?" Selene glances in the direction of the club. "Oh, yeah! That's where we'll be tonight. You're gonna love it."

The exterior of the building both flows with the rest of the resort's design and yet there's something distinct about the way it subtly stands out from the rest. The two-story building blends in seamlessly with the landscape of the property and the view it looks out on. The second floor has a viewing space with mirrored windows, allowing guests to see all around the property, but hides anything on the inside from everything and everyone else. The design gives the building a mysterious feel that conceals more secrets than it reveals.

"Come on." Selene says. "We'll go settle in, get ready for the evening, and then we can meet everyone at the club later."

THE PACKING LIST that Selene gave me for the weekend required shopping and a trip to my esthetician. Somehow I ended up with clothes, if you can call them clothes, that reveal more than they hide and a body that's waxed within an inch of my life.

"You'll look amazing in this," Selene says, pulling out a sheer, deep teal bodysuit from my bag. "The color suits you."

I snatch the lingerie out of her hand before she can get any ideas.

"I have a dress I can wear tonight." I object, stuffing the garment back into the deep recesses of my bag.

"Yes, and when you do, you'll be overdressed for the evening." She snorts.

Selene got me settled in my own room, next door to her and Gunnar still giving me my own privacy, but has been with me for the past few hours while we primped and pampered ourselves to get ready for the evening.

"And what? I'm supposed to just walk over to the club wearing nothing?" I scoff.

"Not nothing. You're wearing lingerie." She says, like it's the simplest thing in the world.

"You realize how weird this is, right? Normal people dress up for going out, not down."

"This is dressing up!" Selene says wistfully. "Trust me. There's something so freeing about being able to exist in your body like this."

"Yes. I know the spiel. 'Everyone has a body.' et cetera, et cetera." I tease.

Still, the idea of wearing nothing but lingerie in front of so many people has my stomach twisting in knots. All of those eyes on you at all times, studying you, judging you? No thanks.

"Precisely," she says. "Really, this is great wisdom I'm sharing. You really should be taking notes for your dissertation. Have you decided your topic yet?"

"No. Nothing is jumping out at me yet. My advisor is breathing down my neck about it, but he always shoots down everything that I suggest. He's just so set in his ways."

My doctoral advisor, Dr. Edwards, is an older white man who's thoughts on the field of psychology are stuck in the past. He's rigid in his thinking and firmly believes that his job is to produce physicians who think exactly like him. Other than that he has tenure, I don't understand how the man is still teaching, much less the new head of the department.

When I interviewed for the program, there was a different

department head who seemed genuine in their interest to develop students and help them grow. The switch makes me feel cheated and lied to though. This isn't the experience that I was anticipating and it's wearing on me.

"Well, maybe this weekend will inspire you." Selene says brightly.

"Maybe. It's just so hard to pick one thing to focus on, you know?" I sigh.

"For sure. But you've got this," she says. "What's your program again anyway?"

I laugh. "I'm in a Clinical Psychology program, Selene. We've been over this."

"Yeah, I know you've told me that. But I still don't know what it means." She shrugs.

"It means I'm studying to become a psychologist." She looks at me blankly. "A therapist, Lena."

"Oh! You should talk with Durante. He's a therapist or something like that. He has his own practice in the city."

My interest perks up. "Do you know what kind of patients he works with?"

"Umm... People?" She teases.

"Like, kids or adults?" I chuckle.

"Adults for sure." She rambles as she gets up to dig through my bag for more clothing options. "He has a lot of patients who are in the lifestyle. He speaks all around the country about it and also polyamory." She pulls out a bright red dress the sales clerk insisted looked amazing on me and spins around. "Oooh. You should do something like that! Like write your paper on kink and the lifestyle or something."

I laugh. "And what, my research is getting spanked?"

"Hey. Don't discount the benefits of a good spanking." She giggles. "No really. You could write about kink and relationships and mental health or something."

"And what? Just pick a couple to be my case study?"

"Well, why not?"

I shake off the idea, saying, "Because I don't know the first thing about kink or polyamory or the lifestyle or anything!"

"Isn't that the point though? To learn about something and gain new insight?"

She says it with such sincerity that I actually take a moment to consider the idea. What would it even look like for vanilla-old-me to dive into the world of kink and polyamory? Am I even capable of going that far outside of my comfort zone? I want to pretend I'm brave enough to say yes, but there's a part of me that hesitates to embrace the idea.

I huff, knowing she's right. "I'll think about it."

"Good! Now," she says, turning to me, hair held up in one of her hands. "Hair up or down for tonight?"

3

BEX

The club itself doesn't typically open until 9 p.m., but we arranged with the owners to come in an hour early to set up for Selene's big night. Resort staff already handled most of the heavy lifting, but the group decided it was necessary for us all to have a hand in making this night perfect for her.

The building that houses the club stands entirely separate from the rest of the resort, with its own parking lot and entrance for the patrons who choose to attend only for a night and don't stay for a longer trip at the resort.

When you first walk into the club you enter into a lobby area, which looks like any other event space or hotel lobby. There's a large check-in desk along the back wall, framed on either side by doors that lead into the club. Two grand staircases hug each side of the room and wrap up against the wall to an alternate entrance on the second floor. Somewhere around here is also an elevator for anyone to use.

The main feature of the space is its art installments, though. When you look up at the high ceilings there are dozens of massive chandeliers surrounded by cages. Each one throws out a warm light that makes the room feel cozy and seductive. Along every wall is another sensual painting depicting mythical moments of lust and love. The floor is a modern glossy dark cement with brightly colored stone inlaid to make it look like geodes of various colors.

Immediately when Alvie and I enter, I spot a tall goddess of a woman across the room.

"Ivy!" I squeal at the sight of the woman. "The club looks great, chica!" I say, looking around at the refreshed space.

Ivy matches my energy as she comes out from behind the check-in desk to give me a hug.

"Girl. Just wait until you see the inside." She giggles. "Juliana and the family went all-out for you all."

Tall and lithe, Ivy le Fleur is a walking Shakespearean nymph. She has an earthy air to her, giving her a grounding presence wherever she goes. The woman is like a walking Xanax and immediately helps settle my nerves about the upcoming evening.

"I can't wait." I say, smiling broadly. "Alright if I go on in?"

"Of course." She says, smoothing back some of my fly-aways before releasing me from her embrace. "The others girls are in full party mode. I think the guy's are a little overwhelmed by the energy."

As she lets me go, Alvie comes into the lobby, arms laden with the supplies I packed in our own bags.

"Good to see you, Alvie." Ivy purs.

"You too, Ivy." He smirks. "Where did they put all of us?"

"Your usual nook. I'll get you checked in for the evening since you pre-paid." She smiles. "Now shoo. You have decorating to do!"

I give her one last squeeze before Alvie and I stride off and enter the main club area through the far right doors.

Like always, a shiver runs down my spine when I enter The Playground.

Despite its size, the club always retains an intimate lounge feeling to it. The lights are dim when you first walk in, but brighten as you near the DJ and dance-floor that are central to the space. The owners pump a signature scent through the air that gives the space an air of seduction that has my pulse thrumming in my veins.

The building is two stories, with most of the playrooms located on the second floor, and from the dance-floor you're able to look up into the bright lights and see the shadows of people moving about the play-space, exploring their most intimate desires.

The first floor is entirely focused on people having a good time. The dance-floor only takes up part of the space, but the majority is devoted to tables, chairs, booths, and private party areas for guests to lounge, chat, and connect with each other.

A dry bar—as the club has a BYOB policy for consent and liability reasons—sits at the back of the main room along the expanse of panoramic windows that have been blacked out from the outside. It gives the space the openness that every exhibitionist craves, but the privacy every patron needs to feel safe and comfortable in the space.

The Playground Club operates on a system that relies on personal responsibility.

Every patron is required to submit an online membership application in order to be registered in the clubs computer system, but it's not as thorough vetting system as some clubs. There's no invasive background check or health screening of individuals. All members are required to agree to the rules and guidelines of the club and everyone is asked to acquire a sponsor before they attend for their first time. It's more of a system so new couples don't feel lost or overwhelmed when they attend than anything, though. There are plenty of couples who show up last minute, complete their membership application, are introduced to members who attend regularly, then complete the BDSM 101 course at a later date.

Membership to the club is a nightly fee, which allows individuals and couples the opportunity to come and go as they please at their own pace and schedule. There's no yearly commitment to membership, nor an expectation that patrons are owed something by the club. Which comes in quite handy when someone acts up or out and their membership needs to be revoked, rare as it is.

My favorite aspect of The Playground, though, is the community Alvie and I have found here. As regular patrons, we have built strong core friendships with others who share similar values to us.

Tonight, we're all gathering to celebrate one of our own and an exciting new step in their relationship.

Passing the dance floor and turning to the right, into one of the private party areas which is connected to a private play room, I am greeted by the familiar faces that make the club feel like home.

"Bex! Alvie!" Elsie exclaims, running over to me to give me a hug and a kiss. "You're here!"

"Hey, girl!" I say, returning her innocent enthusiastic energy. "This looks fantastic."

Looking around at the space, I take in the balloons, streamers, and other decorations that fill the space. There are buckets ready to be filled with ice to chill alcohol and mixers.

More importantly, the space is filled with people I love and adore.

Elsie is a unicorn that our group adopted about a year ago. She's an adorable petite woman who came into the lifestyle wide eyed and clueless, but quickly dug her way into our friend group and hearts.

"Where's Marshall?" Alvie asks from beside me.

Alvie's best friend, Marshall Law, is a single guy and bull, and, since Elsie joined our group, he's been attached like her personal shadow. He's also one of the most observant and intuitive people I know. Which makes for a great lover, I've heard.

"He's helping Val and Holly get stuff out of their truck." Elsie supplies.

"Got it. Gonna go help them, then." He says, turning to head back outside.

"Okay. Put me to work, Elsie." I say, clapping my hands.

"Perfect. Jay dropped off a few bottles of celebratory vodka for the happy couple as a gift. But Chris and Beaux are unpacking the rest of the stuff they brought into the ice buckets. Beaux said Chris went a little overboard and made 200 jello shots for tonight. I think ze had the right idea." She giggles.

"I agree." I laugh, just as ze comes over.

"Hey, Selene." Chris says, giving me a hug and a kiss on the cheek. "Longtime no see."

"It has been a while, hasn't it." I say. "Y'all've been busy!"

"Yeah, well. Beaux just started a new job and you know how that goes." Ze sighs. "He's overworking himself, but I can't get him to slow down. He keeps telling me to come out by myself, and I keep meaning to, but it's just hard to drag myself out of the house sometimes."

I nod in understanding.

"Well, y'all are here tonight. So let's make sure everything is perfect for Selene and Gunnar and we can have a great time together, catch up, and whatnot."

"Excellent!" Elsie cheers.

We settle into a comfortable rhythm as we set up the remainder of the decor and other items for the evening. Soon enough, music starts filtering through the club and members start to trickle in for the evening.

The energy in the room is intoxicating.It's gonna be a great night.

4

NAOMI

Somehow, it took nearly three hours to get ready for the night. By the time we finish, I am ready for a nap, not a night out.

Never in my life has going out to a club involved packing a bag, but evidently this is a necessary part of the evening. Several changes of clothes, shoes, and makeup-for touch-ups, have all been neatly packed away for both of us in matching pink and teal duffle bags Selene got for us.

Despite my protest, I'm ready for the night clad in a body hugging dress that makes me feel like a sausage and wedges which make me fear gravity. Selene insists that I look amazing, but I can't help but be self-conscious about how my tits and ass are threatening to pop out of the garment. I will give her credit though for picking out something that shows off the collarbone tattoos I love. She even had me place highlighter along them to make the floral motif glitter in the light.

Selene chose a stunning red mini wrap dress that drapes over her curves like a Giuseppe Sanmartino sculpture. Her heels are towering and nearly put her at my own 5'6" stature. Her dark hair, streaked with auburn, is curled to perfection and her lips are painted a bright red to match her dress.

Gunnar, on the other hand, is simply dressed in a collared shirt, dress pants, and his nice pair of cowboy boots.

Goddess, I envy men sometimes.

"You sure we have enough stuff?" I ask, looking around at the multiple bags and coolers that are accompanying us for the night.

"Mhmm. If we run out of anything, I'm sure the others will have us covered." Selene replies. "Let's go!"

The trip over to the club takes no time at all from our villas. It's late in the evening, nearly 10 p.m., but evidently very early for our night. I've already been told not to expect to go to bed before 2 a.m. tonight.

Walking into the club itself is like walking into an entirely different world. The entrance leads into an impressive lobby that looks more like an art museum than the lobby of a sex club. There's a line of people in front of us leading up to a check-in desk, but Selene and Gunnar ignore the other guests waiting in line and walk up to the girl behind the desk, clad in a blue baby-doll dress.

"Selene!" The woman cries as she abandons her post to round the desk and give Selene a hug and a kiss on the lips, shocking me. "Hey, baby. How are you?"

"So good, girl. We all good to go in?" Selene asks, returning the hug and placing a kiss on each of the girls cheeks.

"Should be." Gunnar says.

"Yup. You're already in the system and all paid up. I'm guessing this is the single gal we have on the presale list for tonight?"

"Oh, yes! Ivy, this is the bestie I've been telling you about, Naomi." Selene says, turning to face me. "Naomi, meet Ivy."

"So good to meet you, Naomi." The woman says, holding out her hand for a shake which I take. "I hope you have a great time tonight. I won't keep you, though."

"Are you at the door all night tonight?" Selene asks.

"Nope. The girls are back to rotations. Staying at the door all night *sucks*." She rolls her eyes, before stepping back to go around the check-in desk. Then she shoo's us off. "The others are inside and already got you all set up for the night. Your usual place is reserved. And I think one of the owners dropped off a gift on your table earlier, too."

"Perfect." Selene replies and gives the girl an air kiss. "Okay. I'll see you inside."

"Will do." Ivy says as she takes IDs from the next couple in line. "Bye, Gunnar. Have fun, Naomi!"

Selene grabs me by the hand and leads us through the double doors that are off to the left hand side. The handles are the same birdcage design as the chandeliers and somehow gleam in the dark light. Down a short hallway, we come out to the main area of the club.

Stepping into The Playground Club is like entering a different dimension and I stop in my tracks at the sight.

The lights are dimmed to give the space an intimate feel despite the size of the space. People already fill the club, despite it being early in the night, filling up the tables and couches that surround a central dance floor.

The whole first floor has a mix of speakeasy and country club vibes with leather couches and chairs along the edges of the room. Low, intimate tables with seating for two at each surround the dance floor, which patrons have already started grouping and clustering together with other friends.

The bar at the back of the club is buzzing with activity, girls behind the bar-top laughing and flirting with the members who come up for their set-ups.

Looking up through the gap in the ceiling above the dance floor, I can see the second floor of the club and the shadows roaming the level—the play space, according to Selene.

It's shocking... and stunning.

With the confidence of a woman who feels right at home, Selene saunters across the dance floor to a corner decorated to its limits where several people have already settled in, Gunnar on her heels while I have to reboot and trot to catch up with her.

"Selene!" A gorgeous black woman dressed in a purple lacy bra and boy shorts calls out at Selene's approach.

"Zuri! You made it!" Selene squeals and throws her arms open wide.

"Of course. It's been far too long." She beams, embracing Selene tightly. "I've had this blocked off on our calendar for weeks now."

"Awe. Well I'm glad you're here." Selene says, giving the woman a tight hug. "Speaking of which. Everyone, this is Naomi, the friend I've been telling y'all about."

I give a little wave. "Nice to meet y'all."

Introductions to the group happen quickly, and there's no chance in hell that I remember anyone's name at this point.

Without warning, Selene unties her wrap dress and lets it fall down, revealing her own bra and thong set. She tosses the dress over at Gunnar's face before plopping down on one of the couches with her friends.

"Oh. Okay. That's how we're doing this."

"Where's Alvaro and Bex?" Gunnar asks.

"They're upstairs getting set up for their demo. Said they'd be back down in time for cake and champagne later." A petite woman —Elsie, I think—says from next to a massive man who's attention is entirely fixed on her.

"Ooh. Okay. We'll head up there in a minute then." Selene says, turning to me. "This is not a show you're going to want to miss, cariña. But first, drinks!"

AFTER A FEW DRINKS and more chatting with Selene's friends, she grabs me by the hand and we slip upstairs to get a seat for "the show," as she calls it.

The upstairs of the club is just as impressive as the lower level. But here there are two open spaces that flank the opening looking down on the dance-floor below which are occupied by couches and other equipment like a St. Andrew's Cross, Spanking Bench, and more. Behind the open play areas are beds semi-concealed by sheer curtains. Against the wall, opposite the expanse of windows looking out onto the property, are doors that Selene told me lead to different play rooms.

When I've finished taking in my fill of the space, I go to settle on a couch off to the side just as the couple I recognize from the Zoom call, Bex and Alvaro Silva, are finishing setting up their scene.

And *damn* what a scene it is to witness.

I sit there, mesmerized. Watching them together has my whole-body prickling with interest.

I'm leaning forward in my seat, watching the most beautiful women I've ever seen get flogged by a perfectly toned man with skin that glows with a godly light. The call where I first saw them did their beauty a disservice. They look exquisite together, up on the platform.

She's handcuffed to the St. Andrews' cross with her legs spread wide, his body casting a slight shadow over her face as he towers over her, even in her platform heels. Then there's him. He's standing slightly to the side of her, rubbing soft circles into her reddened ass as he tilts his face up to meet her own hazy gaze.

The man leans in to whisper something in her ear and a pang

of longing shoots through my chest at the tenderness which he bestows upon her. The woman melts into him, completely trusting of her partner, and my longing transforms into a green monster at the sight of the two.

"They're beautiful together, aren't they?" Selene's musical voice whispers from behind me.

I jump and face her.

"Alvie and Bex. They're gorgeous together," she says. Gliding around the edge of the couch, Selene comes to sit next to me. "Alvie is good with a flogger in his hand, but you should see him with a length of rope. He's an expert roper. Literally." She giggles to herself. "He's both a kinkster and a cowboy. His specialties are cow hide and rope, in both areas of his life."

I turn back to the couple, watching as the man, Alvie, helps the woman down off the cross.

"You look like you'd like to try." Selene says, bumping into me slightly with her shoulder. "What would it take to get you up on the cross?"

I look over at Selene, who has a mischievous look to her now.

"Selene. You know I could never." I whisper.

"You absolutely could." She nudges me again. "You just have to say yes."

I look back and can't ignore the curiosity that sparks in my chest when I look at the cross.

"I couldn't." I whisper. "I can't."

When the woman on the platform is free from the cross, the man stands before her, rubbing her wrists. He speaks in a low indecipherable tone before leading her to a chair nearby, settling her in and handing her a thermos of water.

Then the man turns to the room. "Would anyone like to try?"

"She would!" Selene calls out.

I look at her, bewildered. "Selene!" I hiss.

"What?" She says, incredulously. "You do! Alvie, she wants to try."

The man looks at me with a raised eyebrow. "I need to hear that directly from her, Selene."

"Oh. Naomi, meet Alvie. Alvie, this is my best friend, Naomi." Selene bounces back and forth between us but my gaze never leaves his emerald eyes.

There's something about him that makes me want to trust him, to abandon the safety of what I know and try something new. To take a risk.

The way he's looking at me, studying me, is like he's trying to catalogue every minute detail of my face and body. His eyes flick around, taking in my body, looking for a lie.

"Nice to meet you, Naomi." The way he says my name has a shiver rolling down my spine and my chest tightening.

"Hi." I breathe out.

"Have you ever topped or bottomed for this type of play before?" He asks, all businesslike.

"No." I breathe out. "Never."

"Would you like to?"

"To get up on the cross?"

"Yes." He says simply, eyes glimmering playfully in the dim lighting.

I look over to Selene at my side who's grinning like the Cheshire Cat.

"If there's anyone in the world that I would trust with my first time, it's Alvie." Selene says quietly, just for us to hear. "Go for it, cariña."

For once, Selene states her case and lets me think without interruption.

Really, I don't have anything to lose here. It's another life experience I get to have, and, worst case scenario, I don't like it? That seems pretty low stakes to me.

I look up at the silver fox who's given me his whole focus and blush. "Yes."

The man grins. "Alright then. You ready to receive your first flogging, then?"

"Yes." I confirm quickly, butterflies fluttering in my stomach. "I would like to try."

The man's green eyes look for something in me, but doesn't seem to find the hesitation he's looking for. I'm not sure if I'm grateful or disappointed at that. But he nods, holding out his hand to me to help me step up onto the podium with him.

A shock of electricity zips through me at his touch. He's so close now. He looks down at me with his jaw clenched, his whole body taut, as he searches my face.

"My partner, Bex," he says, nodding to the woman who's already rising from her chair. "She will help you get positioned."

I nod.

Alvaro's gaze holds me captivated when he looks back at me. Then I'm distracted by a warm touch on my hand, and I turn to find the woman, Bex, smiling at me

"Ready?" She asks.

"Yes," I repeat, blushing at the sight of her clad only in a rust colored harness showing off her full breast with deep rose nipples and a thin thong that wraps around her thick hips and thighs. The bright color contrasts against her tanned skin and dark hair, making her look like a goddess emerged from war.

"Come with me," she replies. "We're gonna get you fastened into the cross first."

I follow her up to the St. Andrew's Cross and let her guide my body into position. She's gentle with her touch as she fastens the cuffs hanging on the cross around my wrists, slipping a single finger under the cuff to make sure it's not too tight.

Every light brush of her fingertips on my skin and reassuring smile she gives me fans a spark in my chest. She's so careful with me, murmuring instructions and praise the whole time that she works with me. As she works, she explains how the scene is going to happen and what I can expect, giving me little tidbits of advice along the way.

"You're all set." She says sweetly. "I'm going to adjust your dress so it's not in the way, alright?"

A quick glance down at my own plump form, squeezed into an awful sausage dress that was crammed at the back of my closet makes the red flush on my cheeks spread to my chest and the tips of my ears.

"You look beautiful, dear." Bex whispers, as if she can hear my own thoughts. Then she rounds behind me to push up my dress around my waist to reveal my dimpled ass. "You're gonna do great."

"Thank you." I squeak as her fingers brush back my blonde hair that had fallen into my face.

With Bex gone, I immediately notice when a warm presence appears at my other side and I turn my head to find Alvaro inches away from me. His hand casually slides to rest lightly on my lower back and I shiver at his touch.

"Hi, Naomi." His voice is low and smooth like a perfectly tuned string bass and hearing my name on his lips has me shivering with pleasure. "So. We will go slow and I'll rotate through a couple of different instruments so you can see what you like. Each time I'll start soft, but if you want it harder, you have to ask. You want to stop, just say so. Talk to me. Understand?"

"Yes. I understand." I confirm.

"Good job." He says, the side of his mouth quirking up in a half smile. "I'm going to start with a flogger to warm you up, just like you saw me use with Bex," he says, walking behind the cross to the table before me that's laden with various tools, many of which I've never seen before.

When he's made his selection, he rounds back behind me and

runs the leather tendrils up and down my legs. The sensation shimmers through my whole body and I relax into the tingling feeling it leaves on my skin.

My whole body is buzzing in anticipation by the time the feeling of the cool leather leaves my skin, and I tense in preparation for the first hit.

"Relax." I hear Bex say from a few feet away. I follow her instructions immediately, my whole body melting at her suggestion.

"Starting with a few hits on either side." Alvaro voices clearly from behind me.

I wait for the first hit for a few seconds, but it doesn't come, and realization dawns.

Use your words, Naomi.

"Yes. Please." I tell him.

"Good job. Keep it up." He replies, and I can almost hear the smug smirk in his voice.

The first hit of the flogger startles me, but it doesn't hurt. It's more like a rippling series of dull thwacks to my ass cheeks. Alvaro is skillful at the placement of each strike, making sure not to hit the same spot in a row. Each hit comes one after the other with very little pause in between and it begins to lull me into a dream-like state.

When the hits cease, I feel Alvaro and Bex both come up close on either side of me. Alvaro's hand goes to my slightly reddened ass, and he rubs in circles where heat from his lashes builds. Bex's fingers are running through my hair, making me slump harder against the cross.

The combination of their touches is lighting my skin on fire with need and for the first time in a long time, there's a craving for something *more.*

"How was that?" Alvaro asks.

All I can manage in my blissful state is to turn to him and smile, my mind still drifting somewhere nearby.

"Do you want more? Harder? Or different?"

I think about it for a moment like I would any multiple choice question, my brow scrunching in concentration as I work through the options.

Do I want more? Yes.

Harder? Different? Also, yes.

My whole body is relaxed in a way I haven't felt in years. A contented peace wraps itself around me as I stand there cuffed to the cross, flanked on either side by a God and his Goddess.

I finally settle on my decision. "D. All of the above," I giggle at my own inside joke.

"Mmm. Adventurous girl." Alvaro hums before stepping around to the table to put down the flogger and pick out my next toy. "All of the above it is then."

Fingers continue to run through my hair, and my attention turns back to Bex who's looking at me with gorgeous hazel blue eyes.

Looking at her this closely brings out all of her unique features. I take in the smattering of sun freckles that dot the bridge of her nose and the dimples that appear when she smiles back at me. I soak in her presence and the smile she bestows upon me.

My body tries to lean into her and when my weight shifts a little too much in her direction, she catches me around the waist.

Her hands are like a brand on my skin, stoking the flame of need that's building in my body.

"You're so pretty." I giggle.

"You're quite beautiful yourself." She replies softly.

My mind is hazy and my filter is completely gone. "I would very much like to kiss you, I think."

"You think?" She smiles that smile that has me melting for her.

"Yeah. I think so."

"Well then we might need to make that happen later."

"Not now?"

"Not now." She glances over her shoulder to check in with Alvaro. "You have other matters to attend to right now."

A large palm skims it's way back to the small of my back and I know that Alvaro has returned. His presence is like a weighted blanket, grounding and comforting me.

"I'm going to give you a few more hits, Naomi." Alvaro says, his hand making small circles on my lower back the whole time. "But harder this time. Speak up if you want to stop."

"Okay." I reply cheerfully.

Bex backs away, but still keeps herself in my line of sight.

The first hit lands harder on my left cheek and my back bows in reflex. But when my body relaxes, I realize it didn't hurt. More than anything it's just the surprise of the hit.

Alvaro continues to flog me, one strike after another. As he gets into a rhythm I start to predict the kind of impact the flogger will have based on the sounds it makes. Lighter strikes come closer together. The more powerful hits have a long pause and a harsh whoosh of the air before they burn into my skin.

But I'm enjoying myself.

My eyes drift closed as Alvaro lands the last few hits on my ass and thighs. And when it stops, I let myself enjoy the contentment that fills me. I float there, in my peaceful state, for who knows how long. It feels like it could be only a second or an hour that I exist in my bliss.

Alvaro's callused hand comes to rest on my shoulder and it slowly brings me back from my wonderland.

"That's all for tonight, Naomi. You did so well." Alvaro says, undoing the cuffs around my wrists that kept me connected to the cross. "I'm going to speak with Bex briefly. Okay?"

"Yes, sir." A shocked expression overtakes his features and he guides me off the cross and to the couch to sit next to Selene again.

"Okay. Just rest for a moment." He whispers into my hair. "You did so well."

I feel Selene gather me in her arms and put a bottle of water to my lips, but I don't really process anything that's going on around me.

But, for the first time in months, I feel *good*.

5

ALVARO

I can feel an electric energy radiating off of Bex.

Bex is not looking at me as I walk toward her, and away from the couch where I left Selene's friend. Instead her attention is focused purely on the brave curvy girl she put up on my cross. If I was another guy, I might be jealous, but instead I take opportunity to admire her incredible body and profile.

Bex's curves are on full display in the leather harness I made for her. I take it in, loving how it hugs her tanned body, toned from hours of leading her outdoor yoga retreats. Her dark chestnut hair drapes over her shoulders in waves created by the french braids she typically keeps her hair in. Her plump lips are curled up in a smile that makes my heart beat fast and my cock thicken for her.

Looking at her now, with a mischievous glimmer in her golden eyes, I know she's planning something.

The girl on my cross, Naomi, has peaked my partner's interest, and I can see the fire of Bex's soul threatening to burn out of control if I don't slow its progress.

"You good?" I ask my wife when I come back to where she stands next to my equipment.

"Yeah, of course. Why wouldn't I be?" She replies breathlessly, turning back to face me.

"There's a look in your eye and I know it means trouble, Bex. Talk to me."

I know my wife, and her heart. She's quick to love, quicker to lust. Right now, I can see that flame of desire being stoked in her.

"I like her." Bex pouts.

"You just met her." I sigh. "You've barely said a handful of words to her."

"Yes, and I liked you when we met, too." She smirks.

"And we were friends for two years before anything serious happened between us."

I've been with my wife for nearly a decade. We met when she was in her early-ish twenties, me in my late thirties, and it was this same eager energy that captivated me as I got to know her. At first, I had a major issue with our age difference, but the way she approaches life so joyfully and unafraid draws you in.

We met at another club in the city—which has since closed it's doors—one night when she was there with an ex. I hated him from the beginning, but it took longer for her to realize how toxic he was for her. Over time she grew close with others in the community and eventually left him. Right after they split she came to live with me until she could get back on her feet. Eventually she moved out, but we kept in contact and continued to visit each other frequently.

"Psh. Longest years of my life." She smirks before giving me a kiss on the lips. "That wasn't my choice and you know it."

It took her those two years to wear me down before I gave in and asked her on a date, but I've never looked back since then.

She's my everything.

"You know nothing about her." I say, shaking my head.

Her little harrumph almost has me smiling, but I squash the inclination quickly. Otherwise she'll be off like a road runner.

"I know she's friends with Selene, and she's adventurous enough to join in on pickup play." She reasons. "And hot as fuck."

"And what? That means you're going to jump into bed with her?"

"I mean, kinda. Yeah."

I sigh and turn to straighten my tools, trying to think of how I can reason with her, save her from heartbreak.

But I come up empty-handed.

"There's no stopping you, is there?"

"Alvie." She sighs. "Just because it happened once, doesn't mean it's going to happen again. History doesn't repeat itself if we don't let it."

My brows furrow at the reminder of the last woman we got involved with.

"This looks like an episode on the goddamned History Channel if I've ever seen one, Bex."

It's been several years since everything happened with her, but the pain of the woman's betrayal still stings.

"You're not pulling a veto, are you?" She asks, genuine curiosity in her voice.

I sigh. "No, Bex. We don't do that. I'm just trying to get you to proceed with a little caution."

"I'll take your caution under advisement."

"Then throw it to the wind, right?"

"Yup," she says, popping the P before bouncing off in Naomi's direction.

Bex has free rein to pursue relationships outside of our marriage, but I've never had interest in pursuing other partners outside of pick-up play and demonstrations.

For me, kink is only sexual with my wife. We started as just a Dominant and submissive dynamic, but that quickly changed once I started actively pursuing a relationship with her.

However, with everyone else I play with it's purely about the artistry and skill of each type of play. There's a beauty to the way you swing a flogger or paddle and the redness that blooms under someone's skin. Binding or suspending someone with something as simple as rope is a feat of engineering that itches the part of my brain that desires to puzzle out problems. There's a connection between the physicality and almost spirituality of BDSM that feels like an extension of myself, one that I will happily engage with others in.

Which is why having Naomi up on the cross was such a surprise.

For the second time in my life, there was a small inkling of something *more* underneath the usual hum of adrenaline that a scene brings.

My hands on her body weren't there just to keep her steady and check in on her body's fatigue. There was a part of me that *desired* to touch her.

I shake off the thoughts of Naomi and focus on on the instruments on my table and the crowd of people who begin clamoring for my attention now that the cross is empty.

Time blurs as each person gets up on the cross to take the impact of one of my toys. I lose myself in the rhythm of swinging floggers, paddles, fire hoses, Hot Wheels tracks, and more with each different partner. I like to pay close attention to the bodies of anyone who gets up onto the cross with me. I want to make sure they feel comfortable and that I don't push them too far. With my experience level, it's easy for me to tell the difference between a shiver of pleasure and anticipation versus a tremor of fatigue or fear. It's easy enough that I keep finding my eyes sneaking over in between partners to where Selene and Bex are sitting on the couch with Naomi between them.

I don't know how much time goes by before I realize that fatigue has taken over and my full energies are no longer on the scene and partner before me. My focus has strayed and my energy fled after such a long time topping for others.

After letting the last person off the cross, I grab a water bottle and let the cool water rush down my throat.

A soft hand on my bicep makes me stop in my tracks.

"Baby you need to take a break." Bex says quietly. "Or stop."

I nod to her in acknowledgement and she turns to let the crowd know I'm done for the night. I begin packing away my tools, grouping them by their purpose, spraying them with a bottle of vodka water to keep them clean, and wiping them down before packing them away in their travel cubes Bex got me for my birthday. I'll condition all the leathers and hang everything up to dry properly when we get home, but this will do for now.

The ritual is grounding and helps steady my breath, but when Bex returns and speaks my heart rate picks up again.

"She's only here for the weekend." Bex says, her gaze searching for something in me that I don't have the energy to give.

"Who?" I sigh, too tired for her vague statements.

"Naomi. She said she came down for Selene's engagement party, then she's heading back home."

"You really want to pursue her, don't you?"

"Yes." She says simply.

I look over at my wife, entirely confident in herself and her feelings, and a bit of jealousy stirs in my chest at her sureness.

I can't keep her from pursing this, it wouldn't be fair of me. I definitely can't keep trying to protect her from potential heartbreak. I have to let her do this on her own.

This is her choice to make, not mine, but she's looking to me for permission and I can't keep it from her.

"Get her number, and invite her to come back for another visit then." I acquiesce.

Bex beams back at me. "Yes, sir."

She gives me a kiss on the cheek before running off to go find the girls again.

I watch her firm, round ass as she practically skips away before turning to finish packing everything up as the crowd breaks up.

I want to believe that this new interest of hers is going to be a good thing, but my naturally analytical mind is skeptical.

The universe is chaotic and unpredictable at times, but it follows patterns. I love BDSM and kinky play because you can try and control and account for some of the chaos. But sometimes you have to let things run their course.

You have to let the chaos win.

6

BEX

January 14 — Thank goodness tomorrow is a holiday

I always tell my yoga students that a large part of finding balance and inner peace is listening to our bodies and the feelings that arise in any given situation. Our intuition, or gut, know far more than society gives them credit for, but they're invaluable.

Living your life in accordance with your values is the most difficult decision a person can make. It takes a strong will and persistence to push back against the expectations that others and society place on us. It's hard work to identify the core attributes that feed our souls. Even more difficult is making these decisions each and every day.

Being your authentic self is exhausting.

Then there are people who come along who feed that part of your soul. They show up in unexpected moments, and just when you need them most. Maybe they're there momentarily and maybe they're there for a lifetime, but it's always with a purpose that contributes to your life.

We don't choose our journeys, but we are the only ones who decide which direction we're headed.

Alvie has been mine since the day he rescued me, even if he didn't realize it yet. When we first met, there was a spark between us, though I wasn't in a place to follow my intuition about him. There were a lot of gut feelings I was ignoring in those days. But then there was a time—one I wholeheartedly believe was predestined—when the domino's fell and Alvie caught me as my world tumbled around me. He was the exact person I needed then, and he continues to be to this day.

My comfort and safety, Alvie is my rock.

He's the heartbeat that matches mine perfectly.

Chemistry and attraction to a person are one thing, but I believe there are a few people in life that our souls are drawn to inevitably. They are the people who make us feel centered and whole.

Alvie has always been mine, my everything.

Now, Naomi calls to me in a similar way.

Being in the same room with both my husband and the curvy blonde who's captured my attention is like being drawn to twin suns, and I already know I'm going to get burned up in their orbit. I'm drawn to her and my heart is skipping in my chest, eager to get back to her.

Turning away from Alvie, I look over to the couch where the woman, Naomi, is leaning with her head propped up on Selene's shoulder, who's petting her hair with a tenderness which makes my heart ache for that same softness.

I grab a water bottle from the ice chest next to Alvie's table of tools and strut over to where the pair are cuddled on the couch. Lowering myself to the couch, on the other side of Naomi from Selene, I take in the gorgeous woman.

She's younger than me, with a baby face that makes me want to cradle her in my arms and protect her from the world. Her straight blonde hair falls around her angelic face, framing doe eyes that match her blue bandage dress and puffy lips that beg to be kissed. Little bundles of flowers are painted into the skin along her collar bones and as I look down her body, there are other small marks along her wrist, hands, and ankles that decorate her body.

I schooch closer to her, pressing my body toward her own full hips so we're nearly touching.

"How are you doing?" I ask her, opening the water bottle cap and passing it over.

"Hmm?" Naomi lifts her head from where it lays on Selene's shoulder.

"How are you feeling?" I repeat with a grin on my face.

She takes a breath in and out, before replying in a soft voice. "Oh. Good. I feel really good."

After her scene with Alvie, I'm not surprised to see that she's floating in her own world. A good scene can give you a high that feels like heaven, or will drop you in hell. I'm glad she's having an experience on the good end of the spectrum.

She's calmed down since her scene and her pulse is no longer thrumming like a hummingbird, but she's still clearly not fully back to herself. I'm close enough to see the sheen of sweat on her skin and I hold back the urge to lean in and lick up her cheek. Desperately, I want to taste her. I want to know what it's like to have our bodies connect and our breath mingle. I want to have her under me begging for my touch as Alvie watches on.

Her energy calls to me and I can sense by the way that she's now leaning away from Selene and into my own body that mine calls to her as well.

"That was your first time, right?" She nods sleepily. "You did really well. Alvie doesn't normally test people so much on their first go, but you took everything so beautifully."

Naomi turns to me with a beaming smile, which I return.

Her innocence is adorable. I want to wrap her up and hold her tight, then unfold her on my bed and devour her bite by bite, scream by scream.

"This is your first time at a club too, right?" I take a risk and slide my hand onto her thigh.

Nature may call people together, but the threat of rejection is ever present. Every person gets to make their own decisions about their time and energy and I desperately hope that she chooses to give me some of hers in return, to choose me.

Naomi glances down to where my hand now rests, but when she looks up, the rejection I was afraid of isn't there.

"Yeah." She breathes out. "I've heard plenty of stories about the club and always wanted to come, but never made it down here. School has just kept me too busy. But I'm glad Selene gave me a reason to come."

"What about Selene?" The woman in question pipes up, leaning around Naomi so I can see her clearly.

"You've always wanted me to come down to visit." Naomi's hand slides down her thigh, closer to my own, as she turns to face her friend.

Taking a risk, I reach out and take her hand, hoping desperately that she won't pull away from the affection, and my shoulders relax when her fingers twine between my own in return.

Her open affection makes my heart warm and my smile grow.

Selene scoffs. "Yeah, but you always had school, or an internship or something. Honestly, I'm surprised that you came this time."

"I wouldn't have missed this for the world, Selene." Naomi says, her head going back to Selene's shoulder to rest.

"What do you think so far?" I ask.

"Great. It's been great. I'm really enjoying myself so far. Everything is so..."

Her brain is clearly offline and I can't help the chuckle that comes out at her bumbling.

"I've been telling you!" Selene says with a little back handed slap to Naomi's side.

"I know. I know." Naomi's giggle is like trilling bells. "And it's just as magical and kinky as you said it would be."

"I'm a little surprised that you got up there though." Selene giggles.

"You made me do it!" Naomi gawks.

"Nobody makes you do anything, cariña." Selene quips back, which earns her a huff of annoyance from Naomi.

"So what made you do it?" I ask, genuinely curious as to what prompted her to go so far out of her comfort zone. "You're a student, right? What made you go from books to BDSM?"

"Excellent question, Bex." Selene laughs as she gets up from the couch when she spots Gunnar. "Y'all have fun. I see a viking that needs attention."

Both Naomi and I laugh at Selene's antics, the sounds blending together like the perfect melody. Our gazes connect and the room slips away. Thoughts flash through Naomi's eyes, but I don't know her well enough to understand what they mean.

"So?" I prompt.

"I think..." She pauses. "I think I just needed to get out of my head. I've always heard from Selene about the benefits of participating in kink, and a part of me has always been curious. So, like, why not?"

She says it like she's still questioning her own choices and a part of me empathizes with the rollercoaster of emotions that she's going through.

"It's definitely a way to get out of your head, for sure. That's part of what brought me and Alvie together."

"Oh?"

"Yeah, I don't know if anyone has studied it or not," I shrug.

"But I firmly believe that there are mental health benefits to kink and BDSM."

"Oh?" She says, perking up a bit.

"Absolutely. I've been to my fair share of therapy, and there's so much about the kinky world that relies on incredible communication and interpersonal skills between all consenting parties. Not to mention the mindfulness and emotional regulating required for so many different kinds of play." I blush. "Sorry. I don't mean to ramble."

"No. Don't worry about it. I'm actually studying Psychology in school. So this is super interesting to me." The way her blue eyes sparkle in the dim lighting has me believing her wholeheartedly. "Selene was telling me earlier that there's another therapist who comes to the club?"

"Yeah. Durante. He's great. His partners too." I look around for the trio in question. "I don't think they made it tonight, but I'm sure you'll meet them eventually."

"I hope so." She smiles.

"Means you're going to have to come back though." I smirk.

"Guess so." She says, blushing bright pink before yawning.

"Here." I tug her hand lightly toward me and she falls easily into my shoulder to rest. "Close your eyes and rest for a bit. Someone will grab us whenever things get exciting again."

Within seconds, Naomi's eyes have closes and her breathing evens out. Out of the corner of my eye I spot Alvie leaving the space with his bag of goodies.

He returns my smile with his own when I look at him and gives me a wink before heading downstairs.

People start to filter out of the open play area, either heading into the private playrooms or back downstairs to the main area of the club, now that the excitement of pick-up play is over.

I curl myself around Naomi, and we sit like that, in comfortable silence, for what only feels like minutes. I don't even notice myself drift off, but when I open my eyes the room has cleared out completely and it's only us curled up on the couch that are left in the room.

Footsteps coming up the stairs alert me to someone joining us and when Alvie's head peeks over the top step, I smile.

He takes the few steps to stand before the couch where we lay and looks down at both Naomi and me with a softness in his expression that has my heart warming.

"We're doing toasts." He says just loud enough for me to hear him over the music coming from the DJ booth downstairs.

He gives me a kiss on my cheek before turning to go back downstairs and I nudge Naomi to get her to wake.

"Naomi. Wake up." I say quietly.

She groans in a way telling me she's not someone who wakes easily.

"It's Selene." Naomi shoots up at her friends name.

"Shit." She gasps, trying to balance herself where she sits. Automatically my hands go to her shoulders to steady her. "Shit. Did we miss it?"

"I don't think so." I say, trying to calm her. "But we should get moving just in case."

I stand, slipping my feet into the slippers Alvie left me in exchange for my heels, and help her rise up as well.

Still a little sleepy, Naomi sways on her feet and I take her by the hand to steady her, which draws out a sweet smile from her. Walking hand in hand down the stairs back to the private party section with all of our friends, we return to smiling faces and glasses of champagne being shoved in our free hands.

Much to my disappointment, Naomi detaches herself from me without a backward glance at the sight of her glowing best friend and slips her way through the crowd to celebrate with Selene and Gunnar.

Alcohol flows freely for the rest of the night as we all celebrate together, everyone raising their glasses each time one of us drunk-enly shouts for another toast to the happy couple.

When "Closing Time" by Semisonic plays, everyone starts packing up their stuff to leave. People start filtering out of the club, and I see Naomi, passed out on one of the couches. I look over to Gunnar who has his arm wrapped around Selene, who's also struggling to stand on her own.

He looks over at me, worry in his gaze when he looks back at Naomi. "Can you help me with her?"

"Of course." I say, standing quickly and making my way over to where the trio were sitting.

"Her bag is the teal one." He grunts out over the music. "Her room key should be in the side pocket with her ID."

"I can get her back to her room. Don't worry." I say, pulling her keycard out only to be surprised that her villa is right across from our own. "She's actually right by us."

"You're sure?" He asks.

"Of course." I reassure him.

"Alright. Night, Bex. Night, Alvie." Gunnar says as he walks away, Selene and bags in tow.

I look back at a sleeping Naomi and giggle to myself.

"I think we tuckered her out, Alvie." I joke, turning to my husband who's laden with our own bags.

He hands me a t-shirt and shorts, which I slip on to cover up the gorgeous body harness he made for me.

"I've got everything for us. Want me to carry her bag too?" He asks.

"Nah. I've got her and her stuff. I think her villa is right before ours. So we can walk together."

He nods.

Approaching the sleeping beauty, I admire how peaceful she looks as she sleeps.

I give her a gentle nudge on the shoulder, hating that I have to disturb her for a second time tonight.

"Naomi."

"Huh?"

"Time to go home." I say quietly, just as the music cuts out and lights come on throughout the club.

She lets out another annoyed groan before forcing her eyes open and squinting just as her eyes take in the bright lights of the club.

"Sorry. I'm not used to being out so late. Or drinking so much." She yawns.

"That's alright." I soothe. "Do you have a sweater or anything you want to slip on over your dress?"

She nods and I go over to her bag to find the garment.

When we have her fully dressed and finish changing her into flats—Cinderella style—I pull her up to stand from the couch.

It's like everything around us fades away as her body crashes into mine. Her form is soft against my own and I get lost in the warm feeling that spreads through me, having her so close.

"Are you sober enough for me to kiss you?" I murmur.

"What?" Her eyes widen, clarity and alertness returning to her gaze.

"Can I kiss you, Naomi."

Her breathing quickens and I lean in, barely a breath away from brushing her lips with my own. "Because I would very much like to kiss you right now."

"You do?" She asks, surprise lighting up her face.

"Yes. I do." I nod, lips brushing so close to her own.

"Well, when you ask so nicely." She smiles.

"I need to hear you use your words, Naomi." I purr. "Do you. Want me. To kiss you."

"Yes. Please. Please kiss me, Bex." She begs.

Hungrily my lips collide with her own. I take her mouth

eagerly, pouring every ounce of need into the connection between us.

She melts under my touch, and I wrap my arms around her waist to keep her from slumping into the floor. Her hands come up to my shoulders and she steadies on her feet, allowing me to caress the rises and dips of her body as my hands move up her soft form.

Reaching up, I cup her face between my hands and pull her into me further. Our kiss turns hot and hungry for each other as my tongue pushes into her mouth. She opens wide for me and her head slants back just enough for me to fully devour her.

She tastes of vodka and cranberry juice, but it taste like heaven right now. I breathe her in as we kiss, clamoring for more of each other with each brush of our lips, and gnashing of our teeth. My hands snake up to the base of her skull and into her hair, where I grip from the base of her locks and pull back, hard.

She lets out a groan that has me moaning in return.

"Alright love birds. Save that passion for the play rooms." A voice calls out.

I pull away from Naomi, a frown on my face, and spot Ivy smirking from the entryway to the party area.

"Us girls can't leave until y'all are all gone, Bex. You know better." She chuckles, turning on her heel.

I look back at Naomi, who's eyes are still glazed over with lust, before darting my gaze over to Alvie, who's been waiting patiently for us.

His eyes are soft and a smile graces his lips, bringing me a comfort I didn't know I needed.

"Where's your phone?" I ask Naomi as I lean down and grab her bag.

"Front pocket." She says, breathlessly.

My heart soars at the sound, knowing that I made her this way. That her blissed out expression is my doing.

I use her Face ID to open up her phone and quickly add my

contact as I sling her bag over my shoulder and take her by the hand. When I have everything saved into her phone, I call myself and then put her phone back in the pocket where I found it.

I give her hand a squeeze and we follow Alvie out of the club and into the lobby.

"Do you know when you might come back for a visit?" I ask as we walk under the chandeliers.

"I'm not sure. I was just here for the party, but..." She's chewing on her lower lip and I want nothing more than to kiss her again to make her stop, but Alvie glances back at us just at that moment and I keep moving forward and out the front doors of the club.

"But now you want to come again?" I say with a wink as we head through the door Alvie holds open for us.

"I mean, yeah." She shrugs, looking a little sheepish. "This has been a lot of fun."

"I'm glad you enjoyed yourself." I smile.

We walk through the property hand in hand toward the villas in silence, Alvie only a few steps behind us.

When we reach the door to her villa, she takes the room key from me and unlocks the door. Turning back to me, she reaches out for her bag and I hand it over slowly, trying to drag out my last moment with her before we part.

She leans inside the villa and sets down the bag just inside the door before turning back to face me again, just as reluctant to let the night end as I am.

"Let me know when you're back at school." I say, stepping in close to her and backing her up against the door frame. "And when you're coming home."

I kiss her again softly before turning to leave.

When I glance back, her fingers are lightly pressing into her lips and I swear there are stars in her eyes.

7

______

NAOMI

Before I fell asleep in my bed, I did remember to choke down some ibuprofen along with two full glasses of water before tucking myself into bed, surrounded by a pile of blankets and pillows. I slept better than I have in years though, my entire body relaxed in a way it has never experienced before. Even waking up, there was no hangover or lingering tiredness from the late night out.

But the morning after her engagement party, I woke up to the sound of Selene pounding on my door. I was then immediately dragged out of my room to get brunch with her and others who were still at the resort.

Much to my disappointment, Bex was not in attendance.

The rest of the day Sunday, we spent lounging by the pool, reading and tanning, or avoiding all sunlight in my case.

Monday came too quickly and now, driving back to school and away from the club, my heart is aching.

The country music blasting through my speakers really isn't helping my mood, but I can't bring myself to turn off the sad melodies. My mind is fixated on the events of Saturday night, me on the cross, meeting Bex and Alvie, and the kiss which had me floating on cloud nine.

Now, trapped in my head with road before me that seems to go on forever, I can't stop my thoughts from straying back to her.

In desperate need of a distraction, I command my phone to call Selene.

"Miss me already?" She says after she picks up on the second ring.

"You know it." I reply, glad she can't see the smile that's snuck onto my face.

"How much longer do you have on the road?" She asks.

I glance down at my dashboard navigation. "Maps says about two hours."

"Damn. You made it longer than I was guessing."

I hear Gunnar's voice in the background, "You owe me twenty."

"Oh hush, you viking. I'm talking to my bestie." She snaps before mellowing out. "What's up?"

"Nothin' much. Just driving and got bored." I shrug, despite her not being able to see me.

"And in your head a little?"

She knows me far too well.

I never told her about how my night ended, which in itself feels wrong, but for now it feels like something I need to keep to myself.

"Maybe a little." I say, my voice trailing off as my thoughts once again stray to the memory of Bex's lips pressing against my own, her hands wrapped possessively in my hair.

"In which case, I'm going to talk your ear off for the next few hours about wedding plans and events." She chirps.

I laugh, fully able to imagine her bouncing around the house she shares with her fiancé as we chat.

"Oh, you laugh now, but I'm going to be a nightmare by the end of this, and you're all going to hate me."

"I could never hate you, Selene."

I love how easy it is to smile with her. There's a reason she's my best friend. She's one of the few people who can lighten my mood, no matter how upset or annoyed I may be.

"Riiight." She says, drawing out the vowel. "First order of business. When's your next school break?"

"Presidents' Day I think." I say.

"Perfect. I'll have decided a date by then and I can show you all the vision boards." She pauses. "You have Spring Break off, right?"

"Yeah, it's..." I reply, pulling up my mental calendar.

"March 11 - 15." She giggles. "I have the University's academic calendar pulled up. Which is perfect because then we can go dress shopping while you're here and still make it to the rodeo at some point."

I shake my head in confusion. "The rodeo? Since when do you go to the rodeo?"

"Since always. It's like a requirement of being a Houstonian. Attendance is practically mandatory."

I sigh, knowing that a rodeo is in my future now, whether I like it or not.

"Please." Selene whines and I can picture her batting her long dark eyelashes at me. "We can get the girls together and get drunk watching hot cowboys and cowgirls compete. Maybe Alvie can get us into the competitor suite."

"Wait. What? Why?" I shake my head in confusion. "How?"

"He's like super important or something in that world. And why wouldn't you want to hang out with hot cowgirls? Or boys, I guess." She says this almost accusatorially.

"Alright then. Does this mean I need to get like a denim skirt or something? Cowboy boots?" I ask, giving in to the path of least resistance.

"Probably." She says, her shrug coming through the speakers

in my car. "Just scoot on over to Highland Park and pick up a pair at Miron Crosby."

My jaw drops. "Selene! Those are like a thousand dollars at *least*. I don't have that kind of money."

Selene and I are definitely in different places in our lives, financially. She's an executive at a tech company and I'm a poor PhD student. Which is normally fine, and even fun sometimes when she surprises me by shipping me luxuries I can't afford on my own.

"Fine." She huffs. "I'll have Gunnar bring me up and I'll buy us both a pair then."

"Selene, weren't we just making wedding plans? Don't you need to save for that?"

"It's fine. I don't need a budget. Gunnar doesn't let me spend any of my own money when we're together. So I'm using my salary to pay for the wedding. I'll just get a white pair while I'm there and we can say it's part of the wedding budget."

"You're a mess." I laugh.

"No. I'm chaos. There's a difference." A deep chuckle comes through underneath her bright voice.

We spend the next two hours going through plans and ideas for the wedding and various other celebrations, everything from color palettes and invitations to cake, music, and venue options.

We hang up as I'm pulling up to my apartment, and just as I park in my normal spot, a notification comes through my dash.

New message from Bex Silva.

A smile spreads over my face at the notification and I quickly swipe to open my messages.

BEX

Get home safe yet?

NAOMI

That was spooky! I just pulled into my garage.
How'd you know?

BEX

Lucky guess it seems!

How was the drive?

NAOMI

Long... but I made it. I'm gonna unpack and then
take a well-deserved nap.

BEX

We really wore you out this weekend, didn't we?

NAOMI

You really did. It's been a while since I've partied
like that. Y'all go hard. :rofl emoji

BEX

We enjoy a good time. No shame in it.

NAOMI

Not at all. If anything, I feel like I need more
weekends like this. I've never slept as well as I did
this weekend.

BEX

Oooh. You had the good kind of sub drop
Saturday, didn't you?

NAOMI

Maybe? I don't actually know what that means.

BEX

It's like when you drop on a roller coaster, you're
up high in the moment during a scene, and then
you come crashing down. Sometimes it's a good
thing like sleeping really soundly, but it can also
be scary if it's the bad kind.

NAOMI

Well I guess I'll just have to avoid the bad kind then.

BEX

It's not an if, but more of a when situation. You'll eventually run into it the more you play and it's just about knowing what you need in those moments.

Do you mind if I add you to a group chat with Alvaro? He's worried now.

NAOMI

Sure!

Bex Silva started a group chat with Alvaro Silva and Naomi Hall.

BEX

Group chat assemble!

ALVARO

Naomi, Bex said you went through sub drop alone last night.

NAOMI

I guess? I just learned what that is.

ALVARO

Are you okay?

NAOMI

I'm good! I feel great actually.

ALVARO

You're sure. I didn't take anything too far?

NAOMI

Really, I'm good.

BEX

Alvie she said she's good. Believe her.

ALVARO

Fine. Know that you never have to do that alone, though. Call someone next time.

NAOMI

Thank you. I'll keep that in mind.

I chuckle at how concerned he sounds. We barely spoke a handful of words between us, but here he is fussing after me like a single dad at his daughters first dance recital.

Bex Silva renamed the group "Bisexual Baddies... Plus Alvie"

BEX

Much better.

NAOMI

😏 I get the first part... why "Plus Alvie"?

ALVARO

I'm not bisexual.

NAOMI

Oh. That makes sense.

ALVARO

I am on the autistic spectrum though.

NAOMI

Good to know, I guess?

BEX

Let me translate.... "I prefer straightforward communication, rules, and boundaries and have difficulties at times understanding others. I'm giving you this information (albeit poorly) so that you have a full understanding of where I'm coming from. My wife likes you (a lot) and I would like to form a relationship with you of some kind as well."

ALVARO

Yes. All of that.

BEX

I'll also warn you that he has a weird sense of humor. Somewhere between dark and morbid and like... dad jokes.

That's what I get for marrying someone over a decade older than me.

NAOMI

haha Can I ask how old y'all are?

ALVARO

45 and 33. How old are you?

BEX

Alvie! It's rude to ask a lady her age.

ALVARO

She just!

BEX

haha

NAOMI

It's okay. I did ask. I'm 25. haha

BEX

Oh man... I could hear that groan from across the house :laughing emoji

NAOMI

What?

BEX

Alvie's gonna have a momentary crisis about how young you are. He did it with me too.

ALVARO

I'm practically a cradle robber.

NAOMI

At least you're not a grave robber.

ALVARO

You're sure of that? You don't know what I do in my free time.

NAOMI

I'm starting to see a bit of this humor you're talking about @Bex. I like it :rofl emoji

Okay. I need to unload the car, unpack, shower and nap. haha I'll talk to y'all later.

BEX

Naps! My favorite. Have fun!

ALVARO

Have a good nap.

NAOMI

Thanks!

Quickly I switch to my messages with Selene.

MINDFUCKMASTER

Thank you so much for dragging me out this weekend. I think it was really good for me.

OVERTHEMOON

I'm so glad!!! All the more reason for you to come back. :kissy face

I put away my phone with a huge smile on my face that doesn't go away for the rest of the evening. My heart feels full as I go through my evening preparing for my return to my normal life tomorrow.

It feels so weird to think of it that way.

I had such a life altering weekend, that returning to school and classes feels like the part of my life that's out of place, not the other way around. It's like this weekend marked a new era of my life and now there's no turning back.

The people I met and experiences I had at The Playground have altered my core being.

But it's leaving me feeling hopeful. Like things are going to get better.

The world is bright and things are *good*.

January 16 — Second week of the semester

Things are absolutely not good and I'm genuinely contemplating murder right now as I sit in my advisors office.

I thought this past weekend was a turning point for me, which was obviously a lie, because returning to school was like being doused in a bucket of ice cold water.

Dr. Edwards' office is stuffy and smells like mildew, a scent which clings to the man himself as well. He's an older white man, who looks and sounds like a dying walrus.

I'd rather be anywhere else than sitting here listening to him reject yet another handful of dissertation topics I'm proposing. Because it's never just a simple "no." It's always more.

"I expect better from you, Ms. Hall." The old man scolds. "Our students are held to a high standard and expected to exceed expectations in this program, not merely get by. Right now you're not even doing that."

"I don't understand." I say, holding back all of my sassy rebuttals that come to mind.

"This is the fourth round of proposals you've brought me, none of which are anything remotely worthy of research, nor writing a full dissertation on." He sighs, disappointment and condemnation dripping in his voice. "Time and time again, you present me with topics that are closer to satire than scholarly." A cruel look overtakes his face. "At this rate, your standing in the program could very likely be in jeopardy."

I know his remarks are nothing personal, if anything they're fueled by his blatant misogynistic attitudes toward women in the field, but nonetheless, the comments sting.

I have no problem with hard work, and I'm more than qualified to be pursuing this path. I've earned my position here and know that I'm worthy of my place in the program.

It's him who's my biggest problem right now.

"What would you advise then?" I ask through gritted teeth.

"I would suggest you take this seriously and find a topic that's truly worthy of study. Something I can confidently put my support behind. None of this nonsense about treating minority groups, or, god forbid, updating practices and procedures to accommodate degenerates."

Tell me what you really think now.

I knew I was taking a risk with these proposals. I had been thinking about studying the first topic, treatment and specific needs of minorities, for a while. Then this past weekend inspired me to think further about how therapists interact with patients who live alternative lifestyles outside of societal norms such as the expectation of monogamy within romantic and intimate relationships. I shudder to think of how this man would react to the mention of BDSM or kink in relation to therapy.

To someone like him, the idea that there could be inherent flaws in how we train therapists is somehow an attack on him and not the field at large. He believes that his specific methods of treatment are the *right* way, which makes everything outside of his experience and expertise *wrong*, just like the patients I'm interested in working with.

His message comes across loud and clear.

Being different is a moral failing by his standards.

And I'm wrong for thinking otherwise.

His grating voice brings me back from my thoughts. "When you have a serious proposal for me, you may return. Until then, leave."

The dismissal is a blessing, and I don't feel like I can finally breathe again until the second that I've escaped his claustrophobic office.

Another painful meeting with my advisor and I'm no closer to figuring anything out than I was last semester. I'm trying to contain my frustration, but it's not working very well.

I leave the building that houses the offices for professors in the social sciences and start my journey across campus.

The University campus is gorgeous with lush landscaping and beautiful Greco-Roman buildings, but none of it really registers as I navigate my way to the parking garage where I left my car.

When I get to my car, I toss my bag onto the passenger side and collapse into the drivers seat. Only when I'm locked safely in the confines of my vehicle do I let the tears fall.

I'm exhausted, too tired for all of this bullshit that comes at me day in and day out.

Those thoughts and feelings of wanting everything to stop

have been creeping back into my mind lately, and I can't fight them any longer. The fear of what I must face next to get through the day is overwhelming and I'm finding myself craving the empty space in my mind where I cease to exist more and more.

Silent tears turn into sobbing breaths until I'm gasping for air.

Everything feels wrong and I'm wrong for thinking there's any value in thinking otherwise.

Once more, it's the ding of my phone with a message notification that snaps me out of my spiraling thoughts.

I take a few deep breaths to calm myself and wipe away the tears that have streaked my face.

BEX

@Naomi, what are you up to tonight? Alvie is abandoning me.

ALVIE

I've told you at least 10 times. I'm going to a meeting.

BEX

See? Abandoning me.

NAOMI

I was supposed to go to the library tonight to start researching my dissertation project. But my advisor shot down all my proposals.

BEX

What? How? It's your project, right?

NAOMI

Yeah. But he has to sign off on everything.

BEX

That's bullshit. I'm sorry.

NAOMI

It is what it is. :upside-down smiley face emoji

But I'm going back to the drawing board.

BEX

Boo. That's no fun.

Just skip that and come hang out with me. You deserve a break.

NAOMI

😂 Totally, I'll be there in like four hours.

BEX

Coming from Dallas? More like 5. We're down in Victoria.

NAOMI

So much more convenient. 😂

BEX

Seriously. Keep me company tonight? Otherwise I'll be all alone. :sobbing emoji

NAOMI

Poor baby. I guess I have to then.

BEX

Perfect. Order food in and we will have a date night since I'm single now.

ALVIE

Don't you dare start, Bex.

BEX

Love you! Have a good meeting. 😘

@Naomi Let me know when you get home and we can hop on FaceTime for our date.

I'm grinning the whole way home, excited for my *date* with Bex tonight.

I go through my routine of checking in with Selene and seeing what chaos she's left in my Discord inbox before hopping in the shower to rinse off the day. Letting myself relax into the pattern of my hair and skincare routine, I slowly start to relax.

When I'm out of the shower, I've checked my messages with Selene once more to find her ranting about how expensive flowers are and whether or not she should have a full band or DJ for the reception.

There's also a message directly from Bex.

> **BEX**
> I'm making pad Thai. What are you ordering for dinner?

> **NAOMI**
> I'll probably just heat up something from the freezer. My stipend doesn't cover eating out much.

Bex Silva sent a payment to your Venmo.

> **NAOMI**
> Bex! You can't do that!

> **BEX**
> I can and I did. Order yourself a treat, Naomi.

> **NAOMI**
> Fine, I'll join you in a Thai food binge.

> **BEX**
> Call whenever, I'm just in the kitchen.

Nerves ball up in my chest. I shouldn't be nervous to spend time with her, but there's something about Bex's sheer confidence that intimidates me a little.

My phone starts ringing before I can build up the courage to press call.

"Hey!" Bex chirps happily when I pick up the phone.

"Hey." I reply, grateful she can't see my goofy smile.

"I could hear you staring at your phone, so I just called." She smirks, setting her phone down so I can see her over the stovetop.

"Sorry."

"No need to apologize." She says, waiving my apology off. "Did you order your dinner?"

"Not yet."

"Do that." She commands.

"Yes ma'am."

She hums in appreciation. "I could get use to that."

The playfulness in her tone makes me giggle and I'm grateful for the reprieve from my terrible day.

There's a comfortable silence between us as I place my dinner order, grab a glass for wine, and settle in on the couch to wait for my food.

"All done?" Bex asks as I set my phone in the holder.

"Yup. Says it will be here in 30 minutes." I reply.

Everything goes silent, but it's not quite comfortable like it was moments ago. This version of quiet is tense somehow, and like neither of us know's what to do next.

"You okay? You sounded off earlier."

"Just a rough day. My advisor is putting a lot of pressure on me to pick a topic for my dissertation, but keeps shooting down everything I suggest." I sigh, letting my head drop to the back of the couch so I'm staring at the popcorn ceiling of my living room.

"Want to talk about it?" She asks carefully.

"Not really? Maybe?" I sigh. "I just... I want to do something meaningful, but I don't know what."

"Tell me what's going on." She says, her voice soothing some of my nerves that have been fraying all day.

I met this woman three days ago. I shouldn't feel this comfortable opening up to her about everything going on in my life, all of my anxieties and fears. Yet, our conversation flows so naturally which makes this kind of vulnerability possible with her.

I talk for the full thirty-ish minutes it takes for my food to arrive, her only responses being small noises of encouragement, empathy, and agreement. By the time I'm opening up my front door to grab my food, I'm feeling lighter having unloaded some of my stress.

"Sorry for dumping all that on you." I sigh to Bex as I unpack the bag of food. "I know that was a lot of shit you probably don't care about."

"Not at all, sweetheart." Bex coos. "It sounds like you needed this."

"Yeah, I think I did." I pause. "Thank you, Bex."

"No problem." She says. "Now, what are we binging tonight?"

I laugh at the shift in her energy and settle into the couch to scarf down my food. We pick a movie to watch on a streaming platform we both have and count down to press play at the same time.

"One."

"Two."

"Three."

8

BEX

Living on a ranch in the country means a lot of my closest relationships are long distance, so things like FaceTime dates are nothing new for me. It's sometimes the only way I'm able to stay connected to my friends when life gets busy. So, I've had plenty of practice timing the start of shows and movies so they start at the exact same moment as my friends, and that's what this feels like.

I didn't mean to call it a date when I asked Naomi to hang out with me tonight. But sitting here with her on the other end of the phone, curled up on the couch in my comfiest pajamas, feels just like the easy comfort I always feel when I'm hanging out with friends.

The movie Naomi picked is a classic I've seen a thousand times about a waitress who's planning to leave her sack-of-shit husband. As she gets closer to following through on her plans, though, she finds out she's pregnant and ends up starting an affair with the new doctor she sees for her condition who's just moved to town.

"Ugh. I hate characters like this. They always remind me of my ex." I say as the husband comes on the screen.

"Oh?" Naomi says through a mouthful of pad Thai.

I put down my own food and turn my attention to the blonde on my screen.

"Yeah. The guy I was with before Alvie was a lot like this guy, a controlling dick who didn't like me having any kind of autonomy or independence."

Naomi stays quiet, but her own focus is now on me as well instead of the movie playing in the background. Part of me hesitates to share so much of myself with a new friend so soon, but I've never lived life half-way and I don't plan on starting now.

I take a deep breath, bracing myself for the possible feelings that tend to arise when I talk about my ex.

"For a long time I thought the attention he paid me was how he showed his love for me. That his involvement in my life was showing me his how he cared." I shake my head, letting it fall down to my chest. "It took me far too long to see how toxic it really was."

It's like a switch flips in Naomi's head as I drag my gaze up to meet her own displayed on my screen. There's empathy in her expression, but something about it feels almost too observant.

"I'm sorry." She says slowly when I don't keep talking. "It can be really hard to see the truth of your present circumstances when you're going through difficult things like that though."

Her words, while true and comforting to an extent, feel almost clinical. Something about the word choice is so particular and calculated. It's as though she's operating based on a script.

"Yeah. Tyler was actually the first person to bring me to a club in the city, before The Playground was even around, and he also introduce me to kink. I think for him, he wanted to show me off as someone that he owned and controlled. He wanted others to see the power he held over me and I let him." I ignore the tickle at the base of my skull, opting to forge ahead instead. "It was actually Alvie and a few of the others in our group who helped me get out of that relationship."

"Really?" Naomi asks.

I nod. "Tyler took it too far one night with an impact scene on the cross and I got hurt. Others in our friend group stepped in and got me help. They moved me out of his place within 24 hours. It was actually Alvie who took me in when I had no place to go."

"That's so sweet of him." Naomi says with a sweet smile gracing her lips.

"Yeah, it really was. He helped me find a therapist and I was able to talk through a lot of different issues that had built up over the course of my relationship with Tyler."

"Did it help?'

I sigh. "It did for a bit, but as I processed more of my trauma and memories of the relationship things got worse for a while."

"What do you mean?" She asks, her head tilting in confusion.

"Tyler was never physically abusive, until the very end. He left a lot of scars, though, which led to PTSD. A few weeks into seeing my therapist I started having panic attacks and nightmares. That's actually how I got involved with Alvie at first.

"There was one night when I woke up after a nightmare, and he found me in the kitchen. He didn't say a word until I was ready to talk. The whole thing was so sweet and I fell apart in front of him. The man has the patience of a saint though. He asked me what I was doing to help with the nightmares and the anxiety attacks but honestly I didn't have a solution at that time."

"How did that lead you to getting involved with Alvaro then?" She asks.

"We started doing kink scenes together and he started to teach me the ropes, literally." Thinking back to those early days with Alvie makes me smile. "It started off with small things like doing breathing exercises while he practiced rope cuffs on me, and it turned into experimenting with things like body, harnesses, and suspension and all sorts of different things."

"Did it help?"

"Yeah." I smile. "The more we played, the more practice I got in just kind of letting go in the moment. It's really taught me to focus on my body and my breathing. It's almost like meditation at this point for me."

"So have y'all just been together since then?" Naomi questions, looking adorable as she listens to me on the other side of the phone.

"No. A few months after I moved in with Alvie I had saved up enough and I got my own place in the city, but we would still meet up every weekend at the club. I think for him it was a purely kink relationship at first, but I fell for him quickly. He's just such a good human, you know?"

She nods and continues to listen to me ramble on about Alvie and I's relationship history and a lot about our dynamic. All the while she absorbs everything like a sponge that's perpetually dry.

We talked through most of the movie about anything and everything. Past relationships, her schooling, my yoga practice, and so much more.

Hearing about how stressful school is for her, I promise to start sending her photos of the horses and other animals on the farm. Especially when she's having a hard day and needs to see something cute.

Eventually lights flash through the windows from Alvaro's truck and I look at the clock, realizing how late it is.

"Alvie just got home. Do you want to say hi?" I ask her, looking up to find the movie ended long ago.

"Yeah, that would be great." She says quietly.

Alvie comes in through the back door, takes off his cowboy hat and comes over to where I sit on the couch to give me a kiss on the forehead.

"How was your date?" He asks. "Are you leaving me for her yet? Should I rent you a trailer and start packing for your move?"

"Still going on." I chuckle. "Say hi to Naomi, Alvie."

Alvie's eyes grow wide, but he dutifully comes around the couch to face Naomi who sits in my screen.

"Hello, Naomi."

"Oh don't be so formal, Alvie. Silly man." I laugh under my breath.

"I'm just being polite." He blushes under his deep tan.

"Hi, Alvaro. How was your meeting?" Naomi asks.

"Brutal. A bunch of rich white men sitting in a circle stroking their own egos." He groans. "If I didn't love the sport so much, I'd leave and never turn back."

"What is it you do?" Naomi asks curiously.

Alvie settles in beside me, pulling my body so it's flush with his own. "I'm on the board of directors for the rodeo and one of the judges for the livestock show. We had a board meeting tonight since we're only a little over two months out."

"That's so cool. How did you get involved in that?"

"Oh, Alvie's a tried-and-true cowboy. He is a champion tie-down roper and has won all sorts of competitions." I say, gushing over my partner and his accomplishments.

Naomi's light laughter filters through the phone. "I have no idea what that means, but it sounds like you enjoyed it?"

"I loved it." A softness takes over Alvie's face. "Still do. It's the only reason I put up with those fools."

An idea forms, and my body vibrates with excitement. "You should come down for the rodeo and see it for yourself! We can show you the livestock show and watch the rodeo events."

"Selene actually had the same idea." She giggles. "She want's me to come down for my next three-day weekend so I can see her vision boards. Then I guess I'm coming down for my spring break, and we're doing the whole rodeo thing after we go dress shopping."

"Wait. When are you coming down next?"

"Presidents' day weekend." She answers with a yawn.

"You should come out to visit us. Or better yet, stay with us!"

Energy surges through my body as the excitement and anticipation of seeing Naomi in person settles in my bones.

"I'll talk with Selene and see what her plans are," she says. "But I'd love to see y'all."

"Then it's settled. You're coming to visit and we'll show you the ranch."

Naomi lets out another yawn and I know it's time for us to end the call, the *date*.

We say our goodbyes and then I sit there with Alvie in silence.

He lets out a little cough. "Uhaul."

"Stahp." I groan, giving him a little thwack on his arm with the back of my hand.

"You know I'm right." He chuckles.

He might be, but it's really too early to tell.

I know myself well enough to know I burn through emotions and interests quickly. I like Naomi, and I want to get to know her better, but I don't want to go too fast.

Alvie gave me his warning at the club and, despite my protests indicating otherwise, I do value his input.

I feel like I'm being pulled in two separate directions. One advises caution and the other urges me to steamroll ahead.

Only, I don't know which to listen to.

February — Sometime between classes

Texting with Naomi is nonstop. I can't help how my heart flutters each time that I get a notification from her. We talk as often as we can. I send her pictures of the horses I train for my therapy program and other animals around the ranch.

I think school is taking more of a toll on her than even she realizes. Every time we talk on the phone and I hear her voice for the first time, I can hear the relief in her sigh as the call connects.

When I ask her for updates on school. Only she brushes me off. I know she's stressed and frustrated, but she's not willing to talk about it much. There's a part of me that admires her independence and how it's pushed her to accomplish everything she has, but I have to grit my teeth whenever I hear a tremor in her voice because of that same independent streak.

Alvie is really only involved in our group text, but he likes to leave me to my own devices when it comes to our calls.

Or he did.

Recently, I've found him lurking in the background when I'm on the phone with Naomi. I'll be in the living room and find him in the kitchen, listening in as I talk with her and he's chuckling at our banter.

We talk about everything, well almost everything. Sometimes it feels like I'm being too open in contrast to her, sharing about some of my past trauma and how it's impacted my life and journey as a yoga instructor.

I started running retreats from the ranch around six years ago and it's grown enormously. We host yoga and meditation instructors from all around the world for both teaching and personal practice retreats. A few years ago we also started running artist and writers retreats, opportunities for creatives to disconnect from the rest of the world and focus on their work without distraction. Patrons and donors from all walks of life have influenced our ranch, and, while it is still a fully functioning working cattle ranch, it's also an oasis for the mind and body that I'm proud to have helped create.

The life I've crafted with Alvie is intentional, and since the moment I met Naomi, I knew we were intended to meet and that she was to become part of our lives. In what capacity remains to be seen, but I know with time, she'll slot right in where she belongs.

I'm putting away my quarter horse, Sour Patch, after a trail ride with our retreat guests when my phone starts buzzing in my saddle bag.

Digging it out of the bag and looking down at the screen, I smile.

The heat of Alvie's body seeps into my own as he comes up behind me, cradling me in his arms. "Naomi's calling."

"I can see that, silly." I snark, turning to face him over my shoulder.

"Are you going to pick up?" He asks.

"Of course!" His emerald eyes looking deep into my own. "Do you want to say hi?"

Alvie tries to hide his smile from me, but I know it's there, even if it is only the crinkle of joy in his eyes that gives him away.

I know this man far too well for him to get away with hiding things from me.

"You like her." He murmurs.

"No." I say automatically.

"You do." A real smirk graces his face. "Pick up the damn phone, Bex."

I press the screen to answer.

"Took you long enough!" Naomi exclaims as the video call connects. "We need outsider opinions."

Things blur as Naomi moves the phone around, though I can't tell what she's doing.

"Hi, Naomi." I soothe, trying to calm her buzzing energy.

"Hi, Bex." She breathes out as she finally looks at me fully through the screen. "Oh. Alvaro."

"Alvie, please. I think it's appropriate." He says flatly, but still with that smile still in his eyes.

"Got it. Alvie it is." Naomi nods before jumping in. "Okay, Selene and Gunnar came up to go shopping."

"Couldn't they just do that here?" I ask.

"Evidently not. We're at a boutique here to get boots. Like stupid expensive boots." She scowls.

"For Selene's wedding?" I glance back at Alvie. "I thought she'd surely be a heels girl for her wedding."

"For the party!" I hear Selene call out in the background. "Heels for the ceremony, boots for dancing our asses off."

"Got it." I laugh. "Okay, what's the dilemma?"

Naomi jostles the phone again before settling somewhere. When she backs up I can see she's in a modern looking dressing room of some kind composed of whites and creams.

"Selene's vision for her wedding is all like sparkly and etherial, right?" She says, as though I have any idea what that means.

"Sure... new info, but we can roll with that." I chuckle.

"Mhh. I'll send you the Pinterest board really quick." A ping comes through on my phone and I swipe to open the message, but Naomi continues to ramble as I scroll through the board. "Anyway. She want's this kind of aesthetic, but we can't decide on boots for the reception."

Alvie leans in over my shoulder to look at the fairytale like inspiration board, and I start to get on board with Selene's vision. Every image on my screen is exploding with color and covered in sparkles of all kinds. If this is Selene's vision, then the wedding is going to be spectacular. And expensive.

"Are you thinking white?" He asks as I switch back to the video call.

"We don't have a dress for her yet." Naomi says, hands on hips as she surveys a row of boxes at her feet. "So we don't know if white is a good move for her and we can't decide on a color either because we don't have one picked for the bridal parties attire yet. Like, what if it's all the wrong things."

"I voted for pink!" Selene appears in the screen next to Naomi in a getup glamorous enough to make Dolly herself proud of. "Hi, Bex! Hi, Alvie!"

"Hi, Selene." Alvie replies. "I'm gonna dip out of this conversation, birdie. You help with shopping dilemmas. I'll finish with the horses."

He backs away, but I glare at him and pout my lips. He closes the distance between us and kisses me on the lips passionately.

"Ew. Gross." Selene mocks as Alvie pulls away.

"Yeah. Like you and Gunnar are so much better." Naomi laughs. "Bye Alvie."

"Bye, Naomi," he says and backs into Sour Patch's stall to brush her out.

"Okay. I'm back," I say, returning my attention to my phone and heading out of the barn. "We were talking about boots."

Our conversation continues my whole walk back to the ranch house, the three of us bantering back and forth as they try on different pairs of boots and look at other accessories in the boutique. Despite the distance, we have fun and my stomach aches from laughter by the time I reach the house.

"I'm home." I tell Naomi as I listen to Gunnar finish up their purchase in the background. "Want to call me again tonight when you get home."

"Yeah." She sighs, clearly exhausted from the shopping excursion.

"Maybe take a nap when you get home?" I suggest.

"Yeah I may do that." She says with drooping eyes.

"You're coming to visit next weekend, right?" Selene asks Naomi and my ears perk up.

"Yeah, I'll be down for the long weekend." She replies.

"Perfect. You can stay with us, then maybe we all meet at The Playground for lunch? Bex, y'all want to do lunch?"

"Of course." I reply.

"Perfect. You can stay with us and we can meet up at the resort for lunch, then stay the night and go to the club?" Selene suggests.

"Yeah. That works for me." She smiles into her camera.

"Me too." I say wistfully.

There's a quiet that settles between us as we look at each other through the phone, both with silly grins spread across our face.

"Okay. We need to get out of here and I'm starving." Selene says, interrupting our moment.

Naomi laughs. "We don't want a hangry Lena on our hands. That's a nightmare."

I giggle. "Y'all have fun."

There's another moment of silence that passes and, despite all the miles that separate us, it feels like I'm a breath away from Naomi.

"I'll talk to you later, Nay." I say.

"Later." She sighs. "Bye."

"Bye."

The call ends and I look around the empty house before breaking out in a squeal.

She's just so *cute*.

ALVARO

February 16 — Thank Goddess for a three-day weekend

Watching Bex over the past few weeks and seeing how she responds to the blossoming friendship she's growing with Naomi is a beautiful sight. Her smile is contagious and the giddiness she experiences with every text and phone call with her new object of infatuation brings light to my heart.

It doesn't feel like it's been that long, but it's been a whole week since I came home after taking care of the trail ride horses to find Bex staring glassy eyed into space, smiling like a cat who got the cream.

I can barely keep up with the messages that fly back and forth between them in the group chat. They talk about everything and nothing all at once. I have no idea how you can talk to someone that consistently. When does anyone have the time?

Since that phone call, Bex has been a schoolgirl with a crush. It's been a while since I've seen her so excited about something.

Our relationship is solid, and I love how we've grown together through the years, through our struggles and changes in life, but Bex is a person who needs novelty.

For a long time, her energy was channeled into helping me build up the ranch and when that was done, then her yoga business. For a while that was enough, but then she became restless, her heart and soul needed something more. So we had discussions about opening our relationship, and Bex started dating again.

It was fun, having her come home and tell me all about her dates. I got to see the highs she experienced when she had a good time, and held her through the lows when she was feeling vulnerable and unsure of herself. I got to be a part of everything, all of the joy, even without being involved in the relationships myself. I found fulfillment in my partner's joy and excitement, which is more than enough for me.

When Bex met Rissa it there was an immediate connection between the two that burned hot and bright. Only, this time Rissa expressed interest not just in her but me as well. Suddenly, there was this person who didn't want just Bex's attention, but mine too.

I was hesitant to embrace anything too quickly with Rissa, but Bex's enthusiasm was always so supportive. I wanted to give the new relationship a chance, if only to just make Bex happy. Only, it didn't feel right, so Rissa and I never developed that part of our relationship. And Bex and Rissa went back to doing their own thing together.

Only, my dismissal of Rissa led to feelings of separation between Bex and me. I could see how conflicted Bex was feeling over the relationship, and while I didn't disapprove of the partnership, I know my rejection of Rissa didn't sit well with Bex. She didn't want to hurt me, but the rift was causing Bex to struggle to balance her relationships.

Seeds of distrust began to sprout and eventually the straw that broke the camel's back came in the form of an unlocked phone, revealing a dozen conversations with different men Rissa was talking to.

Early on in our own exploration with Rissa, there were explicit conversations about what everyone was comfortable with regarding exclusivity, and this breach of trust was a sword through the chest.

Bex cut Rissa out quickly and her heartbreak ate at her for months. It didn't matter how supportive or loving I was to my wife, the hurt was still there. As time passed, the hurt lessened for both of us, but especially Bex. Though I'll never know for sure if it was more the time and distance that helped her heal, or actual forgiveness toward her ex.

For a while I thought things were fine, but then that restlessness came back.

Now? Now it's being channeled through my partner in a way that makes her glow like her true self.

The fear of her getting hurt again, though, is ever present.

So, despite the smiles and soaring high of new love, there's a twist in my stomach every time the group chat goes off, or I hear Bex's phone ring with Naomi's ringtone.

It's that same ringtone that snaps me out of my haze. I'd long since abandoned the finance reports before me, despite the fact that they really need urgent attention.

"Hey, Nay." I hear come from the living room.

I don't even register me rising out of my chair to go and check in with Bex and Naomi as they chat.

When I walk into the kitchen, Bex has her phone on speaker on the counter.

"She canceled?" She ask Naomi through the phone, looking at me with wide eyes as I enter.

"Yeah. Selene called and said something happened with Gunnar. She was unusually tight lipped about it too." Naomi sighs. "I was really looking forward to a weekend away."

Bex glances up at me before looking down at her phone again. "You should come to the ranch then."

"What?"

"Come to the ranch, we can show you around and you can spend the weekend relaxing here!" The excitement building in her voice with each word brings a smile to my heart.

It's good to see her opening up like this, to see her embracing something good again.

"Um... you're sure?" Naomi asks. "What does Alvie think?"

"Alvie agrees." I speak up, taking a few steps further into the kitchen.

"Oh. Okay." Naomi says softly. "Well I'm already packed. So I guess I can leave here anytime."

"Awesome. I'll text you the address." Bex says excitedly.

"Alright. I'll see you soon then."

"I'm really excited to see you." Bex shares with a smile that Naomi can't see.

"Me too." I hear the smile returned through the phone.

"Okay. Address incoming. Text us when you're leaving."

"Will do."

Time passes slowly as Bex and I roam the house looking for things to distract us while we wait for Naomi to let us know she's headed out.

To pass the time, Bex started frantically cleaning the house and I retreated to my workshop to stay out of her way.

I'm lost in my latest project when a text appears on my phone.

NAOMI

I'm leaving now. Maps says I should be there in about 5-ish hours?

ALVARO

Send me your location so I can track you.

BEX

Because that's not creepy at all, Alvie.

ALVARO

I'm trying to ensure her safety.

Naomi Hall shared her location with the group.

NAOMI

I hope that worked.

ALVARO

It did. Thank you.

BEX

See you soon!

And let us know if you stop at Buc-ee's! They
have this salsa I love that I pick up when we stop.

NAOMI

Will do! I'll need to get gas by then and stretch my
legs.

ALVARO

Get gas before you leave. Don't wait.

NAOMI

I have a full tank, but I'll refill when I stop.

ALVARO

Good.

NAOMI

Thanks, Alvie.

BEX

See you soon!

By the sounds of her muttering coming through my workshop

door, I'm pretty sure Bex has cleaned the entire house top to bottom, twice, and is now just pacing the house.

I'm in my shop, working on tanning some leather for a friend's new set of finger floggers that they commissioned from me when my phone goes off for the second time.

NAOMI

I just turned into the ranch. I think?

ALVARO

Just follow the road and you'll come up on the house.

Bex bounds out of the house over to where I'm working.

"She's here! Do I look okay?" She asks, looking stunning as ever in a simple black workout outfit, minimal makeup, and her chestnut hair pulled up in a messy bun.

"You look amazing, birdie." I reply, giving her a kiss on the forehead.

Bex is out of the shop and headed back into the house to great Naomi before I even hear tires pull up.

"You made it!"

10

NAOMI

February 17 — Day 1 of 3 for rest and no school work, kinda

I was exhausted by the time I finished my drive down to Bex and Alvie's ranch. Thankfully, they were so sweet getting me settled into their guest bedroom, right down the hall from their own bedroom. The room is cozy and after finishing the excellent meal they prepared for us, I collapsed into bed immediately.

The next morning, I wake up to a warm presence at my back. Softness envelops me and I turn over to burrow further into the heat that's warming my body.

"I come bearing snuggle worthy tits." Bex says, drawing me out of my slumber.

My eyes flutter open and I look up to find a bright eyed Bex surrounding me. Her dark hair is up in a classic messy bun and her skin is dewy from her freshly applied skincare. With the way the light is filtering into the room, she looks like a goddess who's denied to bless me with her presence.

"And coffee." Alvie says in his deep bass tone that gives me shivers.

Looking over, I spot him standing in the doorway with two

mugs in hand. But it's not the steaming coffee which has me drooling, but rather the impressive cut of Alvie's body. He's clad in a pair of jeans, unbuttoned and hanging loosely around his hips, and no shirt, leaving me free to ogle his deeply tanned frame freely.

"Thanks." I slur out, trying to push myself up in bed only to collapse back into the pillows.

"Oh. Our girl's not a morning person, is she?" Bex chuckles.

I shake my head, my eyes closing against the bright morning light.

"Come here. I make a much better head rest than that pillow of yours." She whispers into my ear as she pulls me into her body.

"Your tits are snuggle worthy, but I'm like an armadillo before coffee." I moan.

"Hard outer shell and soft underbelly?" Alvie asks, his voice closer now.

"Nope. Curl up in my blankets and hide from the world until it leaves me alone." I say, burrowing my face further into Bex's warm breast and inhaling the citrus scent wafting from her skin.

"Well we're not doing that today." Bex's hands move through my bedhead as she speaks. "We're gonna take you around the ranch and then go on a trail ride this afternoon."

"Like with horses?" I glance up, peaking at them both out of one eye.

"Yes. Real horses." Alvie confirms.

"Fine." I huff. "I'll come out of my burrow."

"Oh... tits won't get you out of the bed, but horses will?" Bex scoffs.

"What! They're the closest to a unicorn that I'll probably ever be." I say matter of factly.

Bex and Alvie exchange a look before busting out in laughter.

"What? What is it?" I ask in a panic.

They keep laughing until Bex is gasping for breath.

"Naomi... you *are* a unicorn." She giggles.

"What?"

"In the lifestyle, a unicorn is a single woman who's bisexual." Alvie explains.

My eyes widen, but the soft smile that's snuck onto Alvie's face makes me burst into giggles too.

"Okay. Coffee and breakfast first, then we'll drive you around the property." Alvie says, holding out the mug he'd prepared for me.

"How'd you know how I like my coffee?" I ask.

"Little birdie told me." He winks and leaves the room. "Get dressed! Breakfast in five. I want to be out the door in thirty minutes."

Bex looks over to me and wipes at the side of my mouth where I started drooling after staring at Alvie's ass as he left.

"Let's not keep him waiting. He went easy on you at the club. But his punishments can be a bitch if you're naughty enough." Bex smirks.

I nod into my cup of coffee. "Got it."

The coffee is perfect, and so is this morning.

Everything feels, *right.*

Bex helps me rush through my morning routine so I'm ready to go by the time the smell of bacon comes wafting through the house. We follow the scent into the kitchen to find Alvie fully dressed in a tight fitting t-shirt, wranglers, and socks.

Breakfast is quiet, but pleasant between the three of us. We enjoy our food before stuffing our feet into boots, though Alvie takes one look at the pair I brought and immediately vetoed the pair. Instead digging through a box in their garage to find me a pair of work boots that would fit me.

"There we go." Alvie says after slipping them on my feet like I'm Cinderella. "Now let's get you in the truck."

"Nay get's shot gun so she has the best view." Bex suggests.

"You're sure?" I ask.

"Absolutely."

It takes three tries before I give up trying to get into the truck by myself and allow Alvie to boost me up.

Damn these short legs.

When I arrived the evening before, the sun was already setting and everything was obscured by the quickly waning light. But now, with the sun rising in the east and bathing everything in a warm glow, I'm able to see everything.

As we pull away from the one story ranch style house, I take in its brightly colored shutters and matching door, noting all of the wind chimes and other decorations that ornament the porch. The house is a perfect reflection of Bex and Alvie's personalities, rustic, grounded, bright, and whimsical all at the same time.

The view from Alvie's truck as we pull out of the drive is beautiful. I didn't realize how early it was, but watching the sun rise over the landscape as we journey through the trails on the property from one building to the next is incredible.

A short distance from Bex and Alvie's ranch house is the main barn and both the indoor and outdoor arenas they use for training. They drive me a few miles further down the dirt road and I start to see the full extent of the cattle operation that they have on the ranch. Chutes to guide the cattle through the landscape surround a central barn which then leads out into the pasture. A lot of what Alvie tries to explain to me goes over my head, but the excitement he has when talking about his work keeps me mesmerized.

When we turn to round back to the house, we pass a series of cabins clustered together.

"What are those?" I ask.

"Oh!" Bex exclaims. "Those are the cabins for our retreat visitors."

I turn in my seat to face Bex in the backseat of the truck.

"A few years ago we started hosting retreats on the ranch for guests. Mostly yoga and meditation retreats, but also like leadership gatherings or artistic retreats and other stuff." She explains. "We built cabins so people wouldn't have to camp outside and just to make their stay more comfortable."

"That's so cool." I reply, loving the sparkle I capture in Bex's eyes.

"I'm guessing all of this is new for you?" Alvie asks.

"Yeah. I've only ever lived in cities, so this is a whole new world for me."

"Well, welcome to our corner of paradise then." He smiles brightly at me.

"Have you always lived here, Alvie?" I ask.

"Mhmm." He nods solemnly. "My grandparents worked on this land when it was owned by a family who treated it more like a hobby than a working ranch. When the parents passed and the kids didn't want to take care of everything, they gave my family the opportunity to buy it from them. It was really a community effort, a lot of local families helped contribute to the purchase and so we have a lot of local silent shareholders."

"That's incredible." I breathe out, taking in the land with a new appreciation. "To have a community like that must be amazing."

"Absolutely. We host a few events throughout the year for all the families and other members of the community as a thanks to them. It's always the highlight of my year." He smiles softly.

"And the food is amazing." Bex moans.

I force a smile onto my face, both glad to hear what a wonderful thing Alvie and Bex have found here, yet still a little jealous that I'm lacking the same community.

I want that kind of familiarity and security. The knowledge that I have a support system that will step up for me when needed. Sure, I have my grandma, but she's getting up in her years and while I talk to her often, I do don't get to see her much.

But this? The deep roots Bex and Alvie have? It's definitely something worthy of a little jealousy.

Maybe a little hope too.

Surely if they have found it, I can too.

Right?

SCHOOL HAS BEEN a bitch and coming to the ranch is probably the best decision I could have made for myself.

After a tour around the land, Alvie had to go off and take care of his responsibilities, but Bex stuck around to keep me company. I brought a small embroidery project with me. So we posted up on their back porch and spent the morning on our embroidery and knitting projects while huddled around the fire Bex got going for us.

The day is chilly, but beautiful and the peace and quiet of such a still moment loosens the tightness in my body. Throughout the day I can feel my body progressively relaxing and letting go of the stresses of my daily life.

When Bex comes back outside from grabbing us new mugs of coffee, the peace I momentarily found is broken.

"How's school?" She asks, unaware of the anxiety that's already clawing up my throat at the mention. It must show on my face though because next she says, "That bad?"

I sigh. "It's just been a lot and I don't really feel like I've found my place there yet."

"It must be a lot of pressure."

"That's the thing though, it shouldn't be. I don't think it's supposed to be this hard." I think back to my last advisory meeting with Dr. Edwards and cringe at his cruelty. "Or at least not to the point where I'm finding myself hating everything."

"Do you think it will get better?"

I shake my head. "I genuinely don't know, but I'm not optimistic."

"Well maybe I can be optimistic for you then."

I giggle. "Oh? How are you going to do that?"

"Words of encouragement and cute animal photos of course." She smiles. "Oh, speaking of animals. What do you think about putting together a picnic and going for a trail ride this afternoon, having a late lunch?"

"That sounds like fun." I return her smile, grateful for the suggestion. "Do I finally get to meet the unicorns?"

She lets out a full body laugh that has me laughing with her.

"Absolutely. I'll even let you pick out which one you want to ride." She winks at me and I can't help the blush that heats my cheeks. "Alright, it's almost eleven. So why don't we get everything ready and we can go tack up the horses."

I nod, gather my things, and follow her into the house.

We work in a comfortable silence together to prepare our picnic, and every time I look up I catch her looking at me with a light in her eyes.

I've never felt this kind of attraction to a woman before. My bisexuality has never been a surprise to me, though it took me a while to become more comfortable with being open about it in my teens. Bex has me entranced, though, and I can't help but love the butterflies that fill me each time I catch her looking.

She has a presence that draws you in, brings you warmth, which only makes her physical beauty that much more appealing. It's not just her dark hair and glimmering eyes that draw you in, but her joy and serenity too.

It doesn't take us long to gather up our picnic supplies before we're hopping into a four-wheeler and riding over to the stables.

Walking into the barn makes me feel all warm and cozy. The smell of hay permeates the air and as we pass the various horses stalls they poke their heads out of their stalls to greet us.

Bex leads me over to one stall in particular and a beautiful white horse rears its head, saying hello.

"This is Skittles and I think y'all would be best of friends. She's a two year old American quarter horse. So she's already well trained and gentle as can be." Bex explains. "Aren't you girl?"

The affection with which Bex treats the animal has me smiling.

"She's beautiful." I say taking in the towering horse.

"Isn't she? I thought you might like her coat. She's somewhere between a cremello and perlino white, which very much gives her that unicorn look." She chuckles. "I'm gonna grab Sour Patch and we can take them both to get tacked up."

I laugh. "Are all the horses named after candies?"

"Pretty much." Bex says seriously, turning to walk to a nearby stall as I rub Skittles' muzzle. "Or at least all the mares are because they're sweet as can be. The stallions are all named after more savory snacks like Chex Mix, Cheez Its, and Chewy."

I smile at the silliness of it all and turn back to Skittles.

"Ready girl?" She gives me a neigh and a nod and already I feel a connection to this horse.

It doesn't take us long to get the girls all tacked up, Bex having guided me through the whole process of grooming, adding their blanket and saddle, then putting on their bridle. By the time we're done, the sun is high in the sky.

"Where y'all headed Mrs. Silva?" One of the grooms asks as we bring Skittles and Sour Patch out into main area of the barn.

"I'm thinking we go over the hill toward the pasture so we can watch the cows." She replies brightly.

"Oh, no Mrs. I wouldn't do that." She replies, shaking his head. "The hands said they had some animals over there tearin' up the area and some of the fences."

"Shoot. Well that ruins that plan." Bex frowns.

"Maybe head toward the river and that alcove of trees there? Might see a heron while you're at it." The groom suggests.

"Excellent idea. Thanks!" And immediately Bex brightens again.

The groom hands her a couple helmets and Bex comes over to fasten and adjust it to my head.

"Do we really need these?" I ask.

"Better safe than sorry." She says, shaking her head. "Don't want precious cargo getting injured if something goes wrong."

Bex tries to help me hop on Skittles, and while I love having her hands on me as I try and jump, ultimately a few of the grooms who are around have to help us step up into our saddles.

When I'm seated, she shows me how to hold the reigns in one hand and positions me properly on the saddle.

"The trick is to keep you heels down at all times and move with the horse. Let your body follow her movements and you should be fine." She explains.

"Yes, ma'am." I joke, but it only makes her grin broadly at me.

When she hops up on Sour Patch, I can't keep myself from admiring her ass and how her jeans hug her body tightly, the fabric clinging to every curve.

"Walk on." Bex commands with a little rock of her hips in the saddle, and Sour Patch starts moving.

My own horse takes a step forward before rocking back to her previous position.

"You gotta tell her what to do." Bex calls back when she turns to find me not moving and stops her own horse. "Ask her to walk on and give her a little squeeze with your thighs."

I do as she instructs and suddenly I'm moving forward.

"I'm doing it!" I cry out, smiling broadly.

"Good job!" Bex encourages and when I catch up to her, she gets Sour Patch moving again. "Skittles is a great trail horse, so she'll follow me pretty easily. But to get her to turn, just pay attention to which direction her head is facing. Pull the reigns to the right, and she'll turn right. Shift your hand to the left across your body and she'll turn left."

Bex must nudge Sour Patch again because they pick up speed and Skittles quickly adjusts to the new pace.

"And how do I get her to stop?" I cry out, my heart thundering in my chest at the new pace.

Bex turns back to face me in her saddle. "Tug back on the reigns and she'll slow. Pull back a little harder and she'll stop."

Immediately I pull back on the reigns, trying to get Skittles to slow, but instead she comes to an abrupt halt and I rock forward, unprepared for the sudden stop.

Bex laughs my surprise. "They're a lot more sensitive to our movements than people think initially. When you get more confident we can show you how to use more subtle cues. You good?"

"Alright. Okay. Yeah, I've got this." I catch my breath. "Alright, Skittles. Walk on."

Skittles returns to her original pace and follows Bex and Sour Patch out onto the road.

The trail ride is quiet, with Bex and me chatting lightly as we make our way to our destination. Mostly we spend the time taking in the landscape of trees and brush that surround us, absorbing the beauty of the outdoors.

"It's so beautiful." I whisper as we are approaching a circle of trees with a perfect view of the river.

"Gorgeous."

I look over to Bex, who's already looking at me, and I blush.

She shakes her head. "The Guadalupe River runs from Kerr County and down to the gulf. In the hill country there's a bunch of camps and little hideaway vacation spots, but here we're lucky to have part of it right on the property. So we get it all to ourselves."

We reach the center of the grove of trees and dismount. Or at least, Bex dismounts while I struggle to slide off the horse. Thankfully she catches me when I hit the ground otherwise I would have tumbled backward.

Her arms wrap around me to steady me and I melt into her embrace. I melt into her, letting myself sink into her softness. She's only slightly taller than me by a few inches, but it's just enough to where she's able to lean down and place light kisses along my exposed neck and shoulder that make my spine shiver.

"I like that." I whisper.

"Me too." She says, running her lips up my neck again until she reaches my ear which she nibbles and sucks on, causing me to sigh in pleasure.

"Let's get lunch unpacked. Shall we?" She says, giving me a single kiss in that sensitive spot behind my ear.

Leaving the horses to graze nearby, we set up our picnic blanket and food.

All through our meal, Bex flirts with me, causing my skin to redden into what feels like a permanent blush I won't be getting rid of anytime soon. She sits just close enough to me to where our hands and bodies brush each others and my whole being shivers at each connection.

The sun is peaking through the gaps in the canopy of tree's and we're laying together, me cuddled in the crook of her arm when she turns to me.

"Want to go for a swim?" She asks, a mischievous light in her eyes.

"We didn't bring bathing suits." I reply, wide eyed at her suggestion.

"You have a birthday suit, don't you?" She smirks and my jaw drops. "Come on."

She rises from the blanket and starts stripping her clothes, revealing the lush body I drooled over that first night at The Playground. I'm frozen as I watch her reveal herself to me with no shame.

Her breast, striped with glittering silver stretch marks, hang heavy when she takes off her bra. I'm rising up before I can stop myself, looking at her with need in my gaze.

"You want to touch?" She asks, that same playful look in her eye, daring me almost to act on impulses I would normally ignore.

"Yes." I stutter out.

"What do you say?"

"Please." I rasp. "Please, can I touch you."

"Yes."

My hands reach out from where I kneel, one going to cup the bulge of her belly with the other moving to caress her side.

My hand on her side slides up to cup underneath her breast and my thumb runs along her skin. I love the weight of her breast in my hand, the color of her deep rosy nipples in my sight.

"Fuck." I moan. "Can I taste?"

She nods with a broad smile.

I take her nipple into my mouth, sucking on it with all of the need that's coursing through my body. The taste like sugar and smells like citrus, a combination making me think of sweet lemonade.

Lavishing one nipple with my tongue I suck, nibble and flick at it until she's sucking in air at each movement. I move to its twin and repeat the motions as my hand plays with its partner.

My hand on her stomach travels down to her hip and moves closer to her center. My thumb rests just on her mound and I run my thumb over the bulge of her mound through her jeans.

I let my hand fall from her nipple and bury my face between her breast, breathing in her sweet tangy scent.

I want her, *need her*, like no other woman I've ever been attracted to.

"I want to taste you." I murmur, then gasp and look up at her with wide eyes. "Sorry. I didn't mean to say that out loud."

Bex reaches down to cup my face, a smile still on her lips but lust in her eyes.

"One little nibble at my breast and now you're wanting to sink into my pussy? I love that." Her hand runs back through my hair and grips tight at my root, making me gasp in pleasure. "Don't ever apologize for expressing what you want, Nay. It's a pleasure to be wanted by you. An honor to be needed."

I hold her gaze for a minute before looking to the closure of her jeans.

"Can I?" I ask, looking back up to her.

"Please."

"I..." I pause, gathering my courage. "I've never actually been with a woman before."

My head hangs, anticipating her judgement. But when she brings my gaze back up to meet her own, it's like the fire in her burns even brighter.

"What does that mean, bunny?" She asks.

"Like... I've made out with women plenty, but it's never moved beyond that." I take a deep breath in. "What if I'm not any good?"

"Your worries are valid, but you're wrong, Nay." She smiles at me. "I can't imagine you being anything less than the exemplary student I know you are."

An idea sparks.

"Can you... Can you teach me?" I ask, nuzzling into her soft stomach. "Tell me how to pleasure you? Please?"

My pulse is thrumming quickly in my veins and I wait as patiently as I can for her response.

"You want to be a good girl and do as you're told?" She purrs. "I will happily teach you everything I know."

I look up at her once more, and her expression is filled with heat and desire.

"I'm going to teach you how to touch me until I squirm, lick me until I'm moaning your name, and fuck me until I scream for you."

I gasp, loving the idea of her guiding me at every turn, needing her to tell me how to bring her pleasure.

"Now." She continues. "Be a good girl and help me get out of the rest of these clothes.

Garments fly off her body until she's completely bare before me. My eyes travel down her body, devouring the sight of her, until they stop on her pussy.

The light filtering through the treetops reveal that she's already wet for me, the light glinting off the shiny liquid which has dampened her soft curls.

"Shit, Bex." I grab her by the hips and tug her toward me. Her hands come to my head and bury themselves into my hair. "You're gorgeous."

I bring my face close to her pussy, breathing in the scent of her. My mouth waters at the smell, my need to taste her on my tongue making me pant in anticipation.

"Lay down for me? Please?" I ask, a small tremor, both of need and nervousness, in my voice.

Kneeling back down to the blanket, Bex presses her naked body against my own clothed one and cups my face in her hands before kissing me lightly. Then, she grips me by the root of my hair and stares me straight in the eyes. "I'm going to lead, Bunny. Just follow my instructions and you'll do great."

"Yes, ma'am."

Another kiss, this one more passionate than the previous tender one, consumes me. She kisses like an angel, my own heavenly blessing.

When she withdraws there's a wickedness in her eyes.

"Good girl. Now come here and eat my pussy like you're starved."

11

BEX

My eyes stay on Naomi as I lower myself back onto the blanket and spread my legs wide for her.

She's quick to maneuver herself between my knees. I shiver when her warm hands come to rest on my inner thighs. Her hands run up and down, making the skin under her fingertips tingle with need.

"Yes." She says, her words laced with the same desire that runs through my veins.

"Yes, what?" I grin.

"Yes, ma'am." She breathes out. "May I... May I taste you?"

"No. Not yet. First I want you to kiss and lick your way up." I trail my fingers up my thighs but stop just before my center. "You may get close, but don't touch."

"Yes, ma'am."

She bends down on her knees and and leans down to place a single kiss on the inside of my knee.

"Take your time with me, Naomi. The anticipation is just as important as the act itself." I tell her and she nods in acknowledgement.

Her lips come back down and light a fire under my skin

when they press against the same spot on my inner knee. She switches between kisses, licks and nibbles at my thighs and with each touch I start to ache for her mouth in another area of my body.

As she travels up my legs I start to squirm with need. The feeling of her soft lips against the delicate skin of my uppermost thigh causes a moan to slip through my lips and she looks up at me.

"Don't stop." I say, bringing myself up onto my forearms and staring back down to her. "Move up my body and give me a kiss."

Naomi follows my directions immediately. She lays kisses up my belly and focuses on the purple and silver stretch marks that live there. She stops at my nipples to give them attention and when she flicks her tongue over the pert nubs I groan heavily.

"Goddess. That feels so good. Keep doing just that."

Doubling her efforts at the praise, she continues to circle and flick my nipple with her tongue and mouth.

The sensation rocks through my body, making my desire for her climb.

I want us to lose ourselves in each other, to find ourselves at the center of our own universe.

Looking down at Naomi, how she reverently worships my body, a desire flames in my chest.

"Kiss me." I breathe, and she follows through, her soft lips grazing my own lightly before delving in deeper.

Everything in my body hums in anticipation. I need her more with every breath and pant I let out.

"Use your fingers and spread me wide." I tell her. " Press your fingers into my folds and rub up and down but don't Press your fingers into my folds and rub up and down but don't touch my clit."

"Yes, ma'am." She says reaching down to where I need her.

Her fingers move deftly as they stroke up and down my neatly trimmed folds. Every stroke along the sensitive skin builds up the anticipation and need for her.

She plays with me expertly, and as though she can sense the moment when I need her, most, her fingers slip between my folds and graze up from my entrance to my clit.

Circling her fingers around the sensitive nub, she works my body expertly. Each brush of her fingers against my center makes me writhe and moan.

"Fuck me, Naomi. Use those fingers to fill me up and fuck me like a good girl." I pant.

without hesitation, her fingers travel down and press into my opening. She thrust to fingers in slowly dipping them only into the first knuckle before pulling out again, using a come hither motion, she strokes lightly and teases me with the temptation of her full force.

"Don't be a tease, bunny. Show me how good you can be."

With more force than I'm expecting her fingers enter me fully, and she strokes in and out at a pace that has my breathing turning labored.

I can feel my body heating up with each press of her into me, and every time the palm of her hand grazes my clit I shiver with me and desire.

"More, bunny. Burry your face in my pussy as you fuck me and eat me like you're starved." I pant out.

She follows through with an eagerness that makes up for her lack of experience.

When her tongue makes contact with my clit, I scream out in pleasure. Her mouth is sloppy and wet as she eats me out and nibbles at the sensitive bud.

I never thought such a docile woman would play my body with such vigor enthusiasm that Naomi uses as she fucks and licks me, is a pleasant surprise that has my pleasure building faster.

I can feel myself getting close to the edge. My body is tight with the sensations I recognize lead up to my climax. In my body is taught and ready for the explosion that will send me over the edge of the cliff of my bliss. I'm soI can feel myself getting close to the edge. My body is tight with the sensations I recognize lead up to my climax. In my body is taught and ready for the explosion that will send me over the edge of the cliff of my bliss.

"I'm so close. I'm so, I'm so close. Please Naomi. Make me come." I plead, abandoning any sense of control I had over the moment.

Naomi is in total control now. All of her energy is poured into my pleasure.

When the moment comes, and I am rushing over the cliff of pleasure, I scream out her name and echoes through the woods.

The orgasm is a series of rolling waves that rush through my body like water. Everything tingles with electricity and my body feels like a shocked live wire.

Even after my body settles from the orgasm, Naomi is persistent, and her pursuit of my pleasure. Her mouth continues to lick and suck at my clit as her fingers work slower, in and out of my body.

Small shivers roll through my body as she works me over and soon I'm careening to a second climax. The orgasm hits me more subtly than the first, more like a warmth spreading through my body than an overwhelming sensation that shakes my body, but is no less pleasurable.

"Enough." I pant out, gasping for breath.

Naomi withdraws herself, going to sit on her heels with a pleased expression on her face.

"You're sure you're new to this?" I chuckle.

"Brand." She smirks.

"Well," I sigh, contented. "That was amazing. You did *so* well."

A broad smile overtakes her face, making me smile in return.

"Now hand me my shit so I'm not butt-ass naked while we finish our picnic." I laugh.

She hands me my things and I dress quickly. When I sit back down, I position myself with my legs spread wide and tug Naomi so she's sitting between them. I wrap myself around her like a koala.

We sit there like that, Naomi's head resting back against my shoulder, wrapped up in each other in silence. Sounds of nature filter around us and I match my breathing to the sound of the river's water running nearby.

"Are you okay with everything that's been happening? Do you want to stop? Slow down?"

"No!" Naomi quickly replies. "No. I don't want that. That was incredible. I loved every second of it."

I wrap myself tighter around Naomi, kissing her just underneath her ear.

Naomi turns back to me, eyes shining with longing and need. A quick glance down to my lips tells me everything I need to know and I dive in to consume her.

Our kiss follows the ebb and flow of the wind around us. There are moments of rushing, passionate kisses and softer, billowing caresses of our lips.

Time passes in slow motion as we sit there, wrapped up in each other, until the sun's rays have shifted in the sky and the sky is just beginning its decent for the day.

"We should get going. Alvie should be finishing up with the guys by now. He's probably wondering about us." I say, pulling away from Naomi reluctantly.

"Mhmm." She hums, nuzzling closer into me.

"Come on, sweet girl." I say, giving her a final kiss on the forehead. "Let's go see what the boys are up to."

"Not nearly as much fun as we're having." Naomi chuckles.

12

ALVARO

I'm forty-five and retired as one of the oldest guys on the PRCA circuit, especially for tie-down roping. Pretty sure I broke a record of some sort with my tenure. The multiple NFR Championships under my belt make me one of the best, and, in my retirement, it makes me the best man around to train with.

This weekend, a group of boys came down to learn the ropes and I'm happy to tear into their pride a bit.

We're out at the arena closest to the barns practicing when I spot Bex and Naomi coming back from their trail ride. The closer they get, the more I'm entranced by them.

They're practically glowing with the halo of sunlight coming from behind them. Bex has a gleam in her eyes that tells me there are stories to be shared about their trail ride.

"You teachin' those boy's a lesson?" Bex calls out as they pull up to the arena and settle in to watch.

"About to." I shout.

I go through critiquing each of the guys start techniques, picking apart their strengths and weaknesses. With each start I push them harder, closer to their limit.

It's been a while since I hopped on a horse to show the trainees how it's done. Having those girls just outside the arena with a perfect view of the gate I had the men practice their starts, though? I have a warm envy sparking to life in my chest. Every barking command to the boys has their eyes snapping toward me, and I want it. I want their full attention on me.

Both of them.

Jealousy thrumming in my veins, I exaggerate my disappointment in the guys' performances and have two of the ranch-hands bring up my horse, Pop Rocks, and one of the more energetic calf's we use for practice.

At the sight of me, Pop Rocks tosses her head, and I know she is ready for this. She's retired like me, but I know the familiar heat of approaching an arena and preparing for the seven seconds that push adrenaline through our blood. Those seconds are what make us a legendary tie-down roping team. Pop Rocks' wide brown eyes and head sitting proudly high tell me she feels the same way.

I take her reigns from the ranch hand and toss them back over her head. With one step and a swing of my leg, I seat myself on Pop Rocks' back. Her front hooves stomp in joy and anticipation and I lean down to scratch along her mane where she likes it.

Besides Bex, this horse is my best girl.

Looking up, I see my wife and Naomi's full attention on me. They've dismounted from their mares and are hugging the edge of the arena with a perfect view of the gate where we wait. Bex is smirking at me knowingly, and I wink at her. Naomi is looking at me wide eyed and even from far away I can see how her chest rises and falls with her quickened breaths.

A light squeeze of my thighs around Pop Rocks' barrel is all she needs to trot toward the pair.

"Gonna show the guy's how it's done?" Bex calls out as we approach.

"They need a little reminder of how it's supposed to be done," I say, chuckling when I turn back to see the trainees and several of the ranch-hands swing up onto the arena's railing to watch. "Gotta show 'em why they're here."

"Why's that, Old Man Silver?" Bex laughs.

"Well, I'm the best there is. They need a humblin' every once and a while." I laugh, nudging Pop Rocks into a full trot.

I try to focus on warming up Pop Rocks a bit as we trot around a few times, doing a few simple circles and serpentines across the arena. Passing by the boys is no problem, but the girls have me sitting a bit straighter in my saddle as I pass them each time.

"Jefe," One of the ranch hands calls out. "el ternero está listo para funcionar." (Boss, the calf is all ready to go.)

I rock my hips and Pop Rocks transitions into a smooth canter toward the girls. I pull out my stopwatch from where I tucked it into my button up and hand it off to Bex.

"Time me, Birdie. I'll finish in less than seven seconds."

Bex gives Naomi a look and cackles. "He said it, not me."

Naomi's laugh rolls over me and I chuckle with them.

"Only time I ever finish that fast is with my mare. I like to take my time with pussy." I wink and turn away, fully aware of the dropped jaws I'm leaving behind me.

I head back to the guys at the start gate and several of them holler at me.

"Gonna show us how it's done, old man?"

"Gotta put us in our place, gramps?"

I chuckle at the old man jokes.

"Nah. Old Man Silver's is doin' it for them buckle bunnies." One of the guys yells out, and I hit him with a glare.

"Call my wife a buckle bunny one more time, boy, and see what trouble it gets you into." He, at least, has the common sense to look a little ashamed.

Back outside of the ring, a ranch hand pulls up the rope with an orange flag attached. Two of the boys are holding the calf back in the chute.

I lean down to give Pop Rocks a final pat and whisper to her. "Make me look good?"

Pop Rocks tosses her head in response, her eyes connecting with mine with a hard determination in them.

I glance over to the girls and see Bex explaining something animatedly to Naomi before turning back to me.

A small tug back on her reigns backs Pop Rocks up against the calves chute at an angle. Someone hands off my lasso and rope to me.

I sink into the ritual of getting settled into my saddle. I secure the end of the lasso around my saddle horn, close to the pommel. Reigns in my left hand, lasso in my right, tie-down rope in my teeth. My feet are securely in the stirrups, heels down, and weight firmly on the ball of my boot.

A small signal has the boys releasing the calf, which comes sprinting out the chute.

The orange flag drops with the rope sending Pop Rocks galloping forward at full speed. I lean forward with her movement and bring up my lasso to make a few controlled rotations above my head. My eyes are firmly on the calf as it sprints. My body senses the moment when I need to toss the loop like it's second nature. The rope goes around the calf's neck and my left hand pulls back on Pop Rocks' reigns, signaling for her to stop and hold firm.

I'm already flying out of my saddle when the calves' momentum stops and they are pull back. My feet connect with the ground and I'm running for the calf, hands skimming down the spoke of my lasso as I move. My hands slide to the animals neck and flank and I flip it onto it's side. Straddling the calf, I pull up its back legs in one quick swoop, and pull the rope from my teeth with my other hand. The rope's loop goes around one front heel and I tug it back to where my other hand holds the back legs.

Muscle memory has me looping the rope around the limbs

three times and finishing off the tie with a half-hitch hooey knot. I push up from the calf and throw my hands in the air.

Cheers erupt from the guys, but I ignore them as my head looks up to meet my wife's gaze.

"Boy's! Time!" She calls out.

"Seven point-fuckin-two!" They cheer.

She dips down between the metal arena bars and comes barreling toward me.

"Seven point two!" She cries as she crashes into me, Naomi close behind.

Naomi looks excited, but a little confused.

Bex turns to her, gasping. "In comp, that would be a world record. Not bad for Old Man Silver."

Naomi's jaw drops, and her gaze smashes into mine. I hold the moment as long as I can before one of the ranch hands get's my attention.

"Buen trabajo, jefe." He says. (Nice job, boss.)

"Gracias, hombre." I say, turning back to his voice to find the calf already free and being guided back where it belongs by two of the other guys on their horses.

I scoop up my rope from the ground and go back to Pop Rocks and undo the lasso on her saddle before giving her a rub on her muzzle.

"Thanks, girl." I give her a kiss. "Maybe we should come out of retirement." I wink at her and she gives me a neigh and chomps at her bit.

"Don't think I didn't hear that, Alvie." Bex says.

"What? I'm kidding." I laugh with a look to Naomi, which Bex clearly doesn't miss.

I hand off Pop Rocks to the ranch hand and he hops up to take her on a short trot around the arena to cool off before putting her back into her stall.

"That was amazing. You looked incredible." Naomi breathes out when I walk up to her and Bex.

"And that's what makes him a champion." Bex rolls her eyes.

"Why the nickname Silver then?" Naomi asks genuinely.

"Because before retirement I was the oldest guy on the circuit for several years." I huff, annoyed at the reminder. "But in all the years that Bex and I have been together, I don't think she's ever gotten quite as good at explainin' rodeo ropin' to anyone like I can."

"That's not fair. You're literally sitting on the damn horse for the whole thing. I'm in the stands. Cut me some slack." Bex says sternly.

I turn back to the guys, and then address the women. "I'm gonna wrap up with them and then head in to shower. Sound good?"

Bex shoves me playfully. "Go on. Brag and boast in front of the boys. You know you want to."

I shake my head. "I'd rather get my praise from some very pretty girls in private, Birdie."

The guys are buzzing with energy when I approach them, and I receive several slaps on the back. A quick glance over my shoulder back at the girls reveals two gorgeous, voluptuous rear ends retreating from the arena. I watch them out of the corner of my eye until they pass between the metal bars and are headed back to the house.

When everything is wrapped up and I'm finally back at the house, I find Bex and Naomi cuddled on the couch doing crafts of some kind, something with yarn or thread.

Naomi does a double take when I enter and is immediately on her feet to greet me.

"So. How does it work?" she asks.

I chuckle. "You gonna turn into a buckle bunny if I tell you?"

Naomi gives Bex an adorable look which says she's completely out of her depths.

"A girl who chases after rodeo cowboys." Bex laughs.

"No?" Naomi says hesitantly.

"Promise?"

"Yes, she promises, Alvie. Just get on with it." Bex rolls her eyes.

I love seeing her when she's sassy like this.

"So you want to know about ropin'?"

"Yes?" Naomi says, her voice tipping up at the end in a question.

"Be sure, bunny, because there's no going back after you've had a cowboy."

Naomi's cheeks flush as she nods.

"Tie-down roping is a competition inspired by the method that we use to gather cattle, mostly for medical treatment or branding when chutes and pens aren't available." I take a step into her space. "It requires horse and rider to be completely in sync, working together to catch and tie-down a runaway calf, which is always allowed a head start. When the calf gets a certain distance away, we go after it together. You saw the rest."

"Is it always so..."

"So what?" Bex says, coming up behind Naomi.

"Hot?" Naomi replies with a glance over her shoulder to Bex.

"You like that?" I purr into her ear. "The idea of having me throw you down and tie you up tight. Don't you, bunny?"

"Yes." She says breathlessly, caught between me and my wife.

"Be sure when you answer me."

"Yes. I want that."

"Have you ever played with bondage before?" I prowl further into her space and she steps back, bumping into Bex.

"No." She's panting between Bex and I.

"We'll start with beginner cuffs. Harnesses and suspension

take patience and I don't want to put you in a position that is hard to get out of for your first time. Is that okay with you?" I ask.

She nods before remembering. "Yes, Sir."

A rumble comes out of my throat at the honorific. I don't deserve it, yet she's so willingly putting it out there for me.

"Bex, you're comfortable with all of this?"

Bex's hands, previously resting on Naomi's arms to steady her, move to circle around her waist.

"Absolutely. She's going to look so gorgeous splayed out over our bed, hands cuffed above her head, while we play with her." She brings her lips right beside Naomi's ear. "Is that what you want? Do you want to be bound while we play with you?"

"Fuck yes." Naomi says enthusiastically. "I've wanted your hands back on me since you helped me off that cross."

"Go shower off the day, Naomi." I say. "We eat dinner. Then we can play tonight."

Naomi lets out a small whine that has me grinning.

"Patience, bunny."

TEASING Naomi throughout the evening has been pure pleasure for me. I love seeing how she responds to Bex and my touches. She's so responsive to every brush and graze of the hand as we cuddle on the couch. I don't think that anyone followed the movie we were watching at all.

I can't wait to have Naomi tied up, ready to be played with.

We set up Naomi in her own bedroom for the weekend, but. I know Bex would rather have her in our own bed, snuggled with her.

Touch isn't my favorite thing in the world, but there are times when it's an excellent way to connect with someone. It's always been a big part of Bex's needs and I've done my best to fulfill that for her, but seeing how she interlaces herself with Naomi is a whole new level. They're like two serpents intertwined with each other.

We're finishing up our movie for the evening when Naomi gives the two of us a look filled with longing.

"Please stop teasing me." She pants.

"Oh, but it's so much fun, bunny." I joke, smiling at her adorable pout.

A glance at Bex tells me she's ready to let the evening move on to more exciting activities. I rise and stand before the two women who are looking up at me with admiration in their eyes.

"I think if we're going to let this night progress, we need to have a chat."

Naomi's eyebrows crinkle in confusion.

"Tonight, Bex and I are going to tie you up and play with you. But nothing sexual is going to happen between any of us until we've all been tested. Understood?"

"Yes." Naomi responds, nodding enthusiastically. "I can go to the campus clinic when I'm back and ask them to run tests."

"We'll go to our PCP as well to get panels done." Bex says. "I don't want this to be a one time thing and I want us to all know that we're taking all the steps we need to ensure our health and safety."

Naomi visibly relaxes at Bex's words. "I think I needed to hear that. Thank you."

"What? That safe sex is important to us?" Bex asks.

"No." She pauses, fiddling with the edge of her shirt. "That you don't want this to be a fling."

Bex smiles.

"Do you... Do you feel the same?" Naomi asks, looking up at me with doe eyes.

"I want you and Bex to explore your relationship to the fullest, and I would like to be included. It isn't necessary for me to be intimately involved though. I don't think I'm ready for that." I explain.

Naomi's head drops and a part of me feels guilty, but honesty is truly the best policy.

I don't want to mislead her.

I'm simply not a person who can jump in head first like my partner.

Bex is her own person and a hurricane all her own. I don't move as fast as she does.

"Relationships are different for me, Naomi." I say, using my finger to tilt her face up to face me. "I want to explore with you and show you new things in the world of kink, but I like getting to know people before forming sexual relationships with them."

"Okay. I can respect that." She says, strength coming back to her gaze.

"Do you want more?" I ask out of curiosity.

"I... I think so? I like you, both of you. I want to see where that goes."

"Thank you for your honesty." I say, smiling. "Now, birdie, I think we should spend some time tying our bunny up. Shall we?"

"Oh, I definitely want that." Bex says as she untangles herself from Naomi and stands beside me.

The two of us looking down at Naomi has her looking meek like the bunny she is. I can't wait to make her twitch and squirm.

"I'll grab water." I say, turning toward the kitchen. "We need to make sure you stay hydrated so you can scream out for us."

I leave the girls to make their way to the bedroom and take my time in the kitchen gathering water and a few other essentials.

Entering the bedroom, I'm left breathless at the sight before me.

Bex has stripped down to her lacy undergarments, while Naomi stands in the center of the room in a bra and panties set made of simple cotton. Something about it gives her a whole new level of innocence that has a part of me clawing to have her kneel at my feet.

"I wasn't sure what would happen. I dressed for comfort. Sorry." Naomi pouts.

"Don't be sorry." Bex says.

"You look incredible." I confirm.

I take my time setting down everything on the dresser, giving myself time to steady my breath and calm the spike of unexpected desire flaring in my chest.

Going over to the armoire where we keep our supplies, I ask. "What do you want to have happen tonight. Do you want to set any limits?"

"No pain." She answers quickly. "Other than that, I'm not sure."

"Bex?"

I can hear the gears turning in my birdies mind as she thinks through all of the things she likely wants to do to Naomi as I pull out two lengths of rope.

"I really want to trap our bunny in ropes, tie her to the bed and burry my face in her pussy until she's screaming."

I turn around to find Bex and Naomi pressed close together, barely a breath from each other's lips. Naomi's chest rises and falls quickly.

"Naomi. Is that agreeable to you?" I ask and she nods. "Words, bunny."

"Yes." She breathes out.

"Excellent." Bex smirks and places a light kiss on Naomi's lips.

I walk over with my offerings for Naomi in hand. "Nylon or hemp rope tonight?"

"I don't know the difference." She replies, looking between the two.

"Mostly texture and grip. Here, feel." I hand over the bundles of rope.

She takes each bundle and her eyes snap to the hemp when I hand it over.

"You like the hemp. I thought you might." I smirk.

"I like the texture." She smiles sweetly, but there's heat in her eyes.

"It's my favorite as well." Bex says.

"Okay." I take the ropes from Naomi and toss the nylon on the chair in the corner. "I'm going to tie you in a simple pair of cuffs. Don't move. Don't try to help. Just relax while I tie you. Understood?"

"Yes." She replies and I hold back the urge to call her a good girl.

Unbundling the length of rope, I straighten it out and find the bite of the rope in its center.

"Hands out before you and fist them." Naomi complies as Bex moves behind her and unclasps her bra.

"I think we should remove this before we get too far, don't you think?" Bex croons, slipping the bra off.

Bex lets the garment fall to the floor and I marvel at the volume of Naomi's breast as they fall from the confines of her bra.

"Fists out before you." I remind her as Bex takes the weight of Naomi's breast into her hands and starts to knead them.

Naomi responds immediately and I smile at her eagerness.

Slowly I place the rope across her wrists so the center sits between her fists before wrapping each end twice so it circles her whole wrists. I take my time with each movement, letting my fingers trail over her skin and causing her to shiver under my touch and the texture of the rope.

When I'm done, the rope lays loose and flat, carefully aligned in their five lines atop her wrists with the tails falling to the floor.

"When you tie with rope, you layer things to distribute pressure evenly. That way you're not straining any muscles or nerves. You don't want to put undue stress on any particular part of the body." I explain, crossing the tails of the rope under her fists and bringing them up and around the opposite sides from where they started. "You want everything to lie flat. Things should only twist when you want them to."

I exchange the ropes between my hands and drape them so they fall perpendicular to the five rows that hold her wrists. Then, carefully, I wrap the end of each rope around, moving toward her wrists until there's a small gap between the rope and her skin.

"There. They feel secure?" She nods and I take hold of the center column of wrapped rope.. "Good. If they're too loose, there's less," I pull forward on the cuffs. "Control."

Her eyes widen as she's forced to step into my space and her breath quickens.

"Are you ready for my wife to make you scream, bunny?" I smirk, glancing over her shoulder at where Bex stands with a smile on her face.

"Yes." Naomi whispers.

"Good. Listen to her well and if you need to pause or stop, just say the word. Stop means stop." I tell her.

"Get on the bed and lay down on your back." Bex commands and Naomi jumps to follow the instructions. "I hope you like over-stimulation."

Naomi gets on her back on the bed and Bex has her spread her legs wide before crawling between them. I go up to sit by Naomi's head and admire how her eyes flutter closed as Bex drags her nails up Naomi's thighs.

Watching them together is intoxicating. Bex finishes undressing Naomi ,and, as promised, buries her face into her pussy.

I keep my eyes trained on Naomi's face as Bex plays her body like an instrument. I drink down each minute furrow of her brow, parting of her lips, and arch of her neck that Bex draws out.

Though her wrists are bound, Naomi's hands are free and

when she reaches for Bex's head, I snatch her by the rope cuffs and force her hands above her head.

"No touching, bunny. Just feel." I whisper into her ear and she whines in response.

I lose track of how many orgasms Bex wrings from Naomi's body, but the begging she does is like music to my ears.

"Please no more." She pants out. "Please."

"One more," Bex says, coming up for a breath of air. "Give me one more."

Naomi whimpers, but acquiesces.

The final orgasm shatters her and I let go of her wrists where I've held them above her head, allowing her to curl into herself as she shakes with aftershocks.

Bex comes up with a satisfied grin on her face before she slides off the bed to grab baby wipes to clean Naomi up.

Looking over at the woman curled into a ball, I reach over to brush her hair back out of her face.

"You did so good, bunny." I soothe, but she lets out a keening noise. "Are you okay?"

She nods and I don't press her for words, knowing from experience how overwhelmed she is after having Bex's mouth on her for such a long time. A tenderness thaws in my chest and I reach to gather her in my arms and untie the cuffs from around her wrists.

She's so soft and pliant in my arms, warm and comforting.

Bex comes back and cleans up Naomi as well as gives us all water. I help tip the bottle so Naomi can take sips.

Quickly, Naomi's breathing evens out and she falls asleep.

I crawl out from beneath her and get up to go to the bathroom as Bex curls up with the exhausted girl.

Looking back at them cuddled together brings warmth to my chest and a lightness to my mind that's been evading me recently.

I'm so fucked.

13

BEX

March 6 — Three sleeps until Spring Break

The rest of that weekend was easy and carefree between the three of us. Sending Naomi back to school, though, was a lot more difficult.

There's a drop from the high of having her around and I'm struggling to wade my way through the emotions that are roiling in my stomach. We talk every day and the group chat is busy as ever, Alvie is even chiming in more than normal. There's still an ache though because of the sheer distance between us.

Of course, Alvie is the first to notice, but, thankfully, he gives me space for the better part of the week.

It's not until the next Wednesday night when we're getting ready for bed that he breaks the silence between us after my fourth sigh in as many minutes.

"You want to talk about it?" He asks patiently as he washes his face.

"Yes. Oh my goddess." I collapse beside him on the bench beside the vanity.

Alvie laughs. "You could have asked."

"I know. I just…"

"It's okay." He says, pulling me up and into his firm body so he's cradling me in his arms.

"I just miss her. This is so silly!"

"It's not silly at all, Bex." Alvie smirks. "You're allowed to get excited about a new relationship and it's normal to want to spend time with that person to continue to build that relationship. All things considered, you're doing great."

"Well that was…" I trail off, surprised by his words.

"Straightforward?" He says smugly.

"Yeah."

"It's why you love me, though." He says, nuzzling into my hair.

"One of many reasons." I huff. "I just wish that this wasn't so hard. And I'm worried about her. I think school is taking more of a toll on her than she's letting on."

"Well, she'll be back in a few days for her spring break. We'll be able to spend a whole week with her then." He reassures me.

"We?"

"Well… yeah. I presumed she would be staying with us again. That's what y'all talked about, right?"

"Yeah, I was hoping so. We didn't make definitive plans because she didn't know if she would be staying with Selene and Gunnar." I fiddle with the edge of my nightgown. "Also, I didn't know how you felt after that our weekend with her here."

Alvie lets out a rotund laugh. "What would leave you with the impression that I didn't think the weekend went well? We all get along and we had a great time."

I free myself from his hold and make my way into the bedroom, crawling in and picking up my knitting.

"Yeah, but my brain makes me doubt sometimes. And I'm never quite sure where you stand with things."

"Then ask." He says, following me to the bed.

I hesitate before my desire to know takes over. "How are you feeling? About her, me, us, all of this?"

Alvie shrugs as he climbs under the quilt and reaches for his book. "I think you and Naomi have a really special connection which I would like to see grow between the two of you." He pauses. "Naomi and I are developing a friendship that I would like to see through as well. I don't have romantic feelings toward her, and I don't know if I ever will, but I enjoy her company."

"Okay."

"Okay?" He asks with a raised eyebrow.

"Yeah." I tilt my head to the side. "You're not one to be pushed into things. So I'm not going to try. But thank you for being honest with me."

He grabs hold of my thigh under the covers and squeezes. "Anytime, birdie."

Leaning over he gives me a kiss on the forehead and settles into bed.

When I finally notice that Alvie has already passed out, I put away my knitting supplies and reach over to put his book back on the nightstand before snuggling into the crook of his arms.

My mind wanders back to Naomi, worrying about how she's doing. There's something niggling at me that says something isn't quite right, but I push the thoughts to the side, instead focusing on my breathing until I fall asleep.

I don't know how much time has passed, a few hours at least with how dark it is outside, when chimes wake me from my slumber. I'm pressed up against Alvie's warm body, and it finally registers that the sound is our phones blowing up with notifications, despite the do not disturb function.

"Fuck. Make it stop." Alvie groans from beside me.

Pulling myself from his warmth I drag my phone over to me and find twelve new messages from Naomi in our group chat. Each one longer than the next, with increasing panic shown in the frequency with which they appear on my screen.

I bolt upright in bed at the sight of Naomi's clear panic on my screen.

"Bex?" Alvie says wearily.

I don't even bother responding or even reading the messages in their entirety before pressing call on the video chat button.

The line rings twice before she picks up, and the sight of her breaks my heart.

Her eyes are rimmed red and puffy, her breathing coming in shallow, panting breaths.

"Nay? What's wrong?" Fear and concern shake my voice, which has Alvie pulling himself out of bed and turning on the bedside lamp.

"I... I can't... I can't..." She cries.

"Breathe for me, Nay. Breathe." I say desperate to help, but she can't seem to center herself. "Nay, where are you? Are you safe?"

She nods and I let out a sigh of relief.

"Are you alone?" I ask.

Another nod, but her breaths are still erratic.

"Naomi, I need you to breathe with me." I say, but she doesn't seem to be responsive.

Alvie takes the phone from me. "Bunny, stop. Hold your breath for three seconds with me." He commands, and while she struggles to contain her breath, she does try. "Breathe in and out with me, Nay."

His arm wraps around me, drawing me tightly into his body and I breathe with the two of them until Nay is inhaling and exhaling easily on her own and her tears have slowed.

My heart aches for her and I desperately wish that I could take her into my arms and tell her that everything is going to be okay.

When she's finally breathing by herself again, Alvie and I wait for her to speak, but the silence drags.

"Naomi, talk to us. What happened." I beg.

Her hiccuping breaths are lighter, but she manages to talk through them. "I can't. I can't do this anymore. I'm so tired. I don't want to be here anymore."

I grab my phone back from Alvie and mute the phone while it's facing the ceiling.

"Text Durante. See if he's up." I tell him and he reaches for his own phone.

I bring the phone back to my face and unmute the line. "Baby, where do you not want to be?"

"Here." She sniffles. "I just want it to stop. I want time to stop. I don't want to do this anymore."

"Naomi. I need you to answer me honestly, are you thinking of harming yourself?" I ask, dead serious.

She lets out a coughing sob and nods.

"Bunny, we need to call in help. Is there anyone local you can go to?"

She shakes her head.

"Okay. If I walk you through things, can you follow instructions?"

"I think so." She chokes out.

"Grab a bag. We're going to pack you up and you're coming here early. Okay?"

"What?" Her eyes go wide. "But, I have class tomorrow."

"Not anymore." I say.

Her silence speaks volumes, but after a few moments she uncurls herself from where she's balled on the ground and gets up.

The next two hours are a blur of activity. I walk Naomi through the emails she needs to send to cancel classes and inform her advisor of a personal emergency. We pack her a bag and get her in her car in one piece. Each step seems to ground her more and more and by the time we get her on the road she's seeming much calmer, but quieter.

Alvaro leaves the bedroom at one point to talk with Durante and make some kind of arrangement with him.

I stay on the phone with Naomi the entire five hour drive from her apartment to the ranch, pacing in the living room the entire time in my pajamas. I walk her through her stops at Buc-ee's, getting gas and snacks. I talk to her the whole time about what's going on at the ranch and the plans we have for next week with the rodeo being in full swing.

By the time that she's turning off of Highway 87 and onto the dirt road that leads to the ranch entrance, I'm bleary eyed, but my heart is still racing.

I need her here with us. I need her safe.

Finally, her headlights pull up in front of the house and I end the call, sprinting outside to meet my girl.

14

NAOMI

March 7 — Fuck it. Spring Break sprang early

Sunlight is just peaking over the horizon when I arrive at Bex and Alvie's house.

Bex comes sprinting out of the house and she's at my drivers side door, pulling it open, before my car fully rocks to a stop.

I scramble out of the car and into her arms. Within her grasp, I break down all over again despite being on the phone with her for over five hours. Sobs wrack through my body and I cry out all the tears that I've been holding back for the past five hours.

A large warm hand on my shoulder draws my attention away from Bex, and to Alvie who's standing beside us.

He takes my hand and guides both of us inside where the smell of breakfast meat and pancakes wafts through the space.

"I'll grab your things in a bit, but first we're all going to sit down and have breakfast together." He says simply as he pulls out dishes from the cabinets and starts to fill a plate with food. "You're going to drink three glasses of water and a glass of orange juice.

You're going to finish everything on this plate, and if you want more you're going to ask. Understand?"

The way he looks at me is full of strength and fire. There's a determination there that warms my heart, because it's for me. He's concerned and taking care of me the best way he knows how.

"I understand." I say as I sit myself down at the kitchen island next to Bex.

Placing the plate before me, he says, "I'm glad you're here, bun."

"Me too." I say with a small hiccup.

Alvaro goes about serving both Bex and himself before sitting down at the island with us. Breakfast is quiet but comfortable, though I know a confrontation is coming.

I'm dreading having to explain what happened tonight. I don't know what triggered everything. Or rather, I don't want to think about *who* triggered everything.

My brain is as scrambled as the eggs in front of me.

"I'm sorry... I shouldn't have..."

"Yes, you should have and you did." Bex interrupts, reaching for my free hand. "Let's eat breakfast, and then we can curl up with some tea and talk, okay?"

"Yes, ma'am."

Breakfast is quiet, but my anxious mind is swirling less. When we finish, I offer to help clean up, but Alvie and Bex settle me into the couches in the living room with a blanket and tea.

I love seeing the peace and ease with which they move around the kitchen together. They fit so well together and the sight of them makes my heart ache.

I want that. I want the peace that comes with partnership. The security of being *loved*.

Bex turns around and at the sight of me scurries over.

"Nay, why are you crying."

"I don't know." I lie, and she wipes away my tears that won't stop.

"Do you know what you need? Or do you need suggestions?" She asks.

"Suggestions." I hiccup.

Bex looks over to Alvie, who's joined us on the couch and is sitting on my other side. He doesn't touch me, but even his presence at my back is reassuring.

"I think you need sleep first." He says. "More water. Then I think you need to talk to someone."

I let us sit in silence but he breaks it. "A professional, bunny. "

More tears leak out. "I am the professional, Alvie. I shouldn't need help."

"Everyone needs help, Nay." Bex says.

"I don't." I say stubbornly.

"Okay. Okay. Let's get some sleep, I think we all need it." Alvie soothes. "We were supposed to have some friends come over to dinner tonight, do you think you would be up for that?"

"It might be a nice distraction." Bex suggests. "And they're chill. You don't need to perform for them. We're just grilling on the porch and drinking wine."

"Yeah, that sounds like it could be nice." I acquiesce.

Alvie is the first to stand and he pulls me up and into his arms for a hug.

"It's going to be alright, bunny." He affirms as Bex closes in behind me, giving me neck kisses that make me shiver.

When we all pull apart to go to bed, I'm feeling a little lighter but exhaustion kicks in.

Settling into the center of their massive bed immediately has my eyes fluttering closed. Other than the shifting of the mattress, I don't even notice the couple folding me between them until Bex's head is on my chest and Alvie's hand is holding mine.

My mind settles as their comforting presence envelopes me and I settle into a deeps slumber.

I WAKE up alone in the bed, and glancing at the clock I've clearly slept the day away. I hear noise and voices coming from down the hall. Music is playing from somewhere in the house and has me pulling myself up.

Someone set out a set of towels for a shower.

I take the towels and go into the bathroom to rinse off the stress of the night and the sleep in my eyes.

Coming out of the shower I feel better, but my exhaustion isn't quite gone. I settle in on the bench before the vanity and just stare into the mirror.

I don't know how much time passes as I sit there staring at my sallow complexation and the dark circles under my eyes.

"Bunny." Alvie's voice comes from the doorway and I finally focus my eyes on him in the mirror. "You need help."

I freeze, hoping we aren't about to repeat this morning's conversation, but when I realize he's motioning to my damp, unkempt hair, I nod in appreciation.

He grabs the hairdryer that's been sitting in front of me along with a round brush and without a word, starts drying my hair. The ritual is calming, causing my eyes to flutter closed. I relax into the feeling of warm air as it blows through my strands of hair and onto my scalp.

When Alvie turns off the dryer I open my eyes to find that he's curled my hair with the round brush and given me soft waves that frame my face.

"Before mamá passed, she would have me style her hair every week for church." He smiles at the memory. "I got pretty good. I do my nieces hair when I see them too. They're out of their pigtails and braids phase now, but they love having me curl their hair and feeling like grown-ups."

I smile for the first time in what feels like forever and his own widens.

"I like seeing you happy."

The phrase is so simple, but it shakes me to my core.

"Thank you."

"Your welcome... for the blow out. But don't ever thank me for treating you as you deserve." He tucks strands of hair behind my ear. "Let's get you dressed. Our friends will be here in a bit for dinner."

My body tenses at the mention of the strangers coming over, but Alvaro's touch slides down my arm and my tension is replaced with tingles making me feel safe.

He leads me into the bedroom and picks up the dress that's been lain out on the bed. He gestures for me to slip off my towel, but he doesn't even glance to my body. His gaze is firmly fixed on my face and something about the small gesture makes me smile.

"Hands up." He instructs, and I lift my hands over my head.

His extra inches over me allow him to easily slip the dress over my head. When he moves behind me to do up the zipper, his fingers skim up my bare spine and makes me shiver.

But when he comes back around in front of me and kneels before me, I almost crumple before him. He takes the panties that he had draped over his wrist and has me step in one foot at a time. Pushing up my sundress, he pulls the garment up my body but when they're settled around my hips he pauses with his hands gripping my hips.

The whole time, his gaze was fixed on my own, but now he's studying where my belly hangs over the panties.

"I'm going to kiss you." He informs me, his gaze once again meeting my own.

I suck in a sharp breath, my lips tingle at the thought of his own tangling with mine.

Instead, he pushes my dress up higher and lowers his lips to caress my belly apron. I shiver when his warm lips connect with my skin. He just stays there, lips on my skin, burying his face into my fat.

Instinctively, my hand goes up to run through his hair and his eyes come up to meet my own again.

"Tighter." He whispers, and I tighten my grip.

He goes back to kissing my skin, tracing my stretch marks with his lips, *worshiping me.*

I feel treasured and tears start to track down my cheeks.

When he notices, he rises quickly to wipe them away.

"What was that for?" I ask.

"Beauty deserves to be acknowledged." He says simply, tucking hair behind my ear once again. "You need to remember that you're valuable. If you need the reminder, then we're here to be that for you."

I choke in a breath and nod. "Thank you."

"Don't thank me for being honest." He smiles. "Come on. Our guests should be here soon. Let's go pour you a glass of wine, shall we?"

He takes me by the hand and leads me out to the open space with the living room and kitchen where Bex is preparing dinner.

A charcuterie board is lain out on the kitchen island and Alvie goes over to make a plate, which he hands to me before reaching for the wine glasses.

"Red or white?"

"Red please." And he nods and pours me a half glass.

"I'm gonna go into the workshop for a bit." He says, handing me the glass, and turning to head to the garage. "Y'all have fun."

Bex turns around and her eyes light up when she spots me, sending warmth down my spine.

"You're glowing, Nay." I blush. "Come over and taste this for me."

I round the island and am hit with the aroma of Italian spices and the rich pasta sauce that's bubbling on the stove.

"We're having lamb, pasta and grilled veggies." She shares.

"Sounds delicious." My tummy growls and she lets out a little laugh.

Silence settles between us as Bex works on the meal until I can't stand it anymore.

"I feel really bad."

"What why?" Confusion lacing her tone.

"I managed to shower, but I couldn't get myself ready. So Alvie did."

"So?"

"I just... I should be able to do that kind of thing myself. It just feels so stupid that I can't even get myself dressed."

"That's not stupid at all. Everyone needs help sometimes, Alvie stepped in."

"He was so..." She waits for me to finish. "Reverent? The way he did it, with so much care. I don't feel like I deserve that kind of attention."

"Oh, bunny." Bex sighs, putting down her cooking utensil and facing me completely. "That's just who he is. He wants to take care of people, it's his first instinct when he see's people hurting. He wants to solve something, even if it's as small as helping you blow dry your hair."

I shiver at the memory of his lips on my tummy and how he touched me like I was precious.

"After breaking up with my ex, he helped put me together too and get me back on my own feet. It's how I got my nickname, birdie. He doesn't like seeing you feel broken."

I jump at the sound of the front door opening and spin around.

"We're here!" A melodic voice calls out. "And we brought goodies!"

"Ah! Finally! What are your offerings for our table madame?" Bex cheers.

"Homemade tiramisu and a few bottles of dessert wine." The plump petite woman replies as she makes her way over to Bex.

Reka is a petite Asian woman, barely reaching my shoulders in her flats. Her body is supple and full like my own, with prominent hips and breast that any bisexual would be happy to admire. Her dark hair flows over her shoulders, framing her round face and bright eyes.

"Naomi, this is Reka. Reka, Naomi." Bex says as the woman opens her arms, offering a hug which I accept. "These peeps were at the party but I don't think y'all got introduced."

"Nice to meet you, Reka."

"Likewise." She says.

"Where are the guys?" Bex asks.

"Alvie's light is on in the workshop and the guys went straight there." Reka explains. "I'm sure they want to talk leather and lashes."

"I'm sure you do too, Mistress." Bex winks.

I look between the two women in confusion.

"Reka is a switch. She has one partner that she submits to and one that she dominates." Bex explains with a cheerful laugh in her voice. "And I know you love a good flogger in your hand, Reka."

Reka just grins with a glint in her eye which tells me she enjoys a lot more than just holding a flogger in her hand.

Deep voices filter into the room and I glance over my shoulder to find Alvie coming in from the workshop with two other men.

The black man towers over everyone in the room, and, while his bulk should be intimidating, the soft sweater and smile he wears gives you a feeling of safety around him. His hair is short and cropped close to his skin, and there's scruff framing his face. His whole appearance gives off an air of calm strength.

In contrast, his companion is a white man with a milky complexion, contrasted by a dark head of hair and a bright smile. He's tall, though a few inches shorter than the other man. His energy on the other hand is slightly more anxious and it's clear that he's Reka's submissive by the way he seeks her out in the room and his shoulders droop on finding her.

"Naomi. This is Durante" Alvie calls, gesturing to the tall black man before turning to the other. "And this is Symon."

"Hi." I smile and wave back to them.

"Alright! Let's get everyone a drink and we can hang out until dinner is ready."

Bex and Alvie's friends are delightful and the evening passes in a blur of stories, life updates, and a lot of laughter.

Turns out Durante is the psychologist who runs his own practice everyone has been telling me about, and we hit it off immediately. I also learn he's Reka's dominant, while he confirms that Symon is her submissive, and that his practice specifically caters to clients who are in the lifestyle.

After dinner, we talk more privately on the front porch about his experiences as a practitioner but I sense when the conversation turns and I tense.

"I don't want to overstep, but Alvie called me this morning." His face grows concerned and I hate it.

"I'm fine."

"No, I don't think you are, but you can and will be."

"I don't really want to talk about it." I snap.

"I know." He says with the same patient tone I give to my own patients in clinic. "But when you do, I'd be happy to connect you with someone who can help."

I drop my head, feeling the full force of my shame from last night.

"I'm going to give you my number." He offers, drawing my attention back to his face. "I can't be your professional because of our personal relationship. But I'm here when you're ready."

"Thank you," I say quietly.

Durante leaves me to my own and I take a moment to gather myself.

When I rejoin the group everyone is still in a lighthearted mood and it brings a smile back to my face.

Durante doesn't bring up our chat at all and I appreciate the confidentiality.

When the trio leave for the night, the positive energy is still thrumming through my veins and I feel better, lighter.

"You're still smiling." Bex says.

"Yeah, they're fun." I reply.

"They're really good people." Alvie agrees as he does the dishes.

"I talked with Durante." I say, getting a little quieter.

"Oh?" They ask together.

"He offered to connect me with someone."

Bex hesitates before speaking. "That's good. Right?"

"Yeah, maybe. I don't know if I'm ready, but it's nice that he offered."

"He's really good at his job. Him and his colleagues speak all over the country about mental health and working with clients who live non-traditional lifestyles." Alvie chimes in.

"Is that who I am now? Someone living a non-traditional lifestyle?"

"If you want, the possibility is there for you to embrace." Bex says, coming over to sit by me on the couch. "I know Alvie and I are married, but that doesn't mean I, we, don't care about you."

A moment passes between us and a smile breaks out on her face. "I can very easily see myself falling for you. And... when you're ready, we can talk about what that means."

My eyes widen at her forwardness, but my heart melts a little.

"The past 24 hours have been a lot, though. So we can talk about that another time." She gives me a kiss on the cheek before rising to help Alvie. "Just sit and enjoy the wine. We'll join you when we're done."

"Thanks." I say.

I watch the pair as they clean up the kitchen and I can't help how my mind wanders to all the possibilities that could happen, what my future could look like. Part of me is terrified about pursuing something so dramatically different from what I thought I wanted for my life. Another is excited about the prospect.

The heart wants what the heart wants, and if Bex get's her way, I think my heart might too.

BEX

March 14 — Spring Break should never end

The week that passes with us all on the ranch is quiet. Alvie drives into the city for the rodeo frequently but we collectively agreed that Naomi needed time to rest before tackling the rodeo. Our priority is her wellbeing.

The plan is to go up and stay with Selene and Gunnar for the last weekend for the Wildcard competition rounds, Finals and the Championship. Alvie will be busy as all get out during the day, but he'll have downtime in the evening.

"I didn't even think about packing for the rodeo." Naomi says, panicking in front of her bag. "What am I supposed to wear?"

"Don't worry. You're what, a size 18/20?" I ask.

"Yeah." She replies, a little surprised I guessed so accurately.

"Perfect. We can raid some of my old clothes then. I'm a 22 these days, but I knew I kept my old wardrobe for a reason." I wink.

Leading her into our walk in closet, I pull out boxes from the back.

"We're the same size shoe, right? 7 wide?"

"Yes. I think the boots Alvie found for me were an old pair of yours." She says, coming up behind me to grasp me by the hips where I'm bent over.

She slides one of her hands down my spine while the other cups my ass. I shiver at her touch before straightening myself and turning to look at her.

"What was that for?" I ask.

"I wanted to touch you, and you look so good bent over like that." She smirks.

"Nay."

"Bex."

"Don't play with me." I warn.

In the week that she's been staying with us, we haven't played, haven't toed that line for fear of it triggering something for her. But now, the lust in her gaze tells me she wants more from me.

"You and Alvie have been driving me nuts with all your touches. You'll play with my hair, massage my body top to toe, cuddle me with your fingers trailing over my body until I fall asleep. But you won't *touch me*. I need you to touch me, Bex."

"We haven't wanted to push you." I sigh.

"You're not pushing. I'm asking." She pouts.

"You're sure?" I ask.

"Yes. I need you." Her eyes almost glisten with what could be tears or need.

I take a step into her body, flashes of the fantasies that constantly run through my mind blurring together in my head.

"You want me to touch you, bunny? You want me to handcuff you to the bed, spread you out before me, eat you out and finger you until you're calling my name?" Her breath catches and she freezes in place. I press my nose into her shoulder and drag my tongue up from her collar bone and to her ear, which I nip at before murmuring. "Or do you want me to strap on a cock of my own and fuck you until you can't see straight?"

Her breathing turns heavy as I wait for my answer. "Both."

"Both, what."

"Both, please."

"Uh uhh. Both, *what*?"

"Both, ma'am."

"That's a good bunny."

"Go strip and get on the bed, I'm going to dig through another box for us." I command.

She practically sprints out of the closet at my instructions, and I chuckle as she leaves.

I walk over to the dresser where I keep my personal toys, not the collection that Alvie keeps in our armoire for pickup play but our more personal items. I select cuffs, a strapless double ended dildo, and a vibrator.

Coming out of the closet, I freeze just beyond the doorway at the sight of Naomi naked on her knees, eyes cast downward.

"Where'd this come from?" I ask, breathless at the sight.

"Do you like it?" She looks up. "I saw it... in porn. I thought..."

"I like it very much, bunny." My voice is breathy. "Very much."

I walk over and guide her up to standing by holding her face before backing her into the foot of the bed.

"I'm going to put you on all fours and handcuff your hands behind your knees. Then I'm going to take this strapless dildo and use it to make us both cum. When you're still shaking with plea-sure, I'm going to flip you over on your back, and continue to fuck you with this vibrator on your clit. You're going to give me at least three orgasms tonight before Alvie gets home, got it?"

She shivers and nods. "Yes, ma'am."

"On the bed. All fours, hands ready to be cuffed."

Naomi scrambles on the bed and I arrange all my supplies on the bedside table so I can grab them easily, as well as grab a bottle of lube out of the drawer.

Her position with her shoulders pressed into the bed, ass in the air, has me admiring the curve of her back and swell of her ass. She's watching me carefully with a playfulness in her eye.

I've been worried about her all week, but I have to trust that she knows what she wants right now. That she's ready.

"You're sure you want this, Nay?" I ask softer.

"Yes, Bex. I want this." She practically growls.

I smirk at her sass and give her a slap to her ass, making her moan.

I climb up on the bed with the cuffs and carefully fasten her wrists into them before binding her wrists together.

Caressing her ass, I reverently give it another thwack. Not too hard to cause pain, but enough to have her gasping again.

Her ass is positioned perfectly in the air. I love the little dimples in her skin and the way her stomach curves into the sensitive area around her hip. Leaning down, I give a kiss to her cheek before pulling back to admire her once more.

My gaze goes down to her pussy, her folds hiding the sensitive bud that will make her moan as I play with her.

I use my fingers to separate her to reveal her center. She's pink and swollen with desire, which only makes me want her more.

My head dips down and I lick her from front to back, making sure my tongue presses in on the sensitive areas of her clit and labia.

The taste of her overwhelms my senses, leaving me hungry for more.

I dive back in, eager to consume her and leave her writhing for me, begging for me to fuck her. I eat her like a woman starved, switching between suckling on her lower lips and stroking her clit with the flat of my tongue.

In minutes I have her moaning for me, rocking back on my face, ready for more.

I pull back. "You want more, bunny? You want me to fuck you

with my fingers and make you come around them when I tell you like a good girl?"

She nods vigorously.

Slowly, I insert my index finger into her channel. I take a moment to marvel at how tight she is around me, how wet and ready she is.

She moans at the intrusion, before begging. "More, please. I need more."

"Oh? Is my little bunny a size queen? Do you want me to stuff you with my fingers and stroke you till you come?"

"Yes, ma'am. Please, I need you to fill me up with your fingers." She pants out, her face buried in the quilt on the bed.

Backing my finger out, I cross it with another and insert them into her once more. Her walls clench around my fingers as they glide in and out of her. When I add a third, her head lifts up and she lets out a guttural moan that echos through the room, but when I pull out she whines in distress.

"Bunny likes being full doesn't she."

"Mhmm." She whimpers.

With my free hand, I reach down to circle her clit and move in slow lazy strokes. When she jumps at the contact, I press down harder on her pert nub and she relaxes into the touch.

In and out my fingers move as I use my other hand to circle her clit. I set a rhythm, keeping my movements steady the whole time I tease her. Each time she gets close, when her ass is writhing in my face and her walls are fluttering around my fingers, I stop, letting her feel the full extent of my torture.

"Please." She begs. "I need it. Please let me come."

Her breath is harsh and her voice is raspy with need. The slight whine in her tone has me feeling sympathy for her plight and when she looks over her shoulder and our gazes connect, I know she deserves it. Not just the orgasm, but the world.

"Come for me, bunny. Come on my hand and I'll let you have my cock." I pur.

It only takes a few more pumps of my fingers and more pressure on her clit before she's screaming in pleasure as she comes. Her whole body is shaking with pleasure and her hands grasp in their cuffed position, trying desperately to cling to something and channel the energy rushing through her body.

As I withdraw from her body, shivers roll through her and she whines with each aftershock which has her pressing her hips back into me.

I take my hands and place them on her ass, circling there as she rides out her wave of pleasure until she collapses into the bed in pure bliss.

"Such a good bunny, coming for me like that." I squeeze her cheeks lightly. "Can you take more?"

"Mhmmh." She groans in affirmation.

"Words, bunny. I need your words." I push.

"Yes, ma'am. I can take more. Give me more, please."

"Such a good girl, saying please." A grin spreads across my face. "Give me a minute to get myself ready for you. Breathe, bunny. Rest and breathe."

She nods and relaxes into the bed.

I grab the strapless double sided dildo which I laid on the bed beside us and run my fingers, wet with Naomi's own arousal over the portion of the dildo that inserts into my own pussy. Coating the bulge with each stroke, I get it ready to fill me up.

When it's ready, I reach down with my free hand and stroke between my own folds to find myself already dripping wet with my own need. Spreading myself open with my fingers, I take the portion of the dildo intended to fill my own center and run it along my folds there.

I shiver in anticipation and press the bulge firmly against my entrance. My head drops back in pleasure at the pressure and I pump it in, little by little, until it's filling me completely.

A moan slips out of my lips when I move forward and my walls clamp down against the intrusion.

"I'm going to fuck you now, Naomi. The only words I want to hear from your lips are 'yes', 'please', and 'more'. Got it."

"Yes." She whines.

Angling the dildo toward her pussy, I slowly press in, taking my time to fill her inch by inch. The dildo, not as thick as my fingers which filled her earlier, but much longer, makes her rock back and forth onto it as I push my way into her.

"That's it. Take my cock like a good girl." I moan, the part of the dildo inside of me rocking against my walls each time Naomi's pussy sucks in the dildo and pushes it out again.

Each movement from Naomi has a corresponding reaction that shifts the pressure points in my own channel. I'm full and panting with need by the time that I pick up my rhythm and start to truly fuck her.

Soon the rocking movement between us syncs up and with each motion our pleasure grows. It doesn't take long before we're both teetering on the edge, ready for our dive into bliss.

"Please. Yes. More please. I'm so close." Naomi screams.

"Come for me, Nay. Come on my cock."

Naomi rocks back on the dildo and screams as she comes. Her shivers of pleasure echo through the dildo and shortly after her crest, I'm following her over the edge.

With the dildo still inside of both of us, I collapse on top of her, no longer capable of holding myself up. But the echos of our pleasure has me rocking gently into her as I lay on top of her warm body.

"So good. So, so good." I praise her as I pull myself back up and pull out of her.

My hands stroke along her, caressing each curve and dip of her body.All the while, my pussy flutters and grips the dildo tightly until my body relaxes enough for it to slide out of me on its own.

I spend the next hour following through on every promise I made her. I have her on her back and I'm fucking the dildo into her pussy with the vibrator on her clit, her voice hoarse by the time Alvie walks through the room.

"Oh. Someone's been up to a little fun, haven't they?" He says, walking over to the side of the bed.

I just grin at him as Naomi continues to writhe and moan.

"Hi, birdie." He says, giving me a light kiss on the lips before sitting on the bed next to Naomi's head. "How's our bunny doing?"

"She's working on orgasm number four here. Think you can help out?"

His smile is brilliant and he leans down to whisper into Naomi's ear.

"You're doing so good, Naomi. Listening to your body and doing exactly as my birdie wants." He kisses her temple tenderly. "Come for us when you want, beauty. Come all over her cock. Show us how good you can be."

I try to keep up an even rhythm with the dildo, but I'm distracted by the way Alvie moves his hands along her body. He plays with her nipples and caresses her curves. When he reaches her pussy, he takes her palm and presses down on her pelvis just above where I'm holding the vibrator.

Just as he does, Naomi screams and pushes the dildo out of her along with liquid that squirts all over me and the mattress.

"FUCK!" She screams. "Fuck. Fuck. Fuck. Fuck. Fuck."

I keep the vibrator on her clit and insert two fingers to press up into her g-spot and she gives me another gush of liquid.

"Stop! Enough! Please!"

Immediately, Alvie and I both release her and I toss my toys to the side.

Alvie drops his face down to meet her, "You did so good, bunny."

"Kiss me." She gasps out, but Alvie hesitates. "Please." She cries, and I can see how the rejection is hitting her in her current mental state.

Quickly I crawl up her body, covering hers with my own and take her lips in a frenzy. Our kiss is frantic and messy. Need and desire coursing through both of us.

When our kisses slow and turn tender I feel the bed shift and Alvie leaves us alone.

"He..." Naomi starts.

"Shhh. He's had a long day." I sigh. "We can talk about it later."

"Okay."

16

———

NAOMI

March 15 — Still Spring Break

I slept like a baby last night, which is amazing.

It also means that I didn't get any packing done and I'm scrambling to go through boxes of Bex's old clothes to find things to wear.

Alvie is waiting patiently in the living room for Bex and I to finish packing for the weekend.

Every time I pass him, he glances up from beneath his glasses to follow me moving through the house. I love how he tracks my movement, how he pays attention to me even though I don't think he wants to.

When Bex and I finish filling up our three bags with everything we need, Alvie takes them out to the truck without a word.

"Is he okay?" I ask Bex as she's locking the door.

"I think he's feeling conflicted. He'll talk to us when he's ready."

"Conflicted about what?"

"You, Nay." Bex turns and walks away, leaving me dumbfounded.

The drive into Houston is pretty quiet, only the sound of drawling country voices filtering through the speakers. When we reach the outskirts of the city, Bex suggests that I send Selene a text to let her know we're on our way to their place.

MINDFUCKMASTER

Just passing through Katy. We should be at your place in an hour-ish.

OVERTHEMOON

Bitch, I know. I have your location, remember?

You gonna tell me why you were driving through central Texas at 3am last week though?

"Shit." I whisper, but Bex hears and looks over her shoulder at me. "Nothing. I'm fine."

MINDFUCKMASTER

Sorry. I kind of had a crisis and drove down early.

OVERTHEMOON

I heard.

MINDFUCKMASTER

What? Heard from who?

OVERTHEMOON

Alvaro called me that night. I just figured you'd tell me in your own time.

MINDFUCKMASTER

I'm sorry. I've been avoiding talking about it.

OVERTHEMOON

And avoiding me is.... part of that?

MINDFUCKMASTER

No! Never! I'm not avoiding you, I've just been in my head a lot lately.

OVERTHEMOON

Fine, but when you get here, we're all going to get manicures without the guys before we go to the rodeo. We can talk then.

MINDFUCKMASTER

Okay.

I love you, Lena.

OVERTHEMOON

Love you to, cariña.

"Selene?" Bex asks.

"Yeah. Evidently we're getting manicures when we get there." I pause. "And *talking*."

"Oh. Ominous." Bex chuckles.

"Yeah, evidently someone called her about last week and spilled my business."

Alvie's brow furrows. "She's your best friend. She deserves to know when you're hurting. People are allowed to show up for you when you need them."

"I know." I sigh and lean into the window to gaze out for the rest of the drive.

We arrive without incident and immediately Selene tackles me before loading me in her convertible, Bex having chosen to stay back to take a nap, to whisks me off for pampering at a spa and gelato.

The private club Selene takes me to, and specifically their spa, is nicer than any place I've been to. Normally I just go to one of those nail places in a strip mall when I treat myself to pampering, which isn't often with my budget.

"Hi, Ms. Selene." The attendant greets us cheerfully when we walk into the spa lobby. "We're ready for you whenever you would like to go back."

"Thank you so much!" Selene replies. "And you have everything down for me and Naomi, right?"

"Yes, ma'am. Appointments are set up for three. Manicures and pedicures for you as well as your massages, which we can either accommodate you in the same room or separately." She informs, and my jaw drops.

"Lena, I can't afford..."

She cuts me off. "You deserve this, Nay. I'm taking care of everything."

"Thank you." I say, tears welling in my eyes at her kindness.

I've never been comfortable with the treats and present Selene likes to send me when I'm at school, but the thoughtfulness of every gift always makes me feel warm and fuzzy. I know she's financially well off, but the joy she gets from treating me is worth the bit of guilt that pops up every time she sends me a book I've been wanting to read, crafting supplies, or, at a few points, ordering my groceries for me when my budget was tight.

She turns back to the staff member. "Our third won't be joining us though. She needed sleep more than a spa day... can't relate." She laughs. "But I'll be tipping for the staff who were scheduled for the appointments if that's alright."

"Yes, ma'am. That's very generous of you, they will be appreciative." The woman smiles at her, before pulling a basket off of the table behind the check in desk and handing it to Selene. "Here are the items you requested. Feel free to get changed in the locker rooms then head into the spa whenever you're ready."

"Thank you!" Selene says brightly.

We change quickly into comfy cotton robes and slip on sandals before taking the hallway into the main spa area.

Walking into the space is like entering a cozy cave with stone walls and floors and dim lighting. The space is warm and smells sweet like eucalyptus and something bright like citrus.

We're greeted in the main area by staff who ask us if we want a beverage and Selene requests water and wine for both of us.

They get us settled in massage chairs and I slip my feet into the basin of warm water at the base of the chair, enjoying the hot water warming me up, as the women set up.

Selene chats with the staff members, catching up with them about their live sand families, while I'm sinking into the comfort of the massage chair. When their conversation dies down there's only a moment of silence before Selene turns her energies to me.

"Okay, cariña. No avoiding this." My body tenses. "Tell me what's been going on. Why'd you cut out early last week?'

I want nothing more than to sink deeply into the chair and avoid this whole conversation, but I know Selene won't let it rest. Not because she's nosy, well maybe a little of that, but because she cares. Which makes me appreciate her all the more.

Working up the courage, I try to find where to start explaining.

"I had a really bad day last Wednesday." I start slowly. "Everything just hit me all at once and it was like I was trapped in a cave that was quickly collapsing all around me."

Turning to look at Selene I take in her compassionate expression.

"I texted and called you..." She cringes. "You didn't pick up."

"Yeah..." There's something she's trying to hide behind her smile, but I just wait for her to explain. "Something... came up, with Gunnar. We... I guess we had our first fight?"

"Y'all fight all the time, Lena." My lips quirk up at the edges and she smiles at my tease.

"We have spats and disagreements, sure. But we've never fought, not like this."

The women around us are absolutely listening in, but being respectful about it. Plus there's no one else in the room, which makes me feel a little more comfortable about talking so vulnerably.

"Sounds like we both did the thing where we got overwhelmed and hid away from each other then." I say softly.

"Yeah. That." She smiles back at me before her expression goes serious. "No more distracting me with my problems though. I'll fill you in later. Back to you."

I frown and roll my eyes.

"What triggered it?" Selene asks softly.

"Fucking Dr. Edwards." She scrunches her face, reflecting my own frustration and anger back at me.

"Fuck that guy."

"Yeah." I sigh. "I was doing okay earlier in the day, but then I met with him and it just pushed me into a spiral that I couldn't get out of."

"So you called me, and I didn't pick up... then?"

"I kind of just rode the wave, but it only made the spiral worse instead of helping me process. I tried everything to get myself to re-regulate: my embroidery project, cleaned my whole apartment while my happy playlist played in the background, took an ice cold shower. None of it was working, if anything it was getting worse."

"Oh, Nay." Selene breathes out. "I'm so sorry I wasn't there for you."

"It's okay... The whole time my brain was able to recognize what was going on, which was a little weird. It was like I was stuck in limbo, trapped between my logical and emotional mind. But when the thoughts got really dark, I got desperate.

"I called grandma, but she was asleep. I tried the hotline, but after like 5 minutes on hold I hung up." I explain.

Selene reaches for my hand with her free one. "So you called Bex and Alvie."

I nod, thinking back to the night and my throat chokes up.

"I wasn't expecting them to pick up, much less do everything they did. But I am grateful and it's been great spending the week with them."

Selene's eyes glimmer with tears that mirror my own. "They're good people, and they care about you."

"You think?"

"Oh, definitely." She nods aggressively. "I don't know how deep it goes, but they clearly care. You have people here, and I'm glad you reached out."

"Me too." I say, glancing away to focus on the art on the walls and soothing music coming through the speakers.

After a few minutes Selene asks. "So what's going on with them?"

"Oh, Goddess. I have no idea." I say, dropping my head back against the head rest and staring up at the ceiling. "There's been a few... things that have happened, but I don't really know where I stand."

"Things?" She asks, her voice lilting up at the end of her question in curiosity.

Glancing at the ladies around us, I can't help the blush that flushes under my skin. "I'll tell you later."

"Holding you to that." Selene winks, before settling back into her chair. "We can chat more over gelato."

I nod and turn my attention back to the women working on my nails. A basket of gel colors is placed in my lap and I rummage through all of the options, selecting a teal that makes my skin look tanner then it really is.

The women work, even adding flower details to my nails, which are more like actual nail art and far fancier than the basic dot flowers I've gotten before.

When they finish up, we're lead to a small waiting area with comfy lounge chairs and a waterfall in the background while we wait for our massages.

Completely alone in the room, I finally work up the courage to tell Selene the details I promised her.

"I told you Bex and I kissed at the club, right?" I confess.

"Yes!" Selene sits up straight in her chair and turns her body to fully face me, enthusiasm lighting up her face. "I'm guessing there's more? What happened over the three day weekend you spent with them?"

"You mean the one you bailed out on?" I chuckle, letting her know there's no hard feelings about it. "Yeah... So, we played together."

"Oh? All three of you? I didn't realize you were interested in Alvie too." She says and my face falls.

"No. Not all three of us. Not really." I sigh. "I'm definitely interested in Bex and Alvie too, but I don't think he wants anything more than a kinky relationship with me."

"Just a dynamic? No sex?"

"I think so." I shrug.

"Is that what you want?"

"I don't know. It feels weird to have Bex and I be headed in one direction that's definitely emotional and physical, but not have the same thing with Alvie." I explain.

"Well you don't have to have it figured out right now." She says.

I let my body collapse further into the lounge chair. "Yeah, I just don't like not knowing."

"Valid." She pauses, waiting for me to say something else, before prompting me. "So what happened then? I'm guessing *something* happened."

My mind wanders, thinking about the fun Bex and I had down by the river and later that night, how they tied me up and made me into a writing mess.

"Oh yeah. Something definitely happened." I smirk.

I tell Selene everything, well... most everything, about both times with Bex and Alvie's involvement in the time with all three of us. Selene is completely absorbed in the details, drinking down ever taste of tea that I give her.

"Damn girl. I knew they were naughty, but you've been holding out on me!" She says enthusiastically."Would have loved to see all that, or joined in." She winks and I blush at the insinuation.

"I don't need to, but I don't think I'll ever fully understand your situation with Gunnar. That's just so... well, I just don't know much about all these relationship dynamics. It's weird."

"It's not weird." She says defensively.

"Oh! No, not weird like that. I just... I'm out of my depths, *that* feels weird." I explain quickly and she softens.

"Maybe look into it more, especially with whatever is going on with Bex and Alvie. You're technically in a poly relationship of some kind with them. It might help to clarify boundaries if you know more about how different poly dynamics work." She suggest.

"You're totally right."

"Just think of it as another research project!" She says gleefully, knowing how much I love research.

Two staff members come into the space, interrupting Selene and I's very necessary conversation to lead us back for our massages.

The next hour and a half is pure bliss and I'm grateful for the strong hands that help work out the knots and tense muscles in my body.

By the time we're done with our spa day and off to get gelato we are fully talked out and caught up, like we hadn't dropped off each other's map for a week. And on the way Selene and I are belting out to her playlist of, and I quote, *The Cuntiest Songs.*

ALVIE TOLD me that the Houston rodeo is the largest in the country, but I really wasn't prepared for the reality of the event.

We arrive at the rodeo venue, which is not just a regular stadium like I thought but a whole expanse of parkland that houses everything including the stadium, an event space, exhibit space, and of course the Astrodome. All of this is surrounded by park grounds where vendors, booths, wine gardens, and a whole carnival are set up.

Everywhere I look are people dressed up in various combinations of denim, boots, and cowboy hats and suddenly I'm grateful for all the time Selene made us put into getting ready.

I ended up in a cropped corset top with floral embroidery decorating the boning channels and a pair of jean shorts that are far too short to be respectable but make me feel hot as hell. The outfit is paired with the fashionable boots Alvie refused to let me wear on the ranch. My hair is curled into perfect waves, my front wispies braided back and adorned with floral hair pins. Selene immaculately made up my face and somehow managed the miracle of getting my eyeliner perfectly winged and even.

Selene is decked out in an all pink outfit which is just as glitzed out and glamorous as Mrs. Dolly Parton herself. Her metallic pink boots, which we picked up on our shopping trip when she visited me, are the statement piece of her outfit and add a bit of sparkle to the softness of her pastel pink off the shoulder style top and deep rose jean skirt.

I can't keep my eyes off Bex though who looks like a goddess in a plain white t-shirt with a lacy black bralette peaking through the sheer fabric. With her denim jeans she's paired a belt with what I learn is one of Alvie's Championship buckles and her scuffed up riding boots. Her hair is down in natural waves from taking it out of her messy bun and she's applied light mascara, blush, and a lip tint which only accentuate her natural głowy appearance.

Easy enough to say that we take the boys' breaths away when we came downstairs to head out.

After we've toured the majority of the rodeo's offerings, Alvie's status as a board member gets us into a private box inside of the stadium that's reserved for donors and competitors, which has an amazing view of the entire stadium.

Alvie and Gunnar get us settled in our private box, complete with our own private buffet and bartender, and then Alvie goes off to fulfill whatever obligations he has to the event.

Bex explains to us that tonights events are the first of two Wild Card events leading up to the Championship, which means we are seeing the best of the best.

The events pass by quickly, and Bex patiently explains each and every event and sharing details of each competitor that she knows. The bartender keeps our glasses full, though Gunnar is vigilant about making us drink water as well, though we do sneak in a couple shots of tequila when he leaves to take a call during the bull riding competition.

When Alvie returns, he takes over giving us the blow by blow about everything, but it seems like every five minutes we're being interrupted by another person who's come in to say hello.

You'd never guess by their casual attire, but each introduction that Alvie makes leaves me more and more awestruck by the sheer power and influence I know these people have. They're executives of major companies, high level donors to the rodeo, and, of course, fellow cowboys and girls who come to catch up with Alvie and Bex.

By the time the tie-down roping contestants are lining up, I am well on my way to wasted and a little exhausted from meeting so many people, but I snap back to attention when the first cowboy lines up for his shot at beating the record, *Alvie's record.*

Hearing the Announcers talk about the man sitting next to me with his hand on my thigh with such admiration and reverence is a heady experience. There's an odd feeling that overcomes me knowing that even though I'm only a play partner to him, he still chose me. Me.

I'm important to this man who's surrounded by some of the most important and influential people in his world.

My heart is pounding by the time that all of the events wrap up and the event staff start transitioning the space for the nights concert and slowly bring out the massive star shaped rotating stage.

During the break, our little group goes out into the main gathering space that's reserved for everyone in our section.

Alvie takes us around, introducing us to more people, but when his fellow cowboy's start coming up to us, he and Bex grow tense.

"I don't like them flirting with you." Bex grumbles as one of the very cute bull riders walks away.

"Oh? You don't like when they smile at me? Linger a little too long when they shake my hand?" I say, stepping a little further into her space, pinning her between Alvie and me. "Or maybe it's when they scan my body with that hungry look in their eyes."

"Yeah. That." Bex pouts.

I laugh in that tipsy carefree way I only can when I've had a bit too much to drink. "Don't worry, I much prefer when you're giving me that look, ma'am."

Reaching out, I brush my fingers down the arm hanging at her side before giving her hand a squeeze and stepping back.

Her smile that I so enjoy returns to her face, but when I look over he shoulder, Alvie's scowl is still fixed in place.

"Any of these guys give you trouble, bunny, and I'll have them by their throats." He rumbles lowly.

A shiver travels down my spine and I find myself enjoying this protective, almost possessive, side of Alvie.

The announcers deep voice comes over the speakers,

announcing that the concert will be starting soon and our group turns to head back to our box.

Alvie walks closely behind Bex and I as we move. When I stumble a little over my own feet, he grabs me by the waist and pulls me into him to steady me before plucking my drink out of my hand.

"Nope. You're cut off." He warns when I turn back to pout at him. "If you're gonna stay for the concert, you've got to drink a bottle of water and eat something."

"Oooooh. Funnel cake!" Selene cries.

"Real food, luna." Gunnar growls. "And water." He says, turning us all around and herding us to our seats in the box with Alvie's help.

"Y'all are no fun." I whine, but I let Alvie direct me into my seat despite my protest.

The guys return with plates full of barbecue, which is way more appealing than my ego wants it to be, and of course, water.

The lights dim and I can see a truck pull out with people in the truck-bed, who I presume are the artist for the night. When the lights come up, there are three men—brothers—standing on the stage.

"Oh my god!" I squeal, turning to Selene. "You didn't tell me who's playing tonight!"

She lets out a full laugh. "I wanted it to be a surprise!"

Alvie looks between us, confused as all get out. "I don't understand."

"Oh man. I had the *biggest* crush on these guys when I was in middle school." I gape at him. "Year 3000 is probably my grandma's least favorite song of all time, I had it on repeat so much."

"It's a classic." Bex chuckles. "I like their newer stuff too."

"Even I'll give you that." Gunnar chimes in. "They're just fun."

"Right?" I squeak. "I was convinced I was going to marry one of them... Maybe I still have a chance with the youngest brother?"

Alvie's eyes narrow at me and Bex's expression flattens.

"What?" I ask.

"Just... no." Bex says.

When the first chords to the bands newest hit fill the stadium, my attention is completely absorbed in the performance.

Selene, Bex, and me dance the night away, screaming lyrics along with each song the band plays. I glance over to where Alvie and Gunnar are standing with wide grins on their faces as they watch us.

The night blows by and by the time the guys are loading the three of us into the SUV I'm exhausted and ready for bed, but still buzzing from the excitement of the night.

The whole drive back, Alvie and Gunnar chat back and forth in the front seats while us girls are cuddled in the back seat.

"I had fun tonight." I whisper into Bex's shoulder.

"Good." She replies with a smile.

I let my eyes close a little and feel the press of her lips to my forehead.

"Mhmm. Forehead kisses. My favorite."

17

ALVARO

Getting the girls inside isn't too difficult. Bex and Selene are able to walk themselves into the house, but Naomi looks so content in her restful state that I make the decision to carry her inside.

When I step through the front door of Selene and Gunnar's place, Gunnar is waiting for me by the door.

"I know those girls are gonna feel like hell in the morning. There's shit to help with that in the kitchen. I'm sure you'll take care of 'em. Make yourself at home." Gunnar says. "We'll be long gone by you likely are up though. Our flight takes off at 6 a.m."

"Yeah, man. Thank you. Where y'all goin' again?" He just stares at me silently. "Right. Not my business. Y'all have a good time though."

I turn away from him as he shuts the front door and walk down the hallway with Naomi in my arms. I pause at the door to Bex and I's room and see my wife passed out on the bed, already stripped down to her bralette and underwear. Naomi shifts in my arms and snuggles in closer to my chest. She's like a bunny with how she burrows into people when she sleeps. I somehow know she will hate waking up alone, so I carry her into our room and place her down on the bed by Bex.

Going in the room next door, I find her bag and pull out her toiletries and pajamas. When I'm back in the room with the girls, Naomi has already curled herself into Bex.

Part of me doesn't want to move her, but another part of me knows she'll regret it in the morning if she slept in her current clothes. Bex has already stripped into her lingerie, which is close enough to how she normally sleeps and I can tell she's removed her makeup too.

I shift Naomi so she's sitting up on the edge of the bed and kneel before her. Like the princess she is, I help her take off her boots before placing her feet firmly on the ground and helping her stand up. I strip her out of her outfit and toss it on the nearby chair, but when I turn back around she's already out of her panties too and in the process of undoing her bra. When they fall free I can't help how I gape at them for a moment before pulling my gaze away.

"Arms up." I instruct and she complies, though my voice is a little shaky.

I pull the nightgown over her body and help her sit back down.

Grabbing the makeup wipes, I peel off her fake eyelashes and start to wipe away her eyeliner and the remnants of her makeup from the evening. As I work down her face I take in her features. Here sitting before me on the bed, she looks so soft and carefree. Her eyes are dazed and quickly falling shut, which does make taking off her makeup easier. With each swipe her natural beauty is revealed, making my heart race.

When I'm done I go to my bag and grab the ibuprofen and my water bottle. I round the bed to Bex first who's just awake enough to take the pills and water from me and chug them down. Then I go back to Naomi who's still sitting on the edge of the bed, waiting for me.

When I approach, she looks up at me with glazed over doe eyes that I want to disappear into.

"Take this." I tell her softly.

Her compliance makes my heart warm and my cock harden.

When she finishes, she hands the water back to me, but she doesn't lie down.

"Time for bed, bunny. Lie down and get some sleep."

She lays down and I tuck the blankets around both of the girls, but when I back away Naomi starts to get back up again. There's a pouty expression on her face.

"Shhh. Go to sleep, bunny. I'll be here when you get up." I give her a kiss on the forehead, which has her eyes fluttering closed. "I'll always be here."

I'm still covered in dirt and grime from the rodeo, so I grab my toiletries from my bag and slip into the bathroom quietly. I go through my routine of brushing my teeth and cleansing my skin before as the shower water heats up. When I get the temperature just right, I stand under the spray and close my eyes, letting the day wash off me as the water runs over my skin.

The image of Bex and Naomi in bed together comes to my mind's eye and I smile, knowing that when I get out of the shower, they'll be intertwined like before.

Those doe eyes come back to me in a flash though and my cock hardens even more.

I shouldn't want her, we haven't had any discussions about any intimate relationships between us. It's just kinky with her, nothing romantic or sexual. She's involved with my wife, not me. Not really.

But my body betrays the logic that my mind is trying to use and my cock thickens. I grip it in my hand, willing it to go away but my body has it's own ideas and my hand pumps my length without my permission.

The tight grip around my cock has me remembering last night. How I watched Bex fuck Naomi with a dildo until she screamed and squirted all over her.

The image shifts and now it's me, fucking into Naomi with my own flesh and blood. I can see how her face would twist in pleasure as I bring her closer to the edge of bliss so clearly in my mind that it feels real.

My hand works up and down my length as I imagine how Naomi and I would join in body and mind. Flashes of her bright smile, her abundant breast and hips, the stretch marks across her stomach, everything about her flashes through my head.

Bex would watch us. She'd lay to the side of us to caress and tease Naomi as I fuck her. She'd kiss her passionately as I drive my cock into her tight channel, my cock enveloped by her warmth.

My wife would reach down to play with Naomi's clit, and, just as the vibrator sent Naomi over the edge last night, the fast rhythm Bex would set with her fingers would drive Naomi over the edge.

Naomi's walls would squeeze me so tightly that she forces me out of her just like she did the dildo and then she'd soak me.

But I'd want more.

I'd bury my face in her pussy, drawing out her orgasm and forcing her to squirt again. The dream of having Naomi cry out my name in pleasure as she comes for a second time is what has me coming to completion.

My eyes open and I take in the sight of my cum on the shower wall.

"Shit." I whisper, guilt coming over me now that the high of my orgasm is receding.

I splash water to wipe away the evidence of my shame before quickly scrubbing down my sinful body.

Walking back into the bedroom to dress is worse than

confronting nightmares, because these women sleeping so peacefully are the queens who will have me on my knees for them.

I pull on my boxers and round the bed to slide in behind Bex. I wrap her in my arms, burying my face in her hair, which still faintly smells of barbecue and hay.

I stay like that for a while, but soon the temptation to reach out to Naomi is too much. She shifts slightly in her sleep, whimpering as though she's embarking on the start of a bad dream, and I reach over to put my hand on her hip.

Immediately she stills under my touch and her whole body relaxes once more.

These women have me so royally fucked.

March 16 — Spring Break for just a little longer

I wake to find Bex and Naomi intertwined like vines. Looking at where they are curled together, conflicted feelings pop up. There's a glow in my chest at seeing them together. They just look so good together, in a way that makes me feel almost out of place.

Forcing myself out of the room, I go into the kitchen and start rummaging through cabinets and drawers to pull out supplies for breakfast. As I'm starting to put things together and pulling out pans, Naomi strolls into the kitchen.

"Hey." She says softly, sleep still in her eyes.

"Morning, bun." I say softly and she smiles. "Coffee? Juice?"

"Juice, please."

I get her a glass of orange juice, some water and her medications.

"What about Bex?" She asks.

I glance toward the hall leading to the bedroom. "She'll get up when she smells food."

The kitchen is quiet as I finish pulling out the ingredients and supplies for a full breakfast. Then Naomi joins me and the energy picks up in the room, energy zipping under my skin.

Just her presence causes something to spark in me. I know we were intimate in a way in the past and I feel a little guilt about jacking off last night to the image of Naomi in my fantasy, but I wasn't expecting it to effect me so much.

She's on the other side of the kitchen island.

"How you feelin'? I ask.

"Physically or mentally?"

"Both." I chuckle.

"Physically? Trash. Definitely hung over from last night. Mentally? I don't know..." She seems to really consider it. "A little confused, I guess."

"You wanna talk about it?"

The hesitation I see in her expression makes me feel helpless.

"Sit down. Drink your water. We can talk later." She follows instructions and sits at the island bar. I pass her the juice.

I go about cracking eggs into bowls for pancakes and put bacon in the oven. We sit in silence as I work to put together breakfast. I catch her glancing up at me and following my movements several times and a few times I catch her bending her neck from side to side, and rubbing at her temples.

"Where does it hurt?" I say, stopping what I'm doing and rounding the island.

"My head is pounding. And my neck is killing me." She groans.

I step behind her where she sits at the island. My hand comes up to her neck.

"Here?" I say, digging my thumbs into the base of her neck.

"Higher."

Applying pressure to the tight muscle, I run my thumbs up

until I hit where I can feel it is tightest. I press in and she lets out a moans that has my cock thickening.

Her head drops forward and I work thorough the muscle in silence.

"I'm going to presume that physically you're hurting because the hangover." I say. "How do you feel about what we're doing, though." I say, breaking the quiet that surrounds us.

"Just..." she hesitates and I hate it. "It's nothing. I'll be fine."

"I'm not going to let you get away with that. Not this time." I say, turning her around on the stool to face me.

"I just. It feels so good to be with Bex like we are? Knowing it's not just a fling makes me feel secure. It's... she's..."

"I know."

"Yeah, she is. But..."

"But..."

"I just," She sighs wistfully. "I wish I understood you more. I want to know you and I don't know how."

I'm taken aback by her honesty and I reach up to cup her face.

"I don't know if you'll let me." She whispers.

"I..." I stutter.

"It's okay. This isn't on you. I'm just trying to be honest."

My fingers snake up to fist her long strands of hair at the base of her neck and tug hard to lift her chin up toward me.

Naomi lets out a shuttered breath and her eyes flutter close. I press in close to her body that's now fully facing me. My lips go to rest next to her ear.

"And if I kissed you right now? Just like this with my hand fisted in your hair? What would you say? How would you feel?" I ask, my own heart beating erratically.

She sucks in a breath.

"Yes." She pants.

"Yes, what, bunny?" I pull back so that my eyes connects with her own blue gaze.

"Yes, I want that... I want to be wanted by you."

Without hesitation, I take her lips gently. She softens in my grip and I use the hand I have fisted in her hair to pull her up to her full height, though she's still much shorter than me.

Hunger takes over and I dive in deeper. My tongue tangles with her own in a fight for dominance. Another tight tug on her hair has her melting into me.

When I pull back to look at her, all I see is the haze of lust and need that's overtaken her.

I release her and both of my hands slide up to cup her by the chin. She's only a few inches shorter than me, but I'm still able to lean down a little and give her a kiss on the forehead before pulling pack.

"I like having you with us, Naomi. You'll never be unwanted here."

She nods.

"I need time. Can you give me that?" I say as I release her and take a step back.

"Yes." She says breathlessly.

Footsteps come padding down the hallway, and I look over to see Bex with a grin on her face.

"So what's for breakfast?" She asks, eyeing the two of us curiously.

I twist in her direction. Out of the corner of my eye, I spot Naomi's expression. It's lighter than before, maybe even a small sparkle in the corner of her eyes.

"Full spread this morning. We're gonna have a sit-down breakfast." I announce.

"Yes, Mr. Silver." Bex says from my side, giving me a kiss on the cheek. "How can we help?"

There's a light in the kitchen that glows between the three of us. As we work in the kitchen together we snack on strips of perfectly crispy bacon and everyone goes about their task, music playing lightly in the background from my phone. Bex is cutting up fruit and Naomi is setting the table and grabbing drinks for everyone. While I flip pancakes and scramble a mountain of eggs for us all.

The sun is just rising around us as we sit down to breakfast at the table.

Everything feels better, *right.*

18

NAOMI

March 18 — Post-Spring Break Hangover is real

Going back to school is physically painful. The ache in my chest as I drove away from Bex and Alvie grew with each mile that added to the distance separating us until it turned my stomach sour too.

I go through my routine the morning after my return, packing my bags for the day and double checking I have all the students work I need for my intro to psychology class I TA. My mind wanders the whole time though. Everything runs together and I end up straightening the same stack of paper over and over until my alarm goes off and I know I need to leave for campus.

The whole day passes in a haze, the rest of the week too. One class blurs to the next, meals run together, study sessions drag on, and sleep evades me every time I try to lay my head down to sleep.

I've spent the majority of my week after spring break preparing for my advisor meeting to discuss my dissertation topic, which I'm not looking forward to at all.

I've finally decided on a topic, but I have a feeling that my nearly seventy-year-old white man advisor isn't going to like my ideas. He's old school and doesn't see the value in innovation like I want to be a part of. He wants students to study the classics and apply them to modern clinical practice. His entire philosophy is a toss in the face of all of the progress the field of psychology has made in the past few decades.

Meeting Alvie and Bex made me realize how important embracing alternate lifestyles and relationship dynamics are. Counselors are supposed to meet clientele where they're at and embrace their individuality when evaluating them and providing them with resources and guidance.

I want to study the needs of communities like those who are in the lifestyle, who participate in polyamory and BDSM activities. I want to study the correlation between these identities and minority groups like BIPOC individuals, LGBTQ+ identifying individuals, et cetera. I want my practice to reflect the embracing nature of this new world that I've found with Alvie and Bex. I want to serve and support them.

I have my proposal binder clutched to my chest when I approach Dr. Edwards' office.

It takes me a moment to gather my courage and knock on the door and immediately I'm met with Dr. Edwards' barking voice. "You're late, miss Hall."

"Sorry, doctor." I say meekly, ducking into his office with my head bent low and my shoulders hunched.

I hate how I bend under his influence. I miss the confident woman that I get to be with Alvie and Bex. The strong woman they know me to be.

"Sit." The man commands in a way that grates against my nerves, polar opposite to how I feel when Alvie or Bex give me instructions. "Now. Have you decided on potential topics, *finally*?"

"I have, I think."

"You think? Or you know."

"I know."

"Alright, spit it out." He growls.

I scramble to open up the binder and flip to my notes for the meeting. I can feel Dr. Edwards' impatience rolling off him in waves.

"I don't have all day, miss Hall." The way he says my name makes my blood boil.

I've worked hard to get here, excelled in my undergrad and masters courses to learn as much as I can. I've put in my observation hours, written paper after paper, and sacrificed time and time again to ensure my success.

"Do you even care?" I snap my eyes downcast.

"Excuse me?"

"Do you give a single shit about this? Me?" I look up to meet his shocked expression. "Do you care what happens to me? Or if I succeed here?"

"It's not my job to *care*, miss Hall." His voice goes cold. "It's my job to break your preconceived notions and incorrect learnings down. It's my job to break *you* down, miss Hall, and reform you into a clinician that I can be proud of."

"So that's what this is about? Your pride?"

He chuffs. "If you're going to exemplify such insubordinate behavior then I suggest that you quit now, miss Hall. Your attitude has no place in my program."

"Oh that's rich." I laugh, full on laugh.

I must be losing my marbles.

"If this is how you're going to treat me, then I want nothing to do with it." I chuckle. "That's actually what I wanted to talk about. I want to write my paper on how clinicians treat patients who live alternative lifestyles and are part of minority groups. I want to help build people up, prepare other mental health professionals to embrace what they don't understand, and implement treatment plans that benefit clients within their existing circumstances."

"It sounds like a lofty goal for such a silly little girl." Dr.

Edwards' lips thin out and his brow furrows. "You're not going to change the whole industry on your own."

I think of my best friend, Selene, and her partner, Gunnar. I think of Bex and Alvie, and all of the others that I've met through the club over the past few months. How they've embraced me on this new path I've found myself on without judgement.

They're the people I want to surround myself with. They're the people who I know will be there for me through the ups and downs of life.

"No. I'm not." I slam my binder shut. "I have a whole community to support me. You're just not going to be a part of it."

Standing, I feel more sure of myself than I have since the beginning of my program.

I turn and head to the door.

"Miss Hall." Dr. Edwards' voice has a warning in it that I don't like. "You're going to fail here. So long as I am head of this department, you will fail. You should expect less from yourself."

It makes no sense to trust so deeply in these people who I barely know, but my gut tells me that this is the right decision.

"Then expect my letter of withdrawal soon. I'll go find more."

I storm out of his office with a fire in my chest. Every student moves out of my way in the halls and on the sidewalks of campus. It's not until I make it to my car when I break down.

MINDFUCKMASTER

I think I just quit my PhD program.

OVERTHEMOON

WHAT?!?

MINDFUCKMASTER

I just… fought? With my advisor. And I think I just quit.

OVERTHEMOON

You think? Or you did?

MINDFUCKMASTER

I did.

Selene's name pops up on my phone screen and I pick up on the first ring.

"Are you okay?" She asks, out of breath.

"I think so?" I reply honestly. "I think I'm still in shock."

"I mean, sure. That makes sense." She goes quiet. "Tell me what you need. Do you want to talk about it? Vent and tell me what happened? Help problem solve?"

Tears stream down my face, but this time it's because of her thoughtfulness.

"All of the above."

"Okay. Let's do this." Her voice is firm and reassuring.

I drive home, despite the tears falling down my face, telling Selene about my conversation with Dr. Edwards and how I stood up to him, which received the cheers I needed to hear. We talk through everything I've been holding back from her for the past few months and admit that I've been afraid to confide in her with all of the good things happening in her life, not wanting to sour her mood.

By the time that I reach my apartment, my brain has shifted to logistical problems instead of the emotional ones.

"Shit." I murmur.

"What?" Selene asks.

"My apartment is provided by the University. I'll lose it when I withdraw."

"You'll come live with Gunnar and me then until you figure things out." She jumps in, her offer making me breathing out a sigh of relief. "We can come up this weekend with the truck and trailer to move the majority of your stuff down."

"Okay. Okay. That sounds good." I say, opening my car door

and heading into the building, using my fob on the door leading inside from the garage.

"Hey, Nay?" Selene asks, her face growing concerned once more. "Do you actually want to stop pursuing your PhD? Or do you. Just not want to do it where you are?"

"I don't know, Lena." I sigh as I unlock my front door. "I just figured out my dissertation topic. And then Dr. Edwards was ranting about how I'll never succeed and it just made me snap. Part of me feels like I shouldn't give up on my education. Another knows I can always pursue another path and figure it out that way."

I take a deep breath in and out as I set down my bags on the kitchen counter.

"Well we can take this one step at a time. First, we get your ass down to Houston!" She squeals. "We're gonna be roomies!"

Doubt creeps into my mind. "This is a good idea, Lena, right?"

"Well of course it is, cariña. I came up with it." She laughs, before letting her voice go soft again. "You good, though? Do I need to worry any more?"

"Nah. I'm good now. Thank you for talking with me."

"Anytime. Okay. Game plan. You need to officially withdraw and start packing. Gunnar and I will drive up tomorrow morning and should be there by the afternoon. We can load everything up Saturday, finish on Sunday, and drive back to our place. Then we go from there."

"Thank you. So much. You really are the best friend I could ask for."

"I know," she says, and I can hear her broad smile through the phone.

We hang up and I look around my apartment, which for the first time doesn't feel like home. It feels wrong.

19

BEX

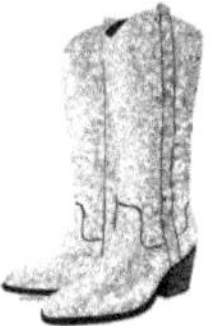

March 29 — Semester-end is coming in sight

"You feeling good about this weekend?" Alvie asks, breaking the silence that's overtaken the playroom.

Over the past hour we've been setting up and we are nearly ready to go through the suspension scene that we plan on expo'ing at the club this weekend.

We do expo's at the club almost monthly when Alvie isn't traveling, but this time almost feels wrong. It's been nearly a week since Naomi left to go back to school and the house has just felt too quiet without her here.

Evidently, a self harm scare that scared the shit out of me and a week and a half in our home was all it took to make me feel like she belongs with us, in our house and in our lives. Which is ridiculous. We just met her and have spent less than three weeks together cumulatively.

"Bex?" Alvie interjects.

"Sorry. Lost in thought."

"Do we need to postpone?" Alvie asks, concern lacing his voice. "You don't seem like you're in the right headspace for this."

"No. Not at all. The club is depending on us for the expo and class this weekend." I huff. "We can't bail."

"We can do without the demonstration. Class will go just fine even if we don't wrap up with a practical."

"No. I want to do this." I say firmly.

"Okay. I'm not gonna push you too hard tonight, though. I don't feel comfortable getting in too far with how you've been acting."

"And how have I been acting, Alvie?" I snap.

He comes over to me and raises my gaze to meet his own with one finger under my chin. "Lost."

My jaw tightens.

"It's okay. You miss her. I do too, a little." Alvie soothes. "We'll go through the scene together tonight, but we aren't going any further than that, got it?"

"I was kinda hoping you'd fuck me out of my own head." I pout.

"Is that what you need, birdie?" Alvie asks. "Do you need me to tie you up and get you off 'til you're exhausted?"

The way he's looking at me has me panting with need. "Yes please."

He raises an eyebrow at me.

"Yes, sir." I repeat with a little too much sass.

"Good girl," he says, sending a shiver of pleasure down my spine. "Okay, we're using nylon tonight."

He cuts off my argument "I know you prefer cotton, but Nylon has nearly three times the tensile strength. No arguing."

"Yes, sir."

Alvie pulls over a plush bench to the center of the room right underneath the anchor point we have installed in the ceiling.

"On the bench." He commands.

I move quickly to the bench and sit on its soft surface, the velvet cool and smooth against my skin.

"You remember everything we discussed, correct?" He says, coming around to face me. "Basic seated suspension. Your hands will be bound behind you. Because of your knee pain you'll remain on the bench while I tie your harness and wrists instead of standing. But I'll take away the bench once we need to get to the actual suspension rig."

"Yes, sir." I say, staring into his bright green eyes.

"Time for my birdie to fly." He winks.

I force my body to relax as Alvie guides my body through the needed motions to tie my chest in a perfect chest harness, called a Shinju.

Alvie's an expert at rope, it's why he's asked to do demonstrations at every club we visit.

I learned very early on in our relationship that Alvie's special interests are rope and leather, in all contexts. He loves the meticulous nature of working with the materials and knows nearly everything there is to know about them. All of his work revolves around the two, from his what he does here on the ranch, and of course his passion for all things BDSM.

Having his hands on me, carefully layering each strand of rope and twisting the strands into the right position to both tightly grip my body, while remaining comfortable enough not to pinch me anywhere, is a mesmerizing process. He's entirely focused on the moment and how each piece of the puzzle comes together as he secures the rope around my form.

The entire time, his hands never leave my body for more than a moment. Even when he reaches for a hank of rope that sits on the small standing tray beside us, one hand stays on me until he has to unwind the bundle and find the bite, the center.

Every time his hands return to my body for the next tie a shiver overtakes my body.

When the chest harness is done, he moves onto tying a simple pair of cuffs around my wrists, which I hold carefully behind my back.

"You ready for the seated suspension? Or do you want to stop here? Nod to keep going. Shake your head to stop." He asks carefully, making sure to maintain eye contact with me the whole time.

This is the one time he doesn't ask me to verbalize every decision and choice I make. We discovered a long time ago that I don't do well with words when I'm deep into a scene. My body relaxes too much, including my tongue.

This time is no different.

Every worry in my head and tension in my body have fled. All that's left is a pure buzzing content sensation.

Alvie helps me rise from my seated position on the bench and holds me tight by the arms until I'm steady on my feet. He checks each of his ties to make sure nothing is too tight, pinches, or has shifted too much for his liking.

"Looks good." He confirms before attaching the chest tie to a support line he ties to the ring overhead, helping with my own balance as my body once more relaxes into the patterns of rope that adorn my body.

Part of what Alvie loves about rope is the technicality of it. There's math and engineering involved in every tie and suspension scene. The process is meticulous and methodical in nature, which satisfies his need for routine and control.

It's why this balances us so well.

While in day to day life my stubbornness leads to playful bickering between us when I push back against his need for control, this is when I let go of that desire to fight. I'm a tool in his chest of toys to be played with.

"Eyes wide open, birdie." He instructs.

I didn't even realize my eyes had fluttered closed, but smile at the sweetness in his reminder. I nod to confirm I heard his instructions and he moves on to the new tie around my hips, a Swiss seat.

"Did you know that the Swiss seat used to be an old school technique used in climbing." Alvie shares. "But you can't use it for suspension alone otherwise your partner will tip over backward."

I smile broadly at his reminder. It's not the first time he's told me this kind of information, either when we're alone or in a class. Nor will it be the last.

He loves the stories behind each and every knot and tie. It's all one web of information that he gets to unfold for anyone interested in listening. And with how his deep voice rumbles as he works, which has my pussy fluttering with need, I *very much* want to listen.

With the seat tied securely around my hips, Alvie checks in with me again. "How are you feeling." He says, tipping my chin up to meet him.

Both of his hands go to rest on my shoulders. "Nod to confirm everything is as it should be, shake to tell me something is wrong. How do your shoulders feel?"

I nod in confirmation as he goes through each pressure point on my body that his mind has catalogued.

"How does your knee feel."

I pause, taking stock of how my body feels and checking in on my knee in particular. "Good." I croak out.

"Excellent. You're doing so well, birdie." He says, giving me a brief kiss on the forehead.

The next lengths of rope go to securing support lines between my hips and the steel ring that will hold all two hundred and sixty pounds of me.

Weightlessness adds to the haze of pleasure I've slipped into. Everything in my body has relaxed to a point where my mind goes fully blank. Alvie leaves me there, weightless and free, for what feels like an eternity.

"Open your eyes." I'm so content and it feels like I have sandbags on my eyes. "Open, birdie."

I shake my head.

"That's okay, birdie." I hear the smile on his lips. "But no orgasms for you if you can't open your eyes."

Immediately my eyes snap open as I whine in protest.

"Ahh. There she is. There's my good girl." He smirks. "You really want that orgasm don't you?"

I nod vigorously.

"Do you want my fingers, or a good fuck?" He asks.

"Fuck." I garble out.

He walks over to grab a water bottle and returns to lift it up to my lips. I gulp down the cool liquid and look him firmly in the eyes.

"Fuck me." My voice is strong this time. "Fuck me hard, sir."

"Yes ma'am."

Alvie tugs his shirt off in that one handed sexy way that men do in the movies, which makes my mouth dry and my pussy wet.

Slowly, he unbuckles his belt and unzips his jeans to reveal his thick cock. He takes his time, pumping his length before coming to stand between my parted legs. He skims the head of his cock up and down my slit and my head drops back with a groan.

Each time he grazes my clit with his cock my hips jolt up and the entire suspension rig gives before pulling taught against my skin once more. Each rub of the nylon rope against my body reminds me of the love and care that he put into supporting me.

That he always puts into supporting me.

After teasing me until he's fully hard, and a lot of whining for his cock on my part, he finally pushes the first few inches into my pussy. The way he fills me feels like being whole after a piece of you being lost for so long.

He starts off with slow strokes in and out of me before he picks up his pace and the thrusts turn punishing. It's like he's losing himself in me, my cunt, and I sink into the feeling of being fucked roughly.

His grip on my hips is tight and the rope rig helps him use gravity to pull him onto his dick, each time harder and deeper than the last.

The orgasm sneaks up on me and before I can warn him I'm coming around his cock. He doesn't give up on his pace though and moments later he's following me over the edge.

"Fuck!" He calls out as his cum fills me.

I love how he feels in me, my cunt pulsing around his throbbing cock as he comes down from his release. He's leaning forward, hands on the support beams of the suspension rig, breathing hard and smiling down at me.

When he withdraws from me my pussy flutters, wanting him to fill me once again.

I can feel his release, mixed with my own juices, running out of me and dripping onto the floor below.

After he's steadied himself, he walks over to grab the package of baby wipes to clean me up. The entire time he goes about the task, his hands drift over my skin in reassuring strokes.

When he's satisfied, he leans down and places a kiss on my center. A flutter of desire runs through my body, despite all the fun we just had.

"You good?" He asks.

"Yes." I breathe out heavily. "Can you untie my wrists first? My shoulder feels tight."

"Birdie, you should have said something." He frowns, walking around and quickly untying the rope around my wrists.

Alvie's ritual whenever we finish a scene is always the same. He cleans me up quickly, releases me from whatever contraption I may be in, settles me into bed or couch with a blanket and water before he goes about cleaning up the play space and the equipment he uses. When all is said and done, he will join me in bed to cuddle and talk through the scene and our emotions when I'm ready.

When he gets me down from the rig, everything goes as normal and I study him as he relaxes into the ritual.

I cuddle in tighter to the blanket that surrounds me, letting my head rest on the pile of pillows that are built up on the bed. Exhaustion sets in and it becomes harder and harder to keep my eyes open.

Just as I'm about to fall asleep, I watch my world slow to a stop as Alvie accidentally steps into the puddle we left in the center of the room and falls backward only to crash into the edge of the bench behind him.

He crashes hard to the ground, his head bouncing off the hardwood floor and in a cartoon it would be comical, but the blood running on the ground is a far cry from funny.

The entire world zooms into focus as I bolt up and out of the bed to crowd next to him on the floor on all fours.

"Alvie?" I say, panic rising in my voice. "Alvie."

It takes me a moment to register the wetness under my hand is his blood, pooling around my hands and knees.

"Alvie!" I screech, reaching to cradle his face and pulling away when I smear red across his scruff. "Siri, call 911."

Time no longer exists as I rush to grab one of the towels nearby to staunch the blood flowing from his head wound. Every moment that he's unresponsive increases my panic more and more.

When the call connects the dispatcher I take in my first deep breath.

"Victoria 911, Where is your emergency?" The dispatcher says.

My mind is racing and it takes everything in me to focus on the questions coming through the phone on the nightstand.

"Off Highway 87. We're at the main house on the Silver Rope Ranch." I say through my tears.

"Okay, to confirm that was Silver Rope Ranch off Highway 87?" They confirm.

"Yes. My husband fell and hit his head." I pant out. "Fuck. There is so much blood."

"Alright, and you said your husband fell and is bleeding? How old is he?"

"Alvie's 45." I say confused by the question, but only able to respond to direct instructions in the moment.

"Is he awake and able to talk to you?" They ask.

"No." I sob out. "He just... he's only been like this a minute or two, but there's so much blood. Please, help me."

"What's your name?"

"Bex. Bex Silva."

"Okay, Bex, you're doing a great job. The paramedics are on the way, but until they get there, I want you to find a clean cloth or towel that you can use to apply pressure to the wound. Can you do that?"

"I grabbed a towel and have it under his head. Does that work?" I ask.

"Perfect. Just keep holding that pressure for me. I want you to tell me if his breathing changes at all before they arrive, but I'm going to stay on the line with you until they get there."

Red and blue lights filter through the windows as emergency services arrive at the house, but everything that follows is a blur. People are rushing in and out of the house, and trying to talk to me, but I'm unable to give them answers. At some point, I dressed in my leggings and t-shirt that Alvie had lain out for me on the bench, but I don't remember it happening.

When they've loaded Alvie onto a spinal board and braced his neck, I'm finally able to snap out of my stupor. I follow as they walk him out of the house.

When we reach the kitchen a sweet firefighter finds me a pair of shoes to slip into as I grab the keys to the truck off the hook by the door.

"You alright by yourself, Ms. Silva?" They ask kindly, as I'm picking up my bag.

I stare at them for a second before responding. "I have to be."

20

NAOMI

I 10 is straight as fuck and it seems never ending with all of the traffic that's crowding the widest highway in America. The road seems to go on endlessly.

Selene and Gunnar were amazing, helping me pack up my apartment to move me out last weekend, but I've been skulking all week, unsure what I'm supposed to do now. So they convinced me that we needed a weekend at The Playground to relax and have some fun.

Plus, I'll get to see Alvie and Bex when we get there because they're evidently doing an expo demonstration of rope suspension this weekend.

I step on my breaks to slow down to a stop on the highway when my car dashboard alerts me to a new text from Selene.

OVERTHEMOON

Alvie's in the hospital.

Selene has shared a map location with you.

I respond immediately using Bluetooth voice to text.

MINDFUCKMASTER

What! When?

OVERTHEMOON

This is the closest hospital to them.

MINDFUCKMASTER

In all caps. Selene I need more information than that!

OVERTHEMOON

I don't *have* more information, Nay. I just know where they're going. So get your ass over there.

I pull off the highway and pull into the Katy location of Buc-ee's and pull up the location that Selene shared.

"Shit" I groan, looking at the map on my screen.

It's going to take me almost two hours to get there.

I bring up Bex's contact and try calling her, but the call just goes to voicemail. I try again, but once more she doesn't pick up.

"Fuck it."

MINDFUCKMASTER

I'm gonna drive straight there.

OVERTHEMOON

Good luck, Nay.

I put my phone down, press start on the map directions, and take my car out of park. It takes everything in me not to speed *too much* as I take off down the feeder road on my new route.

My music is blasting through the speakers, my sad attempt at distracting myself for the next two hours it will take me to get down to the hospital in Victoria.

The drive passes about as quickly as I can hope for, and thankfully no one stops me on my trip.

I pull up to the hospital around nine, and with the sun just setting on the horizon it looks like there's a bright halo of light surrounding the building.

Fear grips my chest as a squad peals into the ambulance only entrance with its lights and sirens on.

I grab my purse out of the passenger seat and speed walk to the emergency room entrance. A sweet looking older nurse greets me at the front desk with a smile.

"Hi, I'm looking for Alvaro Silva? He should have been admitted a few hours ago?"

"Oh. Are you his other daughter? Your sister came in with him earlier. " I blush at the thought. "They're up on the second floor now. Room... 218."

The woman smiles at me. One part of me want's to tear her a new one for making assumptions about my relationship to Alvie, the other, larger, part of me already has me moving in the direction of the elevators.

I get up to the second floor and am greeted by another nurse with white hair.

"Hi. Which direction to room 218?" I ask.

"Oh, Mr. Silva's room. To your left, honey. Your mom went downstairs a bit ago, but she should be back soon."

What is with people making assumptions today?

"Thank you." I say through gritted teeth.

I walk quickly down the hallway, checking the plaques by the doors for the right room. When I find the right one, I don't hesitate at the door and crash through the door.

Alvie is sleeping soundly in the bed, his head wrapped in gauze.

Approaching him quietly I him in as he rests. The rise and fall of his chest calms my racing heart and the quells the anxiety that's been accumulating in my chest for the past two hours.

"I think I should start calling you daddy." I say quietly, taking his hand in my own. "Everyone already seems to see us that way. Silver daddy, maybe."

I let out a small chuckle at my own joke.

"What are you doing here?" A sharp voice comes from behind me.

I turn around to find a very shocked looking Bex starring at me from the doorway of Alvie's room.

"Selene told me Alvie got hurt. I came here as quickly as I could." I breathe out, relieved to see her again, despite the circumstances.

"You decided to just show up?" She says with a raised eyebrow.

"Well... yeah." My voice goes quiet.

Tension builds in the air between us as she takes a few steps toward me.

"You can't be here when he wakes up." Her tone is desperate.

"What? Why not?"

"You just... you're... you just can't. Okay?"

"I don't understand." I say, stepping back and bumping into the edge of Alvie's bed.

"No you don't. Do you?" Bex says incredulously. "You wouldn't know the first thing about what this is like. Seeing your husband like this. Watching him get hurt."

I take a breath and use the moment to truly study Bex. She looks exhausted, as though the past hours have aged her by years. There's a sickening anxiety that surrounds her and permeates the air. Everything about her demeanor is wrong.

It's not her.

"Then help me out understand, Bex." I ask quietly as though speaking to a spooked animal.

"No." She says sharply. "I just. I need you to leave."

The forcefulness and conviction in her tone leaves no room for argument, yet I push back anyway. "Bex. You're not being reasonable."

"Reasonable? You want me to be reasonable?" She cries. "Why are you here, Naomi? Why aren't you at school? I called Selene less than two hours ago and you're here. Why the hell are you already here? Without my permission or request."

"I..." I stutter. "I quit."

"Quit what?"

"I quit school. I'm dropping out." I say, voicing the truth for the first time since I called Selene after my advisory meeting.

Bex's eyes go wide in shock before her brow furrows and her face falls into a staunch frown. "And so what. You decided that it would be a good idea to pick up and come down here, for what? What's your goal here?"

"I don't know, Bex. All I know is that I couldn't do that anymore. I couldn't be there. I couldn't be that person."

"That's fine, Naomi. But why the fuck are you here? Why now?"

"Because I was fucking done, Bex. I was done and I needed out."

"So you left."

"Yes. I left, and I had no where else to go. So I went where my people are."

"And what, we're you're people?"

"Well... yeah." I say quietly. "I thought you were."

"We're not your fucking people, Naomi. We're having some fun, playing around."

Her words hit me like a truck. I knew my relationship with Alvie has been purely based in our friendship and kink, but I thought there was more between Bex and me. I thought we had a connection that was going somewhere.

"I thought we were friends, Bex. Maybe more."

She laughs darkly. "Sure, we're friends. But we've never talked about anything more. I've never asked for anything more than fun from you."

"That's all I am? A bit of fun?" I say, letting go of Alvie's hand I've been clutching and stepping back from the bed.

"Yeah. And this isn't fun, Naomi." She steps in closer, trapping me where I stand. "This is real life. This is what it looks like to be in a real relationship."

"And everything up to now has been fake? Is that what you're saying?"

"No, Naomi. It's all been real, but it doesn't mean anything." She glances over to where Alvie sleeps. "Right now, I need to be with my husband. I need to figure out what the fuck I'm supposed to do here. And I don't need you around to do that."

"Fine. I'll leave." I push past her and head for the door, wanting off of this hells-cape roller coaster.

"I just... I can't deal with you right now. On top of everything else." She says as I approach the doorway.

"So let me help. Let me be here for you." I plead as I turn back to look at her.

"Just..." She sighs. "Just leave, Naomi."

My jaw tightens at her dismissal.

"Okay."

Tears stream down my cheeks as I make my way through the hospital and back to my car. My chest feels like it's been ripped open and my heart torn out.

I should be the one in a hospital bed, being treated for a broken heart.

I thought I meant more to them than that. Could have sworn that there was something more between us, but the stark reality of Bex's feelings being thrown in my face are all I need to disillude myself of that notion.

Just a bit of fun. Nothing more.

Practically a toy to be used for fun and games.

I'm tired of being tossed around, tossed away.

If that's how she feels about me, then fine.

I can deal with a broken heart. I'll move on eventually.

Wiping away my tears, I start my car and pull out of the hospital parking lot.

I'm on autopilot, driving back along the path that brought me here. Hoping that the clock will rewind as I reverse my path.

I'll go back to before, when I was simply driving to The Playground for a weekend of fun with my best friend.

That's all I'm good for, after all.

Fun.

21

BEX

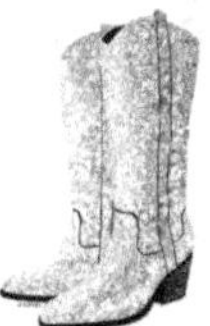

I t takes nearly three hours to get Alvie the scans he needs to determine if there's going to be any lasting damage and I wait as patiently as I can in the waiting room. Which is much more difficult than I would prefer.

With Alvie's medical history, and all of his past concussions from being in the rodeo circuit for so many years, another head injury is not ideal as the doctors keep telling me.

Naomi's appearance at the hospital, seeing her looking at him so sweetly while he slept in his bed, shook me. Part of me regrets speaking to her so harshly, but I didn't need her around distracting me. I needed to deal with this on my own.

Alvie has always been my rock, he's handled the world for me, so that I didn't have to. He takes care of me in every way imaginable.

This is my turn to return that kindness and love. It's my turn to care for my person.

Having her here would just be a distraction, one that would keep me from focusing on Alvie, his needs and recovery.

My mind keeps wandering back to her though. I replay our conversation over and over in my head. The image of her crystal clear in my mind. Her devastation as she left the room was written all over her face.

I should feel guilty, but there's no room in my head for guilt right now.

Focusing on the paperwork in my lap, I try to push the feeling away.

"Mrs. Silva?" I glance up to find a young nurse nervously bouncing on her toes.

"Yes?"

"Mr. Silva is finished with his scans and he's being brought back to his room if you want to go meet him there." They say.

"Thank you." I sigh.

The hospital is quiet considering the late hour and the silence only makes the thoughts in my head feel that much louder.

When I reach Alvie's room, I catch myself outside of the door, suddenly unable to move.

My heart sinks, realizing that I'm going to have to tell Alvie when he wakes up. I can't withhold Naomi's visit from him, and if I tell him she came by to see him, I'll also have to explain why she left.

Will he be mad? Will he understand?

Shit.

Pulling myself together, I force my body to go through the doorway. The sight of Alvie, peacefully laying in his bed with the monitors beeping steadily around him, calms me a bit.

I set the paperwork down on a nearby table and walk over to him where he sleeps.

When I reach for his hand, he stirs, blinking awake. His face turns to me like a sunflower to the sun and I smile when his eyes crinkle at the sight of me.

"Hey, love." I say quietly.

"Hey." He croaks out.

I reach out to grab the pitcher of water by his bed and fill the glass. I put the straw in and hold it to his lips, he gulps down the water. When he's done his head drops back to the pillow propping up his head and his eyes flutter closed.

"Fuck. My head hurts." He groans, eyes fluttering closed.

I giggle. "Yeah, well it seems you've reached the age where you're gonna have to get one of those Life Alert buttons."

He scowls back at me.

"Help! I've fallen and I can't get up!" I mock lightheartedly, before the sorrow takes over. "You really scared me, Alvie." I reach for his hand. "There was so much blood and you weren't responding to me... and... and..." I hiccup.

"I'm sorry, birdie. I'm sorry." He soothes.

"It was so scary, seeing you like that." My voice is small. "I was all alone."

"Birdie." His eyes match my inner turmoil. "You should have called someone."

"I called Selene! On the drive over, I called her." I defend. "Then Nay showed up." I mumble.

"What was that?"

"Nay came to the hospital."

"Where is she?" He looks toward the door eagerly and my stomach drops.

"I sent her away." I mumble.

His gaze snaps back to me. "What? Why?"

I take a step back and turn away, using the excuse of grabbing a chair to avoid facing Alvie when I tell him.

"She was just... she was dropping all of these really intense thoughts and emotions on me and I just couldn't deal. You were still unconscious and I was alone. And..."

"You weren't alone, birdie." He sighs. "She was here to help, surely."

"No." I snap as I whip around, anger surging through me. "She was here for herself and whatever the fuck is going on with her.

Plus," My possessiveness rears its head alongside my anger. "You're not hers. You're *mine*."

Alvie gives me a skeptical look and I turn back to the chair to drag it over.

I don't turn around when I add. "She was here to take over. It's my job to take care of you when shit like this happens. I'm your wife. She's what? Our play partner?"

Alvie's brow furrows. "I think she's more than that, don't you agree?"

"No." I snap. "You're my husband. She had no right showing up here without my permission, trying to fill a role she had no business being involved in."

"Birdie." His voice is a warning. "What did you..."

There's a knock on the door and a doctor and nurse walk into the room.

"Good you're awake." The doctor chirps. "Mr. Silva, Mrs. Silva." They nod to each of us before diving into their update, but I barely process the information they're giving us. Thankfully some of the suffocating emotions that were taking over start to subside the more I listen to them drone on.

My hand tightly grips Alvie's as they talk about his injury, and resulting concussion. I know from past experience, this will take at least a week or two of monitoring his symptoms to make sure that there's nothings super wrong. This isn't Alvie's first, or even his fifth. Being a rodeo star is hard on the body and Alvie's been bucked off his fair share of horses.

Each injury is another time when my heart seizes in my chest and my world stops. Alvie is my rock, he's the foundation that keeps me grounded. I'm not good in a crisis and he's always handled so many of the difficulties we've come up against. So times like these are nearly paralyzing for me.

A squeeze on my hand brings me back from my rambling thoughts.

The nurse is reaching out with a stack of papers in his hand, gesturing for me to take them from him. "Mr. Silva's discharge instructions."

"Thank you." I say quietly.

The doctor nods to each of us. "We'll finish up your paperwork and you should be out of here in a few hours."

"Thank you, doctor." Alvie says.

The duo leave and I turn to put the paperwork in my bag sitting in the chair.

I pray to whatever deity is listening that Alvie lets us move on from our earlier topic, but clearly no one is listening in my time of need.

"We're not done talking about this." Alvie says when my back is turned from him.

"I know." I sigh. "Just... I need a minute."

"Okay." He says. "Have you checked in with her?'

"No."

"Do you plan on it?"

"I don't know."

He sighs and I can hear the disappointment in his breath.

"I will." I pause. "I promise. Just not... now."

22

NAOMI

The two hour drive, which ends up being three with the addition of a number of stops to cry, back to Selene and Gunnar's empty home is the perfect amount of time to let my thoughts spiral into a complete breakdown.

Everything is suffocating and each breath that I try taking in feels like sand being poured down my throat.

When I arrive at the house, I leave Selene's texts unanswered and instead let myself in, greet Beef Cake, and immediately crawl under the covers to cry.

Time floats by in a daze and tears continue to stream down my face and soak the pillow under my head.

Even cuddles from Beef Cake, who seems very in tune with my distress, does nothing to cure the ache in my chest.

Bex's rejection was a direct hit to my heart and has me drowning under an ocean of mixed emotions.

My fingers itch to text in the group and ask for support, but that's in direct conflict from Bex's clear order to stay away.

I'm not needed there.

I'm not wanted.

The anxiety of not knowing how Alvie is doing only adds to the mountain of crushing emotions that's settled on my chest.

When the tears slow and my breathing is steadily matched with my calmer heartbeat, I'm able to draw myself to sit up in bed and take stock.

I feel my way through my body, letting myself embrace my tension headache, the weight on my chest, my clenched hands, and locked knees. With each recognition of discomfort and stress in my body, I take the time to focus my energies there and attempt to relieve some of that pain. Slowly my body starts to relax again, and while the emotional pain is still present, the physical toll of my heartbreak is lessening.

Laying back on the mountain of pillows I hid in, I just stare at the ceiling.

Time has no meaning when you have a broken heart. Hopes, dreams and plans that I made in my head are dashed. The future I pictured in my head is now a fantasy.

All of that potential is gone.

In its wake is a bone chilling hopelessness that swarms my body and soul until I'm floating in nothingness.

Without school or any kind of schedule at all, time passes in a mixture of moments broken up by sleep.

I know the long weekend is over when Selene walks into the bedroom where I've hidden all weekend.

"Nay?" Selene whispers as I uncover myself from my blanket and pillow pile.

Her gasp tells me all I need to know about my appearance.

"Nay. When was the last time you ate, or showered?" She asks, but I can't do anything other than stare at her. "Never mind. Gunnar!"

Gunnar's head is next through the doorway and his deadpan expression somehow makes me feel even worse than Selene's exuberance.

"Order Italian for us tonight from that place off San Felipe we like." She commands.

"Sure..." He trails off. "What do you want?"

"Just get a bunch of shit." She snaps, and Gunnar rears back at her venom. "Shit. Sorry. Just, I trust you to handle it. I'm gonna help Nay."

The way she looks at him in that moment, with such trust and admiration, makes my tears, which I previously thought had dried up, come back with a vengeance.

"Oh, Nay." Selene says, rushing to my side. "We thought you stayed with them. I had no idea. We would have come home sooner if we knew."

I nod into her shoulder when she embraces me.

"Let's get you cleaned up." She gives me a tight squeeze before rising and taking my hands to drag me out of bed.

Selene and Gunnar coddled the fuck out of me in the following days, checking in on me and making sure I was at least alive.

It's reassuring to have people around. It staves off the feeling of being physically alone, but the emotional loneliness is overwhelming.

Time passes in a blur and nothing feels real.

To go from the high of love to the low of loneliness is brutal.

They say women are trapped in gilded cages made by their oppressors.

What happens when your heart is bound in chains that aren't of your own choosing?

ALVARO

April — Probably

Bex is hyper vigilant over the next week as I'm healing. I keep telling her that I'm fine, and honestly the effects from the concussion really aren't that bad. Every time I try to shake her off though, she just get's this furrow in her brow that tells me she doesn't believe me.

I've been hiding in my workshop to try and avoid her mothering. But even there she's restricted me from using any of my heavy duty tools and won't let me touch any of my leather conditioners or dyes that may have fumes, even though I always wear a respirator when working with those materials.

Bex asked me not to bring up Naomi until she's ready, but as time passes, there's an itch for me to reach out to her. I worry about her, just as much as I'm worrying about how Bex is handling their fight.

I'm currently hiding out in my workshop cutting a new piece of leather from Italy. It's a goat leather dyed a brilliant mixture of teal and purple and textured with a holographic finish.

Leather shouldn't make me emotional, but a pang of longing shoots through my chest as I cut.

I turn around to grab the hardware I'll need to assemble everything and when I look back at my work station, it's like I'm hit by a freight train.

This is for *her*.

The pieces lain out on my table are for a pair of cuffs, a handle that will be attached to a chain, and a *collar*. All in Naomi's favorite color.

I don't know when I memorized her favorite color, but looking at the pieces, pieces made only for my bunny, I know things can't stand as they are.

The distance that's pushed in between Bex and I since my return from the hospital isn't there because it's distance between us, it's the place where Naomi fits. Where she belongs, with us.

I toss the hardware on the table and march into the house.

"Bex!" I holler, only to be met with silence.

I check every room in the house, but she's nowhere to be found.

Pulling out my phone I pull up our texts, ready to hunt her down.

BEX

Went out for a ride. Be back in a few hours.

I sigh in relief, but it's like my phone burns in my hand. My fingers itch to take action, to fix this.

Without a second thought I bring up Naomi's contact and hit the call button.

Three rings in I'm sent to voicemail.

"Fuck." I murmur, pressing the call button again.

It only takes two rings this time before I hear the automated voicemail message play.

I pull up my text chain with Naomi, and my heart drops.

There are so many grey texts from her, and so few blue responses from me.

No wonder she's not picking up when I call. I haven't been there for her in the way she needed me, *wanted me.*

She put in the effort and I ignored her.

Well, no more.

That same competitive energy I always feel when I pull up to an arena on Pop Rocks sparks to life in my chest.

This is a competition I'm not willing to lose.

I've set my eyes on a new prize now, her trust.

Her heart will be mine.

ALVARO

> You deserve so much better than how I've treated you, how I'm currently treating you. For that I'm sorry.

> I want to make it up to you, please. But I need to talk to you in order to fix this.

The read receipt comes through and then the text bubble pops up. It disappears for a moment before coming back. Then I breathe a sigh of relief.

NAOMI

> You didn't do anything wrong, Alvie. You've been very clear about how you feel about me.

> If it wasn't for Bex, you wouldn't have anything to do with me. And she's made herself very clear about how I fit into both of your lives.

> I'm done putting myself in positions that only set me up for heartbreak.

ALVARO

I hear you, and your feelings are valid. I regret much of how I've treated you and I will take time to process that on my own. But if you'll let me, I'd like to try to mend what I've broken.

NAOMI

You didn't break anything, Alvie. There was never anything between us to break. I was a play partner for you, a little bit of fun to have with Bex. I get it. We played, you had your fun. Now you're done.

ALVARO

I'm not done.

You make it sound like you're an object, a toy of some kind, to be played with. You've never been that. You're so much more than that. I was too oblivious to see that. Please let me work on changing for the better.

It's a long time before the bubbles pop back up, but no text comes through. I probably stand there in the middle of the living room for a solid five minutes before I give up waiting and slide my phone back into my pocket.

Bex comes home from her ride and we go through the rest of our evening in silence.

It's not until I'm climbing into bed that my phone chimes again and I reach for it impulsively.

NAOMI

Okay. I need some time, but yeah. We can try to start over.

ALVARO

Try?

NAOMI

That's the most that I can offer.

ALVARO

I'll take it.

Thank you, bunny. Sleep well.

NAOMI

You too.

24

NAOMI

Alvie promised me time, but clearly we have different interpretations of what that means.

The next morning I wake up to a picture of a sunrise from him atop Pop Rocks on their morning ride. Then the next day is a photo of the cattle grazing on the land by the river on their property. The day after is a video of Alvie putting some of the new ponies through their paces in the arena.

It goes on like this for weeks, a text every day with something else that makes my heart warm and the fog dissipate, even if it's only a little.

I keep telling myself the tightness in my chest and the tears that lurk behind my eyes are part of the process after experiencing heartbreak, but the clinician in me knows this is more than just a case of the blues. I can feel the cloud of depression setting in, and it feels inevitable.

Selene does her best to keep me in high spirits, but sometimes her energy is too much for where I'm at. She tries her best to make things better, but sometimes it's not possible. Sometimes you just have to sit with the uncomfortable feelings, ride the waves and hope that in the end you find yourself in calmer waters.

The daily text from Alvie helps though. Sometimes it's the only thing that makes me smile that day.

He never sends any words, just the photos and videos. It's like he's checking in with me in his own way. He's leaving the door open for me to step through and talk with him if I want, but there's never any pressure.

His persistence pays off when he sends me a video of a new puppy and the first words he's said to me in weeks.

ALVARO

She needs a name. Any ideas?

I click on the video and watch as a feisty little puppy runs around the arena, burning off energy trying to herd Pop Rocks who's standing still in the center of the arena. Pop Rocks looks like she couldn't care less, all while the pup is having the time of its life.

Another photo comes through of the puppy with its black ears, nose and paws. She actually looks a lot like the dog version of Pop Rocks, both having light gray fur with darker brown and black spots speckled about.

ALVARO

Is Spot too... spot on?

I can't stop the cackle I let out and a huge grin takes over my face.

NAOMI

She's really cute.

ALVARO

She really is.

So... name ideas?

NAOMI

I don't know... names are really important. It has to fit just right.

ALVARO

It's a dog, bunny. Not a child.

NAOMI

Omg! Children are even worse. Like they're stuck with it unless they choose to change it. It' helps shape their whole identity.

What if you scar this dog permanently by naming her something like Karen?

ALVARO

Then we just don't name her Karen...

NAOMI

What breed is she?

ALVARO

Texas Heeler, they're a mix of Australian Cattle Dogs and Australian Shepards.

NAOMI

She looks so much like Pop Rocks. It's like they're meant to be friends. You should name her something food themed. Like with the horses too.

ALVARO

Oh? Like what?

NAOMI

Maybe name her like Cookies and Cream because of her coat? Milkshake?

ALVARO

I like Milkshake. She definitely brings all the boys to the yard. :rofl emoji:

I'll get her a tag for her collar when I go into town.

NAOMI

Doesn't Bex get a say in naming y'all's dog?

ALVARO

She would... if she knew I got a dog.

NAOMI

ALVIE!

DID YOU GET A DOG AND NOT TELL YOUR WIFE?

ALVARO

NAOMI

You're ridiculous.

ALVARO

Bex will be fine.

I wait for another text to come through, but I'm met with silence. Instead I sit there, hyping myself up to ask the question that I've so desperately wondered for the past few weeks.

NAOMI

How is she?

I can practically hear the sigh come through the text bubble that pops up.

ALVARO

I'm not really comfortable talking about my wife behind her back.

NAOMI

That's okay. I just... I think about her and everything that happened a lot.

ALVARO

Do you want to talk about it? I'm a good listener.

NAOMI

I don't want to put you in that position, Alvie.

ALVARO

Just because I'm married to Bex doesn't mean I
always agree with her.

Or that I can't be there to support the other
people I care about, Nay.

NAOMI

Maybe another time? I just need time.

ALVARO

Time is worth as much as what you do with it.
Don't waste it.

NAOMI

Yes, sir.

Thank you, Alvie.

ALVARO

Anytime, bunny.

For some reason, that one word, one endearment, has me grinning from ear to ear.

Alvie continues to send me pictures and videos, and when asked, and sometimes when he's not, he always supplies me with Milkshake content.

For those brief moments each day, the world seems a little brighter, but it almost makes the other times seem that much darker.

We start talking more, though, just the two of us.

He tells me about his family and how he came to inherit the ranch, his career as a competitive cowboy and all that time on the road. He's surprisingly open with me and he never hesitates to answer my questions, even the tough ones.

His respect for both **Bex** and my's boundaries though is impressive. He never asks for information from me and always asks for permission to share any piece of information I've told him with her. While I make a point to avoid asking about her, there are times when Bex sneaks into our conversation, but he's always super respectful about what he shares. And he never pushes me to talk about it.

It's me who caves first on a particularly rough day.

NAOMI

I want to talk about it.

The thought of him not responding already has me crying, but his reply is instant.

ALVARO

Alright. Do you want me to call? I can be free right now.

NAOMI

You are free? Or you can be?

ALVARO

What's the difference?

NAOMI

One implies that you're already free. The other that you're doing something that needs your attention.

ALVARO

The second.

But if you need me, then that's more important.

Do you need me, bunny? I'll leave right now.

My breath stops and the tears start to fall freely.

NAOMI

I need you.

The video call comes through not a second later. Alvie is exiting a room and walking down a hall. He glances down at his screen and his face drops when he sees me on the verge of tears.

"Give me one minute," he says softly. A door swings open and clicks shut behind him, the lights coming on automatically. "Bunny, what's going on?"

I shake my head.

"Use your words, Naomi."

"It hurts. It hurts so much." I gasp out.

"What hurts, baby?" His tone is sugar sweet.

My breathing is labored and I'm trying to gulp down air to no avail.

"She doesn't want me." I sob out.

May — Maybe

After my conversation with Alvie, I decide that it's time for me to start moving forward. Which all starts with a trip to Sally's, of course.

I'm unpacking bags from my shopping trip in the bathroom when the door to the room I'm staying in at Selene and Gunnar's place swings wide open.

"Okay, this is quite enough." Selene snaps. "No more sulking. I've let you have your menty b and now we're done. Got it?"

I jump at her sudden entrance, and sheer volume of her voice.

"Oh, babe. No..." She says, marching over to where I stand with the Sally's bag in my hand. "We don't ruin a perfect natural blonde over boys."

"It wasn't just a boy." I mumble.

"Fine. Girls and others too. You get my point. But..." She

glances down at the boxes on the counter and the scissors in my hand. "A terrible, uneven bob cut and red hair dye are not the answer to your problems, cariña."

I groan at her enthusiasm.

"You need to get out of those pajamas and out of this house."

"I just left the house to run errands." I defend.

"To go about butchering your hair? That doesn't count." She snarks.

"Selene." I say, my voice hoarse from crying on the phone to Alvie.

It's been a rough couple of weeks. Or is it months? I'm not really sure.

Selene and Gunnar were really kind in taking me in after I blew up my entire life, but I knew that their kindness would come to an end eventually. They're a couple on the path to marriage and their own happily ever after. Why would they want to keep a negative Naomi like me around?

"Nope. No arguing." She says, grabbing the supplies from my hands and shoving them back into the bag. "We're going to the club this weekend. It's already arranged."

I jolt at her announcement. "We're what?"

"You heard me. We're going to The Playground this weekend."

Back to the scene of the crime.

If you can call falling in love a crime.

Is that what this was? Love? Is that why it hurts so badly?

"Look babe, it's Memorial Day weekend. It's been over two months and you've barely left your room. I'm so happy to have you here. I've loved seeing you every day and spending time cuddling with you and Beef Cake on the couch... well, when you come out of your room. But nothing has changed since you moved in. Plus, you've been glued to your phone like it's the only thing keeping you alive lately. I'm smart enough to know that you're not only reading smut on that thing. You type louder than anyone I know. So, I know you're talking to someone."

I glance to where my phone sits on the counter, just as it goes off with another notification showing Alvie's name on my screen.

"You bitch!" She shrieks. "You have been talking to them!"

"Not them. Bex said she want's nothing to do with me. It's just Alvie..." I say quietly. "He's been checking in on me."

She raises her eyebrow, snatches up my phone, and waltzes back into the bedroom, plopping herself down on the mattress next to where Beef Cake is sleeping peacefully, or at least he was.

"Ugh. Withholding information like this is a violation of the bestie code, Nay. You're in deep shit for this." Her words are harsh, but her tone is still playful. "Now tell me everything. Don't you dare leave anything out."

I collapse on the bed beside her and within seconds, Beef Cake is crawling onto my chest and pawing at me for cuddles and pets. The massive orange maine coon is the most affectionate cat I've ever met, and has been a solid companion through my entire, evidently, two month depression.

He's easily the chillest cat that I've ever met. Just very needy.

I stroke his soft fur, gathering my courage to speak.

"He started sending me photos after he got out of the hospital. Then we eventually started talking about things." I begin.

"About what happened with Bex?"

"No." I say quickly. "Never that."

"Good. That's smart."

"What? Why?"

"Because you and Bex need to work that out yourself. It's okay to be forming a relationship with Alvie outside of her, you know."

I turn my head away from the ceiling to look at her.

"Is that what this is? A relationship?"

"Cariña, you grin at your phone like a cat who got the cream when he texts." She sighs and lays back on the bed with me. "At the very least, you have a crush on him. But I'm gonna call this like it is. You're solidly in the talking stage with Alvie."

I look back up at the ceiling.

"What does that mean for us though. Bex won't even talk to me, and here I am, talking behind her back with her husband?" I sigh.

"Have you ever talked with them about their relationship dynamic?"

"Not really."

"Then you should have that conversation with Alvie." She looks over at me. "You're not doing anything wrong here. Is it complicated? Yes. But you're not doing anything wrong by being his friend."

"And what if it's not just as friends?"

She looks back over at me where I'm petting Beef Cake. "Do you want it to be more than friends?"

"I don't know."

"Well before you get ahead of yourself with that thought process. Figure out what you want. Go from there. And I'm always here to talk if you want." She sits up abruptly. "Now. Gunnar gave me his credit card and said we should have a girls day. So I fully plan on us spending up to his limit."

"Selene, you don't need his money. You have more than enough on your own." I chuckle. "And I'm pretty sure that card doesn't have a limit."

"Yeah. Sure. But it's more fun to spend his. I worked hard for my own. I want to keep it. And he wants me to do this."

"Well then what's the plan?" I ask, propping myself up on my elbows when Beef Cake scurries off my chest.

"I'm thinking a full beauty routine, I already called ahead for appointments for nails and massages again. I'll ask about getting your hair a trim too since you're clearly committed to it."

She continues to ramble off the plans she's made for our day, including a fancy by-appointment-only shopping trip and a dinner at some restaurant with month long waiting list, while pulling out more appropriate clothing for me to wear.

We hurry through getting me ready and are out the door within thirty minutes.

ALVARO

Have fun today with Selene.

NAOMI

Did you orchestrate this?

ALVARO

I sent her a text that you may need a pick-me-up. That's all. She did the rest.

I smile at his thoughtfulness.

NAOMI

Thank you.

25

NAOMI

Definitely May — May for sure, Memorial Day Weekend

Despite the bulldozer methodology, Selene's decision to go to The Playground was definitely the right choice. Our spa day definitely lifted my mood and prepped me well for her plans, and I finally understand what Selene means when she says that the club is the home of her second family when we settle in at the club that night.

When we arrive, the nights festivities are in full swing. People are on the dance floor, losing themselves in the thrum of the bass throughout the room. The bar is active with people getting their setups and already there are couples heading upstairs to the play areas.

We make our way over to the area where we were for Selene's engagement party, and immediately I spot Alvie and Bex. I wish I could say that I handled it well, but my first reaction to seeing them was to freeze in place, then excuse myself to the restroom.

I'm hiding in one of the stalls, trying to regulate my breathing, when Selene's voice rings through the echoing space.

"Come out, come out, wherever you are!" She sings and I groan. "I know you're in here, Nay. Just come out already."

I sigh and unlock the door, revealing Selene who's scantily clad in lingerie that shows off her full figure.

"Tell me." She commands, her face growing serious.

"I just can't handle seeing them right now." I confess. "It's too much."

"Look..." She sighs. "We're here for you to have a good time. If you want them to leave, I think they would for you. But I think the more badass move is to just enjoy the night without them. Right?"

I look up at Selene in wonder. "How do you do that?"

"Do what?"

"Just... that. This all seems to come so easily to you. Like navigating all this shit and relationships. You never doubt yourself or anything. You're like... an adult. A real one."

A loud laugh bursts out of her. "Take that back! I'm the furthest thing from being an adult. I've just gone through a lot of therapy."

I scowl. "I *am* a therapist, Selene. It's more than that. Don't discount yourself."

"Well then you should know better than anyone, that living in fear and hiding from your problems is never going to help solve them." She says, her expression growing serious before it's overtaken by a broad smile. "So let's go out there and enjoy ourselves!"

I roll my eyes when she holds her hand out to me.

"Come on, Nay. Let's let loose. Lose ourselves in the music and just enjoy the night." I blink at her, registering the sincerity in her voice.

"Fine. But I need a drink first." My head drops back onto my shoulders. "Or four."

Selene drags me back out into the club and over to where Gunnar is sitting with all of our bags. Immediately someone hands me a tumbler with a drink in it and I gulp it down.

Two drinks in, I'm buzzed and starting to relax. Selene and some of the other girls drag me onto the dance floor and we lose ourselves in the music, surrounded by others. My voice goes hoarse with all of the screaming and singing we do on the dance-floor and slowly I start to escape into the ethereal atmosphere that envelops us.

When I start to sway on my feet, either from the alcohol or exhaustion, I make my way over to the couches and plop down by our stuff.

I grab a water bottle from the cooler and down it in a few gulps before grabbing another. When I glance up, my gaze connects with Bex across the small space.

There's something determined about her expression, which quickly flashes to another emotion which appears more distraught.

I knew the time would come when my reprieve is would end.

Now is that moment.

I know she's headed over here to talk with me. She has two drinks in her hand and her focus is entirely on me. It feels like an eternity passes as she walks across the space slowly and deliber-ately, giving the butterflies in my stomach plenty of time to stir up a storm.

"Hey. Need a drink?" She says, offering me one of the plastic cups in her hand.

I raise my own tumbler. "Got one."

"Right..." She tosses back both drinks, shaking off the burn of the alcohol as it goes down her throat before sitting in a chair across from me.

Neither of us say a word as we sit there quietly while the room around us buzzes with laughter and excitement.

Alvie pops up behind Bex's shoulder and I smile at his appear-ance, thankful for the break in our silence.

"I didn't get my daily milkshake picture." I pout teasingly, the alcohol making me braver than I was a few hours ago.

"Wait... how did you know we got a dog?" Bex says, turning back to Alvie who blushes. "Did you say daily?"

"We've been keeping in touch." Alvie confesses. "I knew the Milkshake photos would be appreciated."

"*Daily* photos?" Bex squeaks.

"You said you didn't want to talk about it." He scolds.

Suddenly it's like I'm not even there, they're lost in their own conversation, tension thick between them.

"About *it* Alvie. The *hospital*. You don't just hide something like this from your wife." Bex bites out.

"I'm allowed to have friends, Bex." He says, rolling his eyes.

"Yes. Of course you are. But *secret friends*?"

"It's no secret, Bex. Everyone else knows we're friends. You do too. But you said you didn't want to talk about Nay, and I respected that."

"I'm just gonna..." I say, trying to crawl my way out of the booth and away from their spat.

"No, please don't go." Alvie pleads, reaching for my shoulder as I crawl on the bench seat.

My jaw drops at the sudden touch and the feel of his rough hand on my skin.

"Alvie's right. Don't go. We should probably talk about every-thing...." Bex pauses. "I don't like how we left things."

I scoff, settling back on my knees and looking back at them.

"No really. I feel bad and I want to apologize. I just don't know how." She says.

"Sorry." Alvie says quietly, which makes Bex turn to face him. "You start with I'm sorry."

It's like Bex steels herself when she turns back to face me, but Alvie interrupts.

"Wanna go outside for a bit? It's a really nice night." He suggests.

"Yes. That sounds great." Bex replies. "Naomi?"

I nod and follow them out to the balcony where there's privacy and more seating. The thump of the music fades into the background as the doors close behind us. Alvie goes over to one of the couches and motions for us to join him.

Bex sits next to him on the small couch. When I start walking past them toward the chair at the end, Alvie reaches out and grabs me by the waist and pulls me down into his lap so I can see them both equally.

"You look like you've been caught, bunny," he says, grinning at me.

"You're looking at me like I'm prey, Alvie." I chuckle.

"I won't deny that I want you, Nay. I won't ever do that to myself again." He says softly before placing a kiss behind my ear. "Or you."

I melt into his hold at the small gesture and I let my eyes close to soak in the peace that rolls through me at his touch.

"So..." Bex interrupts.

I pop back up, pulling myself out of Alvie's hold and settle between them on the couch. "Right."

Bex looks me directly in my gaze. "I'm not going to make excuses. I know that I hurt you when I asked you to leave."

"It was more than asking me to leave, Bex." I frown.

"Right, it was so much worse. And for that, I'm sorry." She seems genuinely remorseful. "I was already freaking out because of everything going on with Alvie and I reacted in a way that I'm not proud of."

Alvie's hand goes to my back and he starts tracing my spine up and down, letting me relax into his touch.

"Why didn't you try talking to me sooner, Bex? It's been over two months since everything happened. I haven't heard from you once." I exhale.

"And I haven't heard from you either." She says defensively, her hackles rising before she forces herself to relax. "Sorry. That's not fair. I did tell you to stay away. I should have reached out sooner. I just felt so guilty after and with every day that passed, it felt even more intimidating to reach out. To say I'm sorry."

I sigh.

"I would like to try and mend things between us, because... I miss you, Nay. I miss what we had and I want that back."

"I don't, Bex." My voice is hard. "I don't want what we had. It wasn't healthy for either of us. I never knew where we stood. I know we have fun together, but I need more. I want to know that I'm wanted."

"Oh, Nay." She says, softening in a way that feels too much like pity.

"Don't 'Oh, Nay.' me. I don't know about you, but I can't separate feelings and sex. They're two halves of the whole for me. I don't just want you in the bedroom, Bex. I want you everywhere else too." Gathering my courage, I turn to Alvie. "And you. I don't like the distance that you kept between us before your accident. I've loved our texts back and forth recently, and I do want to be your friend. But I need more from you too, Alvie. I want physical intimacy with you just as much as I want the emotional intimacy we've been building."

I shake myself from both of their touches, stand, and turn to look down at them where they sit on the couch. "I want to share all of myself with both of you, but I need you to do the same with me."

Walking away and not giving them the opportunity to respond is probably immature, but I can't take any more of this conversation. So I run back inside and try to lose myself in the energy of the night.

And maybe a bottle of vodka.

THE NEXT MORNING, my head is pounding and my body is sore, but Gunnar drags Selene and I to brunch and is currently prying us with waffles, eggs, and breakfast meat galore.

"No mimosa's?" Selene groans to Gunnar.

"No mimosa's for you, luna." He chuckles. "I think you've had enough alcohol for a while."

Her little harrumph only makes Gunnar laugh more. I can't help but smile at their antics.

"Okay." Selene says, perking up and turning to face me. "So what happened with Bex and Alvie last night?"

It's my turn to groan.

"No getting out of it, Naomi. She's just going to keep pushing." Gunnar smiles.

"He's right you know." She says, her attention bouncing back to me. "Now spill."

"Not much happened, we just talked out on the balcony for a while. I told them how I've been feeling and we left it at that."

"So... you ran."

"I did not run!" I defend.

"Runner." She snickers, picking up a piece of bacon. "Speak of the devils. Look who just walked in."

My head spins to the entryway to spot Bex and Alvie walking up to the host stand.

Selene is already up and bouncing over to them before I can stop her.

I watch, in horror, as she has some animated conversation with the couple before turning back to us and strutting over like a model who just won America's Next Top Model.

"Look who I found!" She giggles as the trio approaches us. "Bex and Alvie are going to join for brunch. I'm so glad they put us at a table for six this morning."

Gunnar's smirk has me glaring at her and her plotting.

When she sits down next to me, she leans in close and whispers in my ear. "You owe me for this."

"Morning everyone." Alvie says a little too loudly, pulling out a chair for Bex to sit in before settling in next to me himself. "How'd everyone sleep?"

"I would keep voices down this morning, these girls went hard last night." Gunnar chuckles.

"Oh?" Alvie smirks.

"I tried to stop them, but I think they snuck a bottle of vodka out of the cooler when I wasn't looking."

"We ended up turning in early." Bex says, looking pointedly at me.

"What are y'all's plans for the rest of the weekend?" Selene asks before taking another big bite of her waffle.

"We're thinking of checking out early and going back to the ranch today." Bex glances. "Alvie's missing his new puppy."

"Milkshake is an important part of the family now, Bex." Alvie scowls.

"I'd love to meet her sometime." I say, glancing at Alvie before stuffing my face alongside my bestie.

"You should leave with them then!" Selene says, a little too enthusiastically. "You already have a bag packed for the weekend."

"Selene." Gunnar warns with a furrow in his brow.

"What? It would be perfect!" She exclaims.

"We would love to have you stay with us if you wanted to." Bex offers.

"Really?" My head whips in her direction.

"Of course. You're always welcome at the ranch. We can put you up in one of the cabins if you don't want to stay with us in the house."

"Oh oh oh! Nay, this could be perfect. Gunnar and I could go get your stuff and we could come out and stay with you for the week. It could be like a little vacation!"

Alvie laughs. "Yes, of course you're invited to stay too, Selene."

"Ope. Sorry, inviting myself aren't I?"

"Yeah, but it's fine. We would love to have y'all."

"Then it's settled. Gunnar and I will go pack up stuff for the three of us and then come out Tuesday. You'll go out to the ranch today with Alvie and Bex, meet Milkshake and all that."

I raise an eyebrow at her. "Why can't I come pack my own bag?"

"Because I said so." Her face grows serious.

"Okay. Fine." I turn to Bex and Alvie. "Are y'all okay with this?"

"Of course." Bex says, a little too eagerly.

"Okay..." Something has me hesitating, but I push it aside. "I guess I should go pack my bag then."

"Yes. Yes! You definitely should." Selene says, bouncing in her seat. "We'll meet you back at the room."

I side eye Selene as I rise from my chair.

"What? Gunnar has to pay for breakfast." I lift my eyebrow. "Goddess, Nay. Give a girl a minute alone with her fiancé, would you?"

"Fine. I'll see you at the room."

"See you there!"

I pause at the restaurant entryway and look back at the table to find Selene whispering animatedly to Bex and Alvie, but I don't have the energy to deal with that.

26

BEX

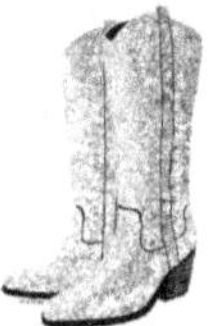

Still May — Officially Memorial Day, unfortunately

The drive back to the ranch was quieter than I would have liked. I try talking with Naomi a few times early on, but then she put in her headphones and we spend the rest of the ride back to the ranch with only Alvie's country station to break up the silence.

Like always, pulling back onto the ranch property has my nerves settling.

I'm home.

And for the first time in a while, it feels like everything is as it should be with Naomi here.

Naomi pulls out her headphones to pack them away as we pull up to the ranch house.

"Do you want to stay with us in the house, or would you rather us put you up in one of the cabins?" Alvie asks.

I look back at Naomi, hoping she'll ask to stay in the ranch-house with us.

"I think I'd prefer the cabin, if that's alright."

My heart drops.

"Of course it is." He replies. "I'll help Bex bring our bags inside and then I'll drive you over to the cabins and get you set up in one."

"Thank you." She says quietly.

I hop out of the truck and round to the back where all of our bags are and grab our suitcases.

"What do you think you're doing?" I hiss at Alvie when we approach the front door to our home. "How are we supposed to spend any time with her if she's all the way out at the cabins. This isn't the plan."

"Plan, shman. This is what Naomi is asking for." He says, unlocking the front door and stepping through with the bags. "Plus, you have two legs, Bex. We can always go and visit her over there, or we invite her to dinner and spend time at the house."

"Fine. But Selene's not gonna be happy with this." I scoff.

"No. *You're* not happy with this. Selene's plot has nothing to do with your needs and everything to do with Naomi's. We're following Naomi's lead here, Bex." He says calmly before closing the front door, leaving me alone in the house.

The rest of the weekend on the ranch passes quietly. Naomi comes over in the evenings for dinner with us, but mostly sticks to herself. Though, she has dognapped Milkshake, who now sleeps with her in her cabin. Then in the mornings, Alvie goes over with breakfast to pick both Milkshake and Naomi up so they can be a part of his day.

I don't like how separate I feel from them, but it's only been a few days. Surely things will change soon.

SELENE

We're an hour out. Any chance you want to pick up BBQ for the group?

BEX

Group?

SELENE

Yeah! Me, Gunnar, Durante, Reka, and Symon are all on our way. Didn't I tell you?

BEX

No... you did not.

SELENE

Oops! Well, they helped us pack Naomi up.

BEX

What do you mean, helped pack her up? Y'all are just staying the week.

SELENE

Well, yeah. Gunnar and me are....

BEX

Selene... what are you plotting?

SELENE

Got to go. Gunnar needs me to drive.

BEX

Liar.

Gunnar hasn't let you drive a car in three years.

Selene...

Selene Aracely Solis de Estrella!

I grumble to myself as Alvie pulls back up to the house and I pounce as soon as I'm through the door.

"We have both Selene and Gunnar on their way, but evidently Durante, Reka, and Symon are coming too!"

Alvie raises his eyebrow at me as I start pacing the house.

"And..."

"Selene's stopped responding to my texts." I huff. "She's avoiding me. And she's plotting."

"That's what she does, birdie." He chuckles.

"She's requested BBQ for lunch." I pout.

"Alright, I'll run into town and grab stuff from Fort's place."

"Will he still be open?"

"It's only 11 a.m. He shouldn't have run out by now." Alvie comes over and puts his hands on my shoulders. "Whatever Selene has got planned, it will be fine. We'll handle it. She may be a hurricane sometimes, but she's got everyone's best interest at heart... most of the time."

An hour later, Alvie isn't back with lunch yet, but two large SUVs and a UHaul truck pull up to the ranch-house.

Selene hops out of one of the SUVs, from the passenger side, and practically skips up to me.

"Bex!" She exclaims. "Where's Naomi?"

"She's down at the cabins." I say, slack-jawed.

"Well that's fine. I just texted her as we were pulling up to the ranch. So she should be here soon." She says, twirling on her heel.

"Selene? What's with the UHaul?" I ask.

"Oh! It's Naomi's stuff." She says simply, just as the woman herself comes down the drive in a 4-wheeler with Milkshake chasing behind.

"Selene!" Naomi calls out. "Why the hell is there a UHaul here?"

"Cariña! It's your stuff! We thought it would be easier to bring it all in one trip."

Naomi's entire face blanches at Selene. "Wh... Why did you... bring all of my stuff?"

"We're moving you in, silly."

"Naomi's staying in one of the cabins right now." I interject, sensing Naomi already shutting down at the sudden change.

"Oh! Okay. We can unload what she want's there and then maybe the rest we keep in your garage or something?"

"Sure. We can do that." I say, glancing over at Naomi worriedly who's now frozen in place.

I jog to catch up to Selene and grab her by the hand.

"What the hell, Selene?" I snap quietly. "You can't just spring this on her, or us. It's not fair to anyone to shove this kind of change on her."

Selene's brow furrows and she glances over my shoulder to where Naomi still stands, Milkshake circling her in concern.

"She needs change. She's stuck in a rut and she's not doing anything about it."

"Fine. But this is a little extreme. Don't you think?"

"No. I don't actually." Selene says, getting more frustrated. "She's my best friend and she needs this. I'm not going to sit here and watch her fold into herself like this. She needs this. She needs *you*."

"You need to talk to her then. Explain and get her on board. Because we're not unloading any of her stuff until she's fully on board." Alvie's truck pulls up just at that moment, pulling my attention away from the frustrated woman in front of me. "We'll eat lunch, and you talk with her before we do anything else."

"Fine." She says with a pout.

I turn on my heel to go to Alvie, waving hello to the others who are unloading from the second SUV.

"BBQ's here!" Alvie calls to the group as he eyes me with concern. "Everyone inside and we can eat."

ALL THROUGH DINNER, I can't keep my eyes from straying to Naomi. She seems more settled than before, but I still need to know how she's feeling about all of this.

Selene's a steamroller when she wants to be, and Gunnar spoils her enough so she gets her way most of the time. I can tell by the way Naomi is smiling that Selene won this round too.

At the end of lunch I start picking up everything and head to the kitchen to clean up. The others go to unload Naomi's stuff into her cabin and quiet descends on the space. So it takes me a while to realize that Reka is still with me.

I'm loading up the dishwasher when she finally speaks.

"How are you feeling about Naomi moving onto the ranch?" She asks.

I rise slowly after placing the last plate in the dishwasher, but can't bring myself to face Reka yet.

"Excited? Worried? Guilty? Name the emotion, Bex."

It takes me a moment before I respond. "The last one... guilty."

"Because of your falling out with Naomi?"

"Yeah. I wasn't kind to her in that moment. I was outright cruel."

"Maybe. But you have to give yourself a little grace. You were dealing with a lot."

"She didn't deserve to be spoken to like that though."

"Is that what's stopping you from fixing things with her? Your guilt?"

I shrug.

"Have you ever considered that maybe your guilt is more about your fear of rejection?"

"Well that would be far to reasonable, Reka." I smirk slightly.

"Symon and I went through the same thing you know." Her eyes glass over for a moment before returning to me. "After his divorce, we had to work through our shit and the hurt we caused each other."

"I remember a little about that."

"Yeah..." Her head drops. "It's hard for me to admit, but I was *angry* with him. I used that anger as an excuse to push him away for a while. But ultimately my anger was what was keeping me from being a good partner to him. From being a good partner for myself."

"I don't understand." I ask, putting down the dish in my hand and turning to fully face her.

She sighs. "When we began reconciling, I had this fear that he was going to hurt me again, disappear again. I'll fully admit that I took it out on him in ways that weren't entirely becoming of me as a partner or a domme. He took it in stride, but I couldn't help but feel like I was failing him somehow."

"And what, I'm failing Naomi?"

"That's for you to decide, babe." She says, hopping off the counter. "Just think about it."

I'm stuck to the spot long after Reka leaves, considering our conversation.

Like... who is my guilt really impacting? Am I punishing myself? Or am I punishing Naomi?

As things currently stand, I'm not helping either of us, but I don't know how to fix this.

I know I want to, though.

I need to.

Because I can't imagine a future without her.

27

NAOMI

Potentially, Mid-June — Semester grades are in, they're not good, and to make things worse, it's hot outside

Two weeks have passed since Selene forcibly moved me onto the ranch. She's an easy person to forgive for most things, but this time took me a little bit longer.

When Selene told me she was kicking me out, it hurt. She pulled me out to the porch and sat me down on the swing with a serious look on her face. There was no hesitation in her voice when she dove in. She was on a mission.

You're not happy, Nay.

Not easy words to hear from your best friend, but true nonetheless. I'd spent the past months wallowing and it was high time for me to start moving forward again. I needed to figure out my shit. Pick a new direction, whatever that may be.

I needed some kind of change to kick me in the ass, and she's right, much as I loath to admit it, this was just the thing to do it.

The question of what comes next haunted me for the first few days that I settled into the cabin.

Since then, I've decided that I don't want to continue my

program up in Dallas, but beyond that I haven't made any plans. I also need to figure out things with Bex and Alvie too and I couldn't do that hiding out in Selene and Gunnar's home.

If I have any hope of finding a path forward, maybe with them, I need to be here.

It helps that I've actually enjoyed being out here. My time spent out in the sunshine and fresh air, or outdoor enrichment time according to Selene, has been great for keeping my depression at bay.

Every morning, I wake up with Milkshake curled at the end of my bed and by the time we're headed out the door for the day, Alvie is waiting outside with a cup of coffee and some baked good that he always says they had extras of because Bex is definitely *not* stress baking for me.

The gesture is sweeter than I like to admit.

Then, every morning, he takes Milkshake and me on a walk around the property, showing us different areas and secrets of the land. Where the pecan trees are located, where I can find wild grapes to pick and turn into jelly, and how to tell where the wildlife is moving around.

I know that by the time I'm awake, Alvie has already been up for hours and completed a multitude of chores on the ranch, but it always warms my heart that he takes the time out of his day to help me start my own.

I love our morning walks, and the talks that come with it. It's nice, getting to know him in that way.

Even Bex and I have started to mend fences.

Alvie and Bex have me over for dinner every night now. In the beginning it was a little awkward considering we haven't figured everything out, but with each day that passes things get a little easier.

Bex and I are able to banter back and forth again without the tension that used to exist between us.

I knew things would take time to sort themselves out, and they have, for the most part.

We still haven't had "the talk" yet. It's just kind of the elephant in the room looming around us.

I'm in the cabin, working on an embroidery project, when I get a knock on my door.

Milkshake hops up from where she was sleeping on the bed and bounds over to the door, yipping to alert me to a visitor.

"Shhh. Milkshake, it's okay." I soothe as I open the door, where I find Alvie standing on the other side.

"Hey." He says.

"Hey." I reply.

"Want to do dinner again?"

"Yeah. That sounds nice."

Alvie waits patiently as I grab my shoes and close up my cabin.

Milkshake jumps straight into the cab of Alvie's truck as soon as the door is open. I struggle to get in myself, but Alvie gives me a little boost before reaching in to fasten my seat belt.

"Do I really need that? We're just going home." I tease.

His eyes crinkle with his smile when he responds. "I've got precious cargo, bunny. Gotta take care of what's mine."

"Is that what I am? Yours?"

"You will be if I have anything to say about it." He says firmly.

The ride back to the ranch house was peaceful between with light conversation back and forth between Alvie and myself. We chatted about how his day went and how my various craft projects are going.

So when we pull up to the house and Alvie looks at me with the most serious expression I've seen from him in a while, I tense up.

"You look like someone shot Milkshake. What's going on?"

"I just don't want you to be blindsided."

"Why would I be blindsided, Alvie." I ask cautiously.

"Bex has kind of been planning an apology."

"And she decided that a random Wednesday night was the best time to do it?" I giggle.

"There's a slideshow." Alvie grimaces and I laugh, opening the passenger side door and crawling carefully from his truck, Milkshake following close behind.

"I'm sure it will be fine." I giggle when I look back at his stricken face.

He scowls and then opens his own door.

I don't bother to wait for him to head into the house, but I can hear the rocks scatter on the drive as Alvie jogs to catch up with me.

"Nay…" He says desperately. "I care about both of you. A lot. I don't one hundred percent know what happened beyond what you've both shared with me, but I can't let the two of you continue on like this." The sincerity in his eyes has me melting for this man that's wormed his way into my heart. "Please just keep an open mind."

"Alvie, you're kind of scaring me."

"No. Don't be scared." He sighs, his head dropping. "Bex is just feeling a little fragile right now. I don't want to watch her heart break. Or yours."

Reaching up, I cup his face in my palms and guide his face down to meet mine.

"I can't promise you a certain reaction." I give him a light kiss, which has both of us smiling. "But I promise I won't run."

"Okay." He says his big hands wrapping around my wrists.

We stand like that for a while, just looking at each other, before he releases me and takes me by the hand. My hand is clasped in his own when we enter the house, and I immediately see what Alvie meant by "planning an apology."

The dining room table is laden with my favorite foods and bottles of my favorite wine. The living room is set up with a massive pile of pillows and blankets that I want to dive into, along with an assortment of snacks.

There, in the middle of it all, is Bex.

"Wow." I breathe out, tears welling in my eyes from the storm that's erupted in my chest. "You did all of this for me?"

Eagerly, she strides over and takes me by the hand, leading me over to the dining room table. "So. I made all of your favorites for dinner so you don't have to choose, then I thought we could cuddle up and watch one of your favorites."

"Even..." I side eye her.

"Yes. Even *that one*." She says incredulously.

"Okay. So you've clearly done all of this for a reason." I draw her to a stop in the middle of the space. "Wanna talk about it?"

"Can we talk while we eat?" She asks.

Alvie puts his hand on my lower back and guides me into my normal chair, before he starts filling my plate with bites of every dish on the table.

"Double of the pasta, please." I chime in, making him smile.

When all of our plates are loaded, Bex looks at me expectantly. I take my first bite and moan, which has Alvie shifting in his seat.

"Moan like that again and this night is not going to go according to plan." Bex laughs.

"Sounds like fun." I tease, but it only get's me a heated look from her that I'm not quite prepared for.

"Don't make threats you're not willing to follow through on."

I put down my utensils.

"I have no problem playing with y'all, Bex. That's never been the issue." I take a deep breath before addressing the elephant in the room. "Our chemistry is great. It's our relationship dynamic that is messed up."

"I agree." She says seriously.

"What?" I'm taken aback.

"I agree." She repeats. "I've been doing a lot of soul searching.

And reading a lot about polyamory, open relationships, and jealousy."

"You've been reading non-fiction?"

"Why is that what you latch on to?" She giggles. "Yes. Non-fiction."

"Okay. So you've been thinking about things."

"Yes." Bex takes a deep breath. "I didn't realize how unfair I was being to you when we started all of this. It was a bit of fun at first, but then it became more, I think, for both of us."

I nod along as she talks.

"Then that night at the hospital. I snapped. I'm not making excuses, but I was just so under-prepared for any kind of serious conversations with Alvie being in the hospital. He's my rock," She says, looking across the table at him with love in her eyes. "I don't know what I'd do without him."

"I understand." My heart cracking a bit at the sight of their connection.

"No. I don't think you do." She continues, turning that same soft look to me. "You're more than a fling to me, Nay. I didn't realize it until I started learning more about it, but the few girlfriends I've had have always been short term situations. I knew that, deep down."

The term girlfriend takes my breath away. Surely she doesn't mean that, doesn't see me that way. Does she? Do I want her to?

"Have you ever heard of hierarchical polyamory?" She asks, and I shake my head. "Basically, I've always seen my relationship with Alvie as paramount to any other relationship I may have had. To a certain extent, other relationships were secondary to anything I had with him. So when you came to the hospital I freaked out because I thought my place with him was being threatened."

"Bex..."

"No. It's okay. I don't want to be like that anymore, Nay. I want to have a relationship with you that feels equal. Where you hold just as much importance in my life as he does. I want you to be a vital part of our lives, not just a piece of them."

Silence fills the room as they let me process.

"And you, Alvie?" I ask, turning to him.

"I feel the same way, bunny." He smiles.

I sit there in shock for a minute before I absolutely lose it and start cackling out of control. Between gasping breaths, I manage to get out. "Alvie said there was a slideshow."

"Oh! Yes! It has graphs." She hops up from her chair, but before she can run away, I grab her by the hand.

It takes me a minute to get my breath back as I try to control my giggles, but Bex waits patiently for me to speak. "I'd love to see your slideshow. But right now, I just want to have dinner with y'all."

The rest of the night feels like how things used to be between all of us, but better somehow.

After cleaning dinner up together, we cuddle up on the couch and turn on one of my favorite movies that Bex loathes, but she doesn't make a single comment about how ridiculous the plot is or how silly the characters are being.

The whole time, I'm snuggled between them and it feels so good to just be comfortable like this with them again. I'm leaning into Bex with my feet thrown over Alvie's thighs, she's playing with my hair and he's rubbing my feet and calves.

"I missed y'all." I whisper as my eyes droop and the credits roll.

"We did too, bunny." Alvie says, squeezing my thigh.

"We really did." Bex affirms.

28

BEX

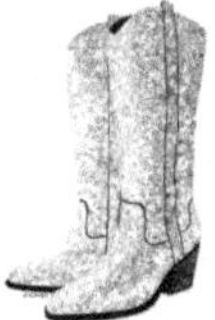

June 14 — A very good Wednesday

Who knew that Wednesday's could be so magical, and healing.

After our initial conversation with Naomi about our relationships, we continue to talk about our lives and relationship. By Friday I'm itching to move things forward.

We're all sitting around the living room, Milkshake at Naomi's feet, absorbed in our own hobbies. We're just siting in comfortable silence together as the record player spins its tune, when I make my announcement.

"I think Naomi should move into the house."

"What?" Naomi chokes on the water she's drinking.

I turn to her, my entire posture serious.

"I want you to move out of the cabin and into the house." I repeat. "You're here all the time and if you're comfortable with it, I don't see any reason for you not to be living here with us. We have the room."

"Bex," Alvie starts.

"No. Listen." I turn back to Naomi who's curled up on the

couch with her embroidery. "I know that a lot has happened between us. But we're starting to repair that. Since you've come to the ranch, things have been getting better. I think it makes sense."

Naomi sets down her project, carefully tucking away the stray threads and needle. She stands and crosses the room to stand before me. She's chewing her lip in that nervous habit of hers. I want to reach up and tug it out from between her teeth.

"Is that what you really want?" She asks softly.

Reaching out, I take her hand in my own. "More than anything." I breathe out. "I just want to be with you."

Naomi glances up, breaking the spell forming between us, and checks in with Alvaro. I don't take my eyes off of her, though.

"We'll put you in your old room so you feel like you have your own space." Alvie decides.

She looks back at me. "Okay. I'll move in. Can we do it tomorrow, though? I'm kinda tired."

"Of course, bunny." I say, my shoulders relaxing at the knowledge that very soon we'll have her close by.

"But not like... too tired."

I raise my eyebrows at her. "Oh?"

"I just..."

"Use your words, bunny. Ask for what you want." I prompt.

"I really want you to fuck me until I fall asleep." She says, closing her eyes to hide from our reactions.

I glance at Alvie, who has a very similar smug expression on his face to my own.

"Naomi, come here." Alvie motions for her join me where he stands and she does. "Is my bunny feeling a little frustrated?"

Naomi nods. "I just..."

"No need to explain, bun." I breathe into her ear, sending shivers down her spine. "Let us take care of you. But first you need a snack. Then we're going to give you exactly what you need."

Naomi pouts.

"You're gonna need your energy for what we have planned." Alvie whispers loud enough for me to hear.

I bounce up from the couch and head toward our room to start pulling out toys, while Alvie leads Naomi to the kitchen.

From our personal collection, I pull out bundles of rope, dildos, and a multitude of other toys that we can potentially use tonight.

When Alvie and Bex walk into the room, their arms laden with water and snacks, Naomi has a beaming smile on her face. The tension between them is palpable with the way that Alvie hovers closely to Naomi.

They set everything down on the top of our dresser and turn to me.

"I pulled out toys for us to play with." I say, smiling back at them.

"And what do you propose we do with these toys, birdie?" Alvie teases.

"Play, of course." I walk toward them and place a hand on Alvie's chest and Naomi's waist, pulling her in closer to my body. "But first I think all of these clothes should come off."

Alvie starts stripping off his own clothes, but I push away Naomi's hands when she goes to take off her top. Instead I take my time, undressing her myself. My fingers skim along her soft skin as I lift the shirt up and off her body. When I remove her bra, I take a moment to run my fingers along the reddened lines where the garment dug into her sides.

"Bex, please." Naomi whispers. "Stop teasing me. I need you."

I smirk at her admission. "I think we should tease her first. Don't you think, Alvie?"

Alvie returns my smirk. "I think that sounds like an excellent plan, birdie. Maybe we tie her up in a harness and see how she likes that."

Naomi shivers as I let my fingers travel down her side, down to her hip.

"Would you like that? Do you want to be bound up like a good little rope bunny?" I ask.

"Yes. Please, ma'am. I want to be good for you." She breathes out.

Alvie immediately goes over to where I've lain out lengths of rope and selects an assortment of nylon ropes in various colors.

Hands on Naomi's hips, I walk her back until she's resting against the edge of our bed.

"I think we should put her in a rope dress, sir." I suggest. "I think she'd enjoy being completely wrapped up for us. Like a present."

"What's that?" Naomi asks.

"It's a tie that covers your whole body." I explain.

My hands shift to cup her breast. "Your breast will be surrounded by rope, adding just enough pressure to add sensation when I do this." I squeeze her. "Or this." I take her nipples in my hand and pinch teasingly.

Leaving her breast I let my hands travel down her side and to the center of her stomach. "There will be ropes here. So we can tug you around." I shift where my right hand is to go back to trace her spine. "And more rope here. To give Alvie a handle when he fucks into you from behind."

Naomi's breath catches.

With my hand still tracing small circles on her spine, I take my free hand and guide it down to her center.

My fingers part her folds and press up, making Naomi rise up on her toes. "And we'll run two ropes here too. Which feels amazing when he pounds into you and the rope rubs in just the right place."

My hand cups her center and I put pressure on her core. "Do you want that, bunny?"

"Yes. Yes. I want that." She breathes out. "Tie me up and fuck me. Ruin me."

Alvie walks over with the lengths of rope in his hand.

I'm pressed together with Naomi. The way Naomi's body responds to my touch is enthralling and I want to burn every moment into my memory.

"You ready, bunny?" He asks as he walks over.

The way Naomi looks at me, with such tenderness in her gaze, has me catching my breath.

"Yes, sir." She replies to Alvie without taking her gaze away from me.

Alvie gives me a small tap on the hip and I backs away from Naomi reluctantly, revealing every curve and dip on her body to both our views.

I take a moment to admire the way that her breast fall heavily against her figure. My hands instinctively reach for the apron of her belly and give it a light squeeze.

"You're fucking incredible." I breathe out and she blushes.

With the hand not holding rope, Alvie guides Naomi closer to himself, leaving me just enough space to slip behind her.

"We're going to tie you up now. Tell us if anything pinches or hurts." Alvie tells her and she nods.

"And when it feels good, bunny." I whisper in her ear.

29

ALVARO

The process of tying the harness around Naomi's curves is slow as Bex and I pass rope back-and-forth between the two of us. I make sure that every light caress of my fingers guide the rope where it needs to go.

Tying her up is erotic and sensual. I love how Naomi's body responds to every touch. She shivers at our contact with some of her more sensitive areas.

When we run rope between her legs and up to tie around the waist anchor that we've secured, she shifts at the new sensation. Her body responds eagerly to the pressure that it applies to her center, and when both of the ropes are secured, cradling her core, I let my fingers dip between her folds.

"You like that, Bunny?" I whisper into her ear before cupping her center. "Grind your cunt into my hand like a good little rope bunny. Take your pleasure for yourself."

She responds eagerly to my command, pushing her cunt down into my hand and rocking back and forth. Her movement coats my hand, making it slick with her wetness. Each rock of her hips into my hand has my smile growing wider. I drink down her mewls and groans of pleasure as she moves.

One glance back to where Bex stands behind her reveals that my wife is enjoying this just as much as I am, maybe even more. Her hands travel over Naomi's entire body as the sweet bunny rides my hand. Bex cups Naomi's breast and teases her nipples, strokes her sides and the center of her spine. Every sensation that Bex adds makes the woman between us moan louder, until her eyes are fully closed, head dropped back, and she's lost to the sensations rolling through her body.

My little bunny works herself on my hand until two of my fingers slip into her slit and she's finally able to grind her clit into my hand. The sigh of relief she lets out has me laughing and I pull away my glistening hand, making her pout in protest.

"You want more, bunny?" She nods eagerly. "Get on the bed on all fours. You're going to eat out my wife while I play with you and scream into her cunt when I make you come."

Bex is already backing onto the bed, propping herself up against the pillows and spreading herself wide.

I turn Naomi around and wrap her in my arms, letting my head rest on her shoulder.

"You see that? You see how pretty and pink her pussy is?" I murmur in her ear. "She's so ready for you. Do you want a taste?"

"Yes. I want to feast on her." Naomi confesses breathlessly.

"Then go." I say, releasing her.

Naomi scrambles from my hold and gets up on the bed between Bex's feet.

Bex is smiling broadly and looks up at me, love in her eyes.

"I adore how you look at each other." Naomi says breathlessly, sitting back on her knees and looking between the two of us. "You really love each other, don't you?"

My breath catches at the sweetness of her statement, and I can tell that Bex feels similarly.

"Yes." I say, my voice mirroring her own breathlessness. "We do."

"I want that." Naomi says, which has me crossing the space between us and taking her hand in my own.

My thumb circles the pulse at her wrist and the three of us sit there in silence for a moment while we let the significance of her desire settle between us.

Bex is the first to speak. "You deserve that and so much more, bunny."

Naomi tries shaking her head but I stop her by taking her face between my hands.

"You deserve everything, Naomi. You deserve a happy and fulfilling life." I give her a kiss on the forehead. "You deserve to be loved unconditionally."

Her forehead drops to my chest and I just hold her like that. Bex comes over on the bed to join us in our embrace.

The three of us sit there, breathing with each other for a while.

"Sorry. I didn't mean to make things all heavy." Naomi apologizes.

"No." Bex interjects. "This is good. This is why I want you here with us. I want you to feel secure enough to tell us how you feel."

Naomi pulls out of our entangled embrace and sits back on the bed.

"I just wanted to get a really good dicking down." She pouts. "And I ruined the whole mood."

I grab her free hand and press it against my hardened cock. "Oh, bunny. You can absolutely still have this dick if you want it."

She nods, some of her delight coming back.

"Tell me you want it." I growl.

"I want it. Give me your cock, sir. I need it." She pants.

"Back on the bed, Bex. Our little bunny said she wanted to be fucked until she passed out."

"Well we can't keep our girl from a good nights sleep, can we?" Bex teases.

"Looks like we have our work cut out for us though." I say,

running my hand up and down Naomi's leg. "Bunny looks like she has plenty of energy to spare."

Bex and Naomi laugh and it's like angels have come down from the heavens. There's a warmth and light in the dim bedroom that makes my heart sing with them.

"I love y'all." Naomi's laughter stops immediately and her jaw drops. "Shit. Sorry. That was a lot."

"No. No." Naomi rises on her knees and moves over until she's pressing herself up against me, grasping my hands tightly in her own. "Thank you for saying it out loud." She looks over at Bex. "If this is going to work, I don't want to be guessing about how you feel about me. I don't want to be doubting my own feelings."

Naomi releases one of my hands and moves to take one of Bex's in her own.

"And I undoubtedly love you. Both of you." She says looking between both of us before her gaze settles on me. "I fell for you both the moment I saw you put her up on that cross. The way you looked at her, and cared for her, told me everything I ever needed to know about you, Alvie. And you, Bex, I knew in the moment that you took to adjust my dress that I wanted to be loved like that."

"You will be." Bex says. "You are. I know I fucked things up, but that was about me and my fears, not you. You deserve to be loved like that." She takes a deep breath. "And I do, I love you."

Naomi squeals and jumps on Bex, smothering her in kisses before pulling back quickly. "You do?" She asks, the look of pure innocence on her face is heartwarming.

"Yeah. Absolutely." Bex says, giving her a kiss on the lips.

I watch as their kisses grow heavier and they start to loose themselves in each other. Watching them together is intimate and heartwarming. The way they cherish each moment with the other is breathtaking.

"On the bed, Bex." I interrupt.

Naomi gives me a look of annoyance before realizing what I'm asking for.

Bex pulls herself away from Naomi and settles at the head of the bed once more. This time she teases both of us as she spreads her legs. Her hands glide up and down her body, caressing every lush curve that I adore, before stopping at her center.

With two fingers, she parts her pussy to reveal her core. "Come taste, bunny."

Naomi crawls up the bed and I watch her round, dimpled ass as she moves. She settles herself between Bex's legs and wraps her arms under Bex's full thighs to give herself a good grip.

There's an appreciative reverence in Naomi's eyes as she looks at my wife, studying the beauty that I've been honored to call mine for so long.

Now, before me, I take in the marvel that is them together and a heartwarming shock overtakes me at the thought that these women are mine.

Mine.

I crawl up on the bed behind Naomi as she dives in and begins eating Bex out. I move my hands over her body in the same rhythm as Naomi uses to play Bex's body. When she uses slow long licks on my wife's core, I let my fingers trail softly and slowly up her spine and across her shoulders. When Naomi picks up the pace, I press firmly into her ass, kneading the supple flesh there. I take every opportunity to graze the most sensitive spots on her body, but I refuse to go to her cunt.

Not until my wife has come undone.

I watch Bex's face as Naomi pleasures her. In the telltale moment of her impending orgasm, when she bites her lips and arches her back, I finally give in to the temptation to let my fingers glide into Naomi's center once more.

My hand slips between her warm, wet folds and I groan in unison with Bex as she comes for the first time.

Naomi doesn't stop though, instead she free's up one of her hands and starts running her fingers through Bex's folds. With each brush of Naomi's fingers, shivers rock through Bex's body.

I press down on Naomi's clit just as she spears my wife with her fingers and both women cry out.

"Like that, bunny?" I tease. "You like getting your reward while you make my wife come?"

As though my words spark a new energy in her, Naomi dives back in with her mouth on Bex's clit and my wife reaches to grasp Naomi by her blonde strands.

"Fuck!" Bex calls out as Naomi fucks her with her hand and eats her out. "Fuck. Fuck. Fuck. Naomi! Alvie! Fuck!"

Watching Naomi pleasure my wife with such enthusiasm and hearing Bex cry out my name as she receives her due has my cock fully hard and desperate to dive into Naomi.

We've never fucked before.

This feels significant.

"You ready for me, bunny?" My hand grasps my cock and pumps several times.

"Yes." I hear her mumble into Bex's cunt.

"Good bunny." I pur.

Using the head of my cock, I part her lower lips and run my tip up and down her slit, gathering her wetness to use to fuck her.

With every graze of her clit and pass against her entrance, Naomi shivers and moans for me.

I tease her like this until her groans turn into almost pained whines of need.

"Ready?" I confirm with a growl. "I'm gonna make you mine now, bunny. *Mine.*"

30

NAOMI

Mine.

The word echoes through my soul and shocks my system.

Alvie's cock is right at my entrance and I'm grinding my hips back into him, begging for him to fill me up. Tingles build in my pussy with each stroke through my folds, but the warm sensation spreading through my body is all due to his words.

Alvie continues to tease me with a few pulses into my entrance, but he never lets himself inside me fully.

"Please, sir. I need you. Make me yours." I beg before chocking on my words as his cock thrusts into me fully.

It's been such a long time since I've been filled by *good cock* and Alvie's is truly a marvel. He feels amazing, like every empty space in my soul is now full. He gives me plenty of time to adjust to his size and I pant louder with each second that passes and he doesn't fuck me.

His hands stroke up and down my spine and he grinds his hips into my ass just enough to feel him twitch inside of me. The moment between us is bliss and pain.

All I want is for him to fuck me.

Take me.

Fill me up and make me his completely.

"Alvie. If you don't fuck me right now, I swear this will be the last time you ever feel my cunt around your cock. Fuck me or get out." I swear.

"You stopped eating your dessert, bunny. Go back to your treat and I'll give you yours." He rumbles, giving my hip dips a squeeze.

Not wasting any time, I lower myself back in to taste the heaven that is Bex's pussy. Just as my tongue connects with her clit, she groans.

Alvie uses that as his cue to withdraw from me. His girth leaves me feeling empty as he pulls out, but my body welcomes him back as he pushes back in. His movement, in and out, continues slowly. The even pace he maintains drives me frantic with need for him.

"More." I moan into Bex's pussy. "Please, more."

"Do you think she deserves it, birdie?" He asks. "Does she deserve to be destroyed by my dick?"

Bex moans loudly in response, lost to the feelings that have taken over her senses.

"Words, birdie." Alvie snaps.

"Damnit, Alvie. Fuck the damn woman." She glares back before letting her head drop back once more onto the pillows behind her.

"You heard the lady." Alvie chuckles as he thrusts into me harder.

Alvie pounds into me with the enthusiasm of a man overtaken by lust. He's brutal in his rhythm and the size of him is near painful. When he finds the perfect spot, I moan and collapse into the V between Bex's thighs.

Immediately Alvie stops and I remember his earlier command.

Pulling my hand free I find my way to her core. Each thrust of

Alvie's hips into my own push my fingers into Bex and I crook my fingers to fit right against the place I know makes her scream out in blissful agony.

I lose control of every muscle in my body as he pounds into me. I can no longer focus on any kind of steady pattern to bring Bex to her climax, but Alvie's movements have my face rocking into her at just the right pace that my tongue presses into her clit steadily with each thrust of my fingers.

"Fuck. You're gonna make me cum, bunny." She groans uncontrollably.

Alvie picks up his pace and I shift my shoulders, allowing me to press up into Bex at the perfect angle to hit that most sensitive hidden spot.

Within moments, Bex is screaming out her orgasm. Her body rocks and shakes as she peaks and her climax takes over. The noises she echos around the room are primal and deep.

My wrist gives out just as her cunt slows its fluttering around my fingers and I pull them out to rest.

My face rests against her core and as though by instinct, my mouth goes to suck and lick at Bex's clit as she comes down from her high. My face is buried in heaven as Alvie pushes into me, making me voice my own incoherent noises.

The feeling of his cock gliding in and out of me is overwhelming and I start to fully relax into the feeling of being fucked now that my task has been taken away from me.

When Bex has gathered herself, she pushes herself up and goes to Alvie's side.

"You going to come inside our girl, sir?" She asks quietly from behind me.

"Fuuuck." He moans. "I love when you do that."

"Mhmm. You like when I nibble on your neck, sir?" She murmurs.

"Fuck yes." Alvie's pace slows as Bex teases him, but it only elongates the sensation of each stroke.

My cunt squeezes around his cock on his next rock into me and he groans long and deep. I feel when his cum starts dripping out of me and onto the bedspread, but he doesn't stop fucking me. He's still hard and with each thrust of his hips, he forces his cum back inside of me.

I don't even have time to grieve the loss of his cock in my pussy when he softens because he pulls out and flips me on my back.

Like a man who's gone weeks without food or water, Alvie eats me out. His licks and light nibbles are frantic and earnest. His movements are consistent enough to where the orgasms that's evaded me starts to build quickly.

"You like that, sir? You like tasting her pussy as your cum leaks out of her? You like tasting you with her?" Bex says from above me.

My eyes open and I find her staring back at me with a sweet smile on her face.

She reaches for my nipples and together the couple play my body like an instrument until I'm singing like a soprano.

In an instant, my orgasm crashes over me in waves. The first peak is strong and devastating like the first hit of a hurricane, then the aftershocks are the whirling winds that continue to wreck havoc on every nerve in my body.

Alvie draws himself up my body and places a light kiss on my lips. The salt and musk of our combine scents is overwhelming and I moan into the kiss, which lasts far too short.

He pulls back, looking me deep in my eyes before rolling to my side and collapsing on his back.

"Fuck." He grunts.

"Yeah." Bex says, giving me a light kiss on the lips before sliding off the bed.

I lay there, staring up at the ceiling fan whirling above us, thinking about everything and nothing at all.

My body is satiated and relaxed.

Water is put to my lips and I gulp it down before taking a few of the bites of food that are offered to me.

I'm happy and exhausted in the best possible way.

There's a sense of comfort that blankets over me.

As I begin to fall asleep, I feel safe.

And loved.

START BACK at the beginning with *Used* and see how one plus one equals three when the ice queen meets her golden retriever in Book 1 of The Playground Club series.

Get your copy!

Can't get enough? Don't miss the passion, healing, and heat of Book 3 in the series, *Cherished*, and fall even deeper in love with our bride and groom, Selene and Gunnar!

Get your copy!

To stay up to date on news, sales, and releases from Shannon Elliot, join her newsletter here:

Join the newsletter!

NAOMI

June 15 — Merry Moving Day!

I don't know where the pastries came from, but Alvie appeared in the early morning hours with baked goods and coffee. Which is what woke me from my slumber and is coincidentally the key to my heart.

"Morning, bunny." He says as he hands me a mug of coffee where I lay sprawled in the center of the bed and puts the box of pastries down at the end. "Sleep well?"

His smirk is endearing instead of frustrating.

"Very." I smile into my cup of perfectly flavored coffee.

"Good." He smiles before going over to Bex's side of the bed. "Rise and shine, birdie."

"Uunh." Bex groans. "I don't wanna."

"Come on." Alvie gives me a wink. "It's moving day."

Bex bolts up and starts scrambling out of bed. "Alright. Let's go. Grab your shit. Get dressed."

Alvie and I both chuckle at the sudden flip in Bex's energy.

Apparently she gets out of bed for more than just coffee... She goes around the room, pulling her athleisure wear from their various homes and throwing them onto the bed.

Alvie crawls into bed with his own cup of coffee and pulls me into his arms as she bounces around the room. We sit there together for a while, just resting and enjoying Bex's flighty nature.

"Selene asked me yesterday if she needs to send one or two invitations to the ranch." I say quietly.

"For her wedding?" Alvie asks.

"Yeah." I reply.

"Her wedding isn't until like eight months, right? She's already doing invitations?" Alvie says louder, drawing Bex's attention.

"She's started putting together the list at least." I shrug, snuggling back further into his chest.

"Well seating us at the reception is going to be a bitch." Bex says as she tugs on her tennis shoes.

"Why?" I say, glancing up at her.

"Well if we're there as the three of us, then who's the odd man out at our table?"

"Oh. She already said she'd seat us with Reka and her guys. Then she'll put another couple with us to fill out the eight-top." I share.

"She already said, bunny?" Alvie teases.

"Oh. Oh!" My eyes widen. "Fucking Selene! She *knew* and she didn't tell me!"

Alvie takes my mug of coffee from my hands to avoid me splashing hot coffee all over our naked bodies and he laughs at my antics.

"Sometimes we just need to figure things out for ourselves, bunny." Alvie says, nuzzling his face into my hair.

"A hint would have been nice." I pout.

"Pretty sure the U-Haul took care of that." Bex laughs as she comes walking out of the closet with clothes for Alvie and me. "You were always meant to be with us, Naomi."

Alvie tucks his head into the crook of my neck.

"And what about the other stuff? Like finances, and families, and kids, and... and... and *school*. Fuck I almost forgot. I dropped out." My heart starts to race as my thoughts begin to spiral and I take in the magnitude of how fucked up my life is currently.

"Shhh..." Alvie says, putting down both containers of coffee on the side table before returning and running his hand up and down my side in a soothing pattern. "You should talk to Durante about going back to school. But we can figure out the rest as we go."

I hide myself in Alvie's shoulder. "Right. Yeah. You're right."

"I can always make another slideshow if you want." Bex jokes.

"Oh! You never did show that to me, you know." Bex's eyes widen and a giddy smile takes over her face before she rushes out of the room. I look to Alvie, confused. "What?"

"You did this." He laughs. "She practiced on me for like a solid two hours."

Bex comes bounding back into the room iPad in hand, and hops onto the foot of the bed.

"So. Polyamory comes in a bunch of different forms. I'll start by explaining where we went wrong, aka hierarchical polyamory. Well at least, wrong for us."

"Bex, it's like 7 a.m." I giggle.

"Yes, and you're going to sit here like a good girl while I go through my presentation." She mocks.

"Can't we do this after we've eaten and moved our bunny in?" Alvie pleads.

I give her my best pouty eyes. "Please? I just wanna cuddle with my partners."

"Ooh. Partners, I like that." Bex says, tossing the iPad aside and crawling up my body until she's hovering over me. "Would you ever consider being my wife?"

She nips at the curve of my neck and a shiver rolls through me.

"Little soon for that, isn't it, Bex?" Alvie says, reasonably.

"What? Maybe a year or two from now. Nay wants to wear her own white dress!" Bex scoffs.

"And we'll wrap that up when the time comes." He replies, calmly as ever.

"We'll have everything all tied up in a nice little bow." I joke.

"I know someone I definitely would like to have tied up right now." Bex purrs, diving in for a passionate kiss.

"Down, birdie. I think our bunny needs food first. We can play more tonight. You can tie up loose ends then." He says playfully giving Bex a kiss on the cheek.

Both of us break out into full body cackling laughter and don't stop until tears are streaming down our faces.

"I love you. Both of you." I say quietly.

They two exchange a silent look.

"We love you too, bunny."

Get your copy!

To stay up to date on news, sales, and releases from Shannon Elliot, join her newsletter here:

Join the newsletter!

ACKNOWLEDGMENTS

To my online besties and the IRL kinky family who made this book possible. I appreciate y'all more than you can know.

Wifey, Becca, you know what you did. I am a better person, and writer, because of you. Thank you for cheering me on and keeping me going when I want to give up.

Becky, I cannot be more appreciative for all of your support. You opened my eyes to dreams that I couldn't have imagined for myself.

Jenna & Hana, you're the bestest for putting up with me and I cannot express how much I value your contribution to this book and series.

To Grace, Halla, and Hanna, y'all are the true MVPs of this team. You keep things running and I am so grateful to have you by my side.

To Whitney & Christine, thank you for making sure I live to see another day so I can keep writing and for answering all my weird nursing questions. Love y'all!

Thank you to Constantina and Gabby for makings sure I don't look a fool when my characters open their mouths!

The Sinner's Playground Facebook Group - Thank you for putting up with all of my @everyone tags and then riding the chaos wave with me while I ask for your input. Y'all really helped bring these characters to life and I appreciate the support.

The staff at Katz's? Y'all are the best. Thanks for keeping me hydrated and fed while I finished this mother fucker.

To my family, thank you for believing in me and supporting me while I go on this new adventure. I couldn't make this dream possible without you. I am so grateful for your endless love.

ABOUT THE AUTHOR

Shannon Elliot resides in Texas, with her fur baby and writes romance that reflects her readers whenever she's not at the dog park or curled up with a good book. Evidenced by her background in theatre, she is drawn to story-telling and the creative process. Shannon believes that diverse and inclusive stories shouldn't be the exception, they should be the rule. Happily ever after is for everyone and she aims to write romances that reflect her readers.

www.authorshannonelliot.com/pages/links

ALSO BY SHANNON ELLIOT

The Playground Club Series

Used, Book 1

Bound, Book 2

Cherished, Book 3

Descent into Darkness Duet

Angels in the Dark, Book 1

Devil in the Dark, Book 2

Standalone Novellas

Heel

www.ingramcontent.com/pod-product-compliance
Lightning Source LLC
Chambersburg PA
CBHW071408300726
48976CB00006B/2026